A sisterhood

Beverly opened the door, and Ro stared at the ZZT living room. It v spidery web of…yarn? Yarn everywhere, weaving chair and table legs, up around lamps and candlestick holders, through the cushions of the couches in vibrant yellow, red, orange, green, blue, every color imaginable.

Beverly climbed up onto a chair, avoiding the stringwork around her feet. "As y'all know," she started, "at Zeta Zeta Tau we are family. Through good and bad, thick and thin. However, there's always that special bond you have with one person in the house. Tonight, we want you to make that connection to your Big Sister. Each piece of colored yarn has a tag attached to it. Find the tag with your name and then follow the yarn until you reach the end and your new Big Sister. Go for it!"

Roni clambered over to the couch along with the other twenty-nine girls, trying to get to the string that had her name on it. The melee of voices blended together in high-pitched giggles and squeals sounding out through the large living room. Roni managed to make out Veronica Van Gelderen on a black-and-white string.

The new members slowly untangled, eventually all meeting up with their strings at the double doors leading into the dining room and lounge. The doors were slid apart just enough for the girls to see that all of their strings converged at the opening.

When they were all sorted out and ready, there almost seemed to be a collective gathering of breath. Roni could barely contain her emotions and anticipation, wondering what waited for them behind the partition.

SORORITY
101

the New Sisters

KATE HARMON

speak

An Imprint of Penguin Group (USA) Inc.

SPEAK
Published by the Penguin Group
Penguin Group (USA) Inc.,
345 Hudson Street, New York, New York 10014, U.S.A.
Penguin Group (Canada), 90 Eglinton Avenue East, Suite 700, Toronto, Ontario, Canada
M4P 2Y3 (a division of Pearson Penguin Canada Inc.)
Penguin Books Ltd, 80 Strand, London WC2R 0RL, England
Penguin Ireland, 25 St Stephen's Green, Dublin 2, Ireland
(a division of Penguin Books Ltd)
Penguin Group (Australia), 250 Camberwell Road, Camberwell, Victoria 3124, Australia
(a division of Pearson Australia Group Pty Ltd)
Penguin Books India Pvt Ltd, 11 Community Centre,
Panchsheel Park, New Delhi - 110 017, India
Penguin Group (NZ), 67 Apollo Drive, Rosedale, North Shore 0632,
New Zealand (a division of Pearson New Zealand Ltd)
Penguin Books (South Africa) (Pty) Ltd, 24 Sturdee Avenue,
Rosebank, Johannesburg 2196, South Africa

Registered Offices: Penguin Books Ltd, 80 Strand, London WC2R 0RL, England

Published by Speak, an imprint of Penguin Group (USA) Inc., 2008

1 3 5 7 9 10 8 6 4 2

CIP Data is available.

Speak ISBN 978-0-14-241018-9

Printed in the United States of America

To sisters . . .

Sarah and Stephanie Keller,
Deidre Knight and Pamela Harty,
Tyler and Riley Knight,
Donna Lee Ward and Doris Jensen,
Danika and Devin Jensen
. . . and my sister, Jennifer Keller.

ACKNOWLEDGMENTS

Thanks to my family...

To my parents, Joe and Lizanne Harbuck, thanks for a life-time of love. To my brother, Jeff Harbuck, and my sister, Jennifer Keller, for the sibling bond, and for not permanently maiming me when you sent me down the laundry chute when I was three (I know...I asked you to do it). To my husband, Mike Gibson, for too many things to detail here.

Thanks to my *writing* family...

To the incomparable Deidre Knight (read her books), the amazing ladies at The Knight Agency, and my TKA Sistahs (read all of their books). Thanks seems to be the weakest word in the English language right now.

To my critique partner, Diana Peterfreund (read her books). Thanks for your patience, wisdom, and speed at IMing.

To my WAC sisters, Jessica Andersen (read her books) and Charlene Glatkowski (read her short stories). For What-If and Writing Days, afternoon check-ins, and rivers of Diet Coke.

To the Buzz Girls (read all their books): Dona Sarkar-Mishra, Simone Elkeles, Heather Davis, Tera Lynn Childs, Tina Ferraro, and Stephanie Hale. Join our fun at *www.booksboysbuzz.com*.

To my "spiritual" advisor, Dr. Mary Pat Kelly (read her books; watch her movies). Thanks for giving me La Santa Madre Teresa De Jesus, patron saint of writers, to watch over me.

To fellow Greeks, Victoria Bendetson and Heather Potter Laskowski. Thanks for the research help and ideas.

To my work chicas (aka The Ladies Who Lunch), Jen Enos, Kathy Walsh, Meghan Marquez, Rebecca Billado, Penny Georgoudis, and Kristin Manning. Thanks for listening and letting me say *"did we talk about my writing?"* when the lunch bill comes.

To my Bama buddy, Jennifer Echols (read her books). Thanks for Sunday Check-ins.

To my sweetie, Wendy Toliver (read her books). We *will* see Kaskade together one day!

To my New York gals, Kwana Minatee-Jackson and Elizabeth Mahon. Thanks for keeping me entertained with e-mails about Bobby & Whitney, Top Chef, and Mama Ty-Ty and her girls.

To my RWA sisters in the New England and Chick Lit Chapters. Thanks for riding along on the journey.

The publishers would like to extend their thanks to Marley Gibson for her contributions to the Sorority 101 series.

SORORITY
1O1

the New
Sisters

CHAPTER 1

Jenna Driscoll studied the pearly white new member pin in her hand. The dime-size pin was shaped like a blooming white rose with three Greek letters in the middle: ZZT. It was crazy to think that only yesterday she'd been officially pinned as a Zeta Zeta Tau at the conclusion of sorority recruitment.

She lifted her gaze from her new jewelry to the dorm mirror in front of her. She'd changed her outfit at least four times, stripping off her smart black pants and finally opting for the low-rise Seven jeans she'd picked up by some unbelievable stroke of good luck at Goodwill in Atlanta. They weren't too tight in the hips and allowed her to wear her insulin pump, which monitored her diabetes, on the inside of her pants. She paired the jeans with a top that showed off her shoulders and neck but was loose at her waist and wouldn't give away the secret of her medical condition. No one needed to know about *that* just yet.

Right before she headed for the door, she clipped her pin onto her shirt.

She couldn't wait to show it to Tiger tonight!

She'd met David "Tiger" Harrison on her first day of classes at Latimer University. They'd bumped into each other (literally). And when they'd run into each other again during the week, he'd invited her to come to the Phi Omicron Chi party this Saturday night.

Just as she grabbed her jacket and small purse, the dorm room door opened.

"Oh. You're here," her roommate mumbled, barely glancing at her.

"Hey, Amber." Her roommate's face was just as sad-looking as it had been when she'd gotten the word a couple of days ago that she'd been dropped from sorority recruitment. It was a heartbreaking crush for her. "I thought you went home for the weekend."

Amber flopped down on her bed with a long, hard sigh. "I did, but my parents were driving me crazy. They wouldn't stop hovering and babying me. It made me feel worse about . . . everything."

Instinctively, Jenna tugged the collar of her jacket over her pin. The motion didn't escape Amber's attention.

"So, which house did you get into?"

"Zeta Zeta Tau."

Amber merely nodded.

"You know," Jenna said optimistically, "I heard that if any houses weren't full, there would be an open recruitment time, and more bids might be offered."

"Only losers go out for open recruitment," Amber said emphatically.

"That's not true." Jenna sighed. "Amber, look, I know—"

She held up her hand. "Don't. Just don't go there, Jenna." She tossed her fiery red hair over her shoulder. "I know you're trying to help, but I'll be fine. Don't cheerlead. Leave that to the Latimer pom-pom squad."

Jenna's heart raced at the tension swirling around the room. When they'd first moved in together, Amber had been so sweet. She even wanted to decorate their room and get matching comforters for their beds. Now she was like a different person entirely. Jenna kept hoping it was only temporary. It *had* to be temporary, right?

She shook off the negative vibes. Her new sisters were waiting for her, and having fun with them tonight would help soothe her nerves. "Look, Amber . . . I gotta go." She hesitated at the door, hating to leave her roommate like this, even if she was in a pissy mood. "Are you okay?"

"Where are you going?"

Jenna bit her bottom lip slightly, wondering how Amber would take this information. "Umm . . . a few new ZZT sisters and I are going to some frat Rush parties."

Amber frowned. "Of course you are. That's just perfect."

Thinking quickly, Jenna blurted, "Do you want to come?"

"I don't think so. I'm not a charity case." Amber turned into her pillows, and Jenna swore she heard a sob. She didn't know what to do. If she stayed with Amber, she'd miss seeing Tiger at the Phi Omicron Chi house.

No . . . I'm not the big sister here, Jenna reminded herself, thinking about her younger siblings in Marietta, Georgia. She'd worked hard to get into ZZT, so she deserved to have some fun. Amber could take care of herself tonight, and tomorrow Jenna would see if she wanted to go get a coffee together or something.

"Okay," Jenna said. "I'll see you later, then. I'll try to be quiet when I get in."

Amber rolled over and faced the wall. "Whatev."

Jenna felt a heaviness in her chest, but she tried her best to ignore it as she walked to the elevator to meet up with her two new ZZT sisters and friends, Lora-Leigh Sorenstein and Roni Van Gelderen. The three of them had been in the same sorority recruitment group together, and now they were pretty much inseparable.

"Hey!" Lora-Leigh said. "How's the Roommate from Hell?"

"Be nice," Jenna scolded. "She's not that bad."

"Yet." Lora-Leigh adjusted one of the half-dozen earrings dangling from her left ear. Lora-Leigh was outspoken and blunt, with a raw sense of humor that Jenna usually loved, except right now, when it was making her even more nervous about Amber.

Roni seemed to read her mind, because she put her hand on Jenna's arm and said gently, "She'll be all right. Just give her some time."

"Thanks," Jenna said, smiling. Tall, beautiful Roni always seemed to know the right things to say.

"Okay, that's enough Amber-angsting for tonight," Lora-Leigh decided. "Now what do you think of the top I made today?" she asked, pointing to her stunning silk azure halter. "Am I ready for *Project Runway*?"

"You're too good for *Project Runway*," Roni said with a smile.

"Ooh, I like the way you talk. Hopefully the guys tonight will like my style, too."

Jenna giggled. "Something tells me your outfit is for more than just random frat guys."

"Yeah, well, if we just *happen* to stop by the athletic dorm for their party later, and we just *happen* to see DeShawn Pritchard there, *la culpa no es mía*." DeShawn was the junior star running back for the Latimer University football team and Lora-Leigh's current "friend with flirt privileges." There was enough chemistry between them to fuel a bonfire, whether Lora-Leigh would ever admit it or not.

Lora-Leigh pushed the "down" button on the elevator. "Well, ladies, we have a very aggressive social agenda this evening. Let's get started."

Jenna's heart raced as the elevator dropped down to ground level. She couldn't believe she was going to her first frat party tonight! Suddenly, she felt a whole universe away from the relatively quiet social life she'd had with her friends in Georgia. Without her parents around to check her curfew (What curfew? Ha!), she was going to step her social life up a notch.

"Hey, y'all! There you are," a girl sang out when Jenna stepped from the elevator into the dorm lobby. It was her new ZZT sister Sandy Cobb.

"Ready to party tonight, Cobb?" Lora-Leigh shouted out.

"You know it." Sandy was tall for starters, but in her three-inch wedge sandals, she simply towered over Jenna. She motioned outside. "There's Danika. She's going to walk over with us." Danika, one of the other new members, waved from the other side of the glass door.

5

"Ready?" Roni asked.

"As ready as I'll ever be," Jenna said, following her friends.

"Which one is Phi Omicron Chi?" Jenna asked when they turned off University Boulevard onto Fraternity Row, which sat on the east side of campus.

"It's six down on the left," Lora-Leigh said without missing a beat. "The big Tudor mansion. They're right up there with the Tri-Os in their alumni funding, so they've got one of the poshest houses."

"For someone who started out being anti-Greek," Roni teased, "you sure seem to be our resident expert."

"Hey," Lora-Leigh said. "Have you forgotten that my currently estranged mother practically branded Tri-O on my forehead in utero? The notebook she gave me to study the Latimer Greek system weighed ten pounds. I couldn't help learning something." She grinned. "Besides, in high school my friends and I used to crash LU frat parties all the time. What else is a small-town Latimer renegade supposed to do with her time?"

Jenna laughed. "How are things going on the home front anyway?" Lora-Leigh's mom was a loyal Tri-Omega and had wanted more than anything for Lora-Leigh to join their sisterhood, too. But Lora-Leigh had opted for ZZT instead, and as far as Jenna knew, her mom hadn't gotten over it.

Lora-Leigh shrugged, letting out a small sigh. "I'm still blacklisted. Every time I call my mom's cell, I get her voice mail. She's doing the Hannah Sorenstein version of mourning, which involves a lot of tearful lunches with her Tri-O sisters.

It could potentially take years of therapy or a dozen seasons of *Dr. Phil* for Mom to recover."

"We'll hope for a breakthrough," Sandy said jokingly.

"Hope for a miracle instead." Lora-Leigh laughed as she glanced over at the Pi Theta Ep house.

Jenna followed her gaze. While the other houses on Frat Row had well-groomed lawns with quiet exteriors, with rushees in dress shirts and ties coming and going, the Pi Theta Ep house was complete chaos. The front lawn of the stucco, tropical-villa-style house was littered with crushed plastic cups and empty beer cans. A group of rushees in sumo wrestler "diapers" were mud wrestling in a toddler pool as the PTE actives cheered them on.

"What are they doing?" Roni asked, looking slightly horrified at the display.

"Welcome to Rush on Frat Row. They call it 'open houses' and 'group activities,' but really it's just one ludicrous display of machismo. Male bonding at its best," Lora-Leigh said. "You've gotta love testosterone, if for its entertainment value alone."

"They're Neanderthals," Roni said.

"Regressing back to the age of primitive man is what the Pi Theta Eps are good at. They're like Latimer's resident *Animal House*. They have the least amount of funding but the most fun. And they throw some killer parties. They're way more fun than the Gamma Gamma Rhos." She nodded to the plantation-style house with the huge white columns in front. "They're so old school—a bunch of sports-coat donning, loafer-wearing academics."

"I almost feel like we shouldn't be here," Roni whispered

as a few rushees passed them by. "Our recruitment was so . . . personal. It's like we're intruding on their agenda."

"Forget your sense of propriety for a sec, Boston." Lora-Leigh rolled her eyes. "Because we *are* their agenda. The more fab chicks the frats have at their parties, the better they look to the rushees. We, ladies, are one hot commodity."

Roni laughed. "Then I'm going to sit back and enjoy being in high demand."

Jenna laughed, too, but the only guy she was really hoping to impress tonight was waiting for her at the Phi Omicron house. When they walked up the steps to the front door, she took a deep breath. Roni must have picked up on her nervousness, because she gave her a quick hand-squeeze and a reassuring smile.

Lora-Leigh led the way, following some rushees as they went inside, and Jenna felt a thrill as soon as she walked into the foyer. The whole house was pounding with music, and at least a hundred guys were crowded into the living room and den. And, even better, a hundred pairs of eyes were turned in their direction, checking them out.

"I've died and gone to hottie heaven," Danika said above the loud music.

"Why didn't we have activities like this during our recruitment?" Sandy asked.

"Now, let us go forth, be flirtful, and partify," Lora-Leigh quipped.

"You heard her." Roni laughed as she pulled Jenna into the living room with Lora-Leigh following. "Come on."

The girls pressed their way through the hordes of actives and rushees, deeper into the house, to a larger denlike room.

A wooden-railed staircase toward the back led upstairs. People sat on the steps, laughing and drinking from red plastic cups. Guys in shirts and ties stood around making small talk with the brothers of the house, no doubt trying to see if they fit in. Much like Jenna and her friends had done last week. Jenna craned her neck for a glimpse of Tiger, but she couldn't make him out in the crowd. The Foxes—the nickname for Phi Omicron Chi—were all wearing shirts with their Greek letters on them, though, so that helped differentiate between the rushees and the actives.

Jenna noticed a trophy case along the wall filled with all sorts of cups, plaques, and awards. Tiger's name jumped out at her on one of the plaques, and on closer inspection she saw it was an award for coming in first at the NCAA championship golf tournament last spring. Impressive. He'd told her he was on the LU golf team, but she had no idea he was that good. She didn't have time to check for his name on any of the other trophies, though, because her view was blocked as another group of girls clustered around the case, giggling like devoted groupies as they admired the accolades.

Roni nudged Jenna and nodded her head at the girls. "Look, they have on new member pins. I wonder what sorority they're in."

Jenna tried not to be obvious as she scoped out the other girls. "I have no clue. I can't make out what's on their pins."

"It's a three. The symbol for Tri-Omega," Lora-Leigh said drily. "The pin that will be emblazoned in my brain forever, filed under 'Parental Disappointment Number Five Hundred and Fifty-three.'"

"Oh," Roni said. "In that case, I *hate* that pin."

Lora-Leigh laughed.

"Jenna!" a voice suddenly called out over the music. "You made it!"

Her heart accelerated as she spun around. "Tiger! Hey!" She smiled and waved, then scolded herself for not being more subtle. She didn't want the whole world to know she was crushing on Tiger. But, with those piercing blue eyes and sandy, flyaway curls, who wouldn't crush on him?

"That's Tiger?" Lora-Leigh whispered to Jenna. "Yummicious. He's like an Adam Brody sans surfboard."

Jenna felt a blush cover her like a blanket of sweat as Tiger walked toward her. But then he stopped a foot away, covering his eyes. "Wait. Don't tell me which sorority. You joined . . . ZZT!"

"Right!" Jenna said. "How'd you know?"

"Lucky guess. ZZT has some of the nicest girls," Tiger said, leaning in closer. "And some of the prettiest."

Jenna laughed. Okay, so that line had been the tiniest bit cheesy. But, hey, she'd take the compliment if he was offering. She didn't dare steal a glance at Lora-Leigh, though, 'cause she knew the sappy-alarm eye roll was probably going off by now. Hoping to divert the attention away from her, she introduced Tiger to Danika, Sandy, and the other girls.

"I'm so glad y'all made it," he said. "I want you to meet some of the other guys." He waved to a couple of guys from across the room, and they nodded, heading toward them. Jenna noticed them both sneaking subtle glances at Roni, but with her modelesque figure and Natalie Portman good looks, how could they not? They introduced themselves as Corey Hock and Chris Stevens.

"Y'all want some punch?" Corey asked, holding out plastic cups to the girls.

"Is it spiked?" Lora-Leigh asked.

Chris smiled. "You know it, but you didn't hear that from me. We're not supposed to break out the good stuff until after Rush officially ends. But since it's over in fifteen, we figured we could bend the rules a little."

"Works for me," Lora-Leigh said with a grin, and the other girls took cups, too.

But when Corey offered one to Jenna, she hesitated. Even though she'd been careful about what she ate today, she'd been jacked up about this party all day, too. And she knew even a little bit of alcohol might set off her 'betes.

"Um, I think I'll take a Diet Coke instead?" Jenna muttered hesitantly, keeping her eyes on the ground to avoid quizzical glances. She was positive an onslaught of questions, or at least a teasing remark about why she wasn't drinking, was sure to come from someone. And if it came from Tiger, she'd be committing social suicide right then and there. *Please don't say anything,* she chanted in her head.

"No prob," Tiger said quickly. "I'll get it!"

Jenna looked up as Tiger grabbed a can of Diet Coke from one of the ice buckets nearby and handed it to her with a smile.

"Thanks," she said, smiling gratefully as relief swept over her.

"Pacing yourself is smart," Tiger said. "You'll be way better off than the rest of us. Once the keg is tapped, it'll only be a matter of time before half the guys here are completely lit. Rush is hard work."

Jenna couldn't help laughing. "From what I've heard, the guys have it a lot easier than we did. No preference cards, no bid night, no door songs, no ice water teas. Guys just get invited to join the frats and then show up if they want to."

"Our activities are definitely different from sorority recruitment," Tiger said. "We're having a Texas Hold 'Em poker-a-thon later this week. The Psi Kappa Upsilons have a paintball tournament. And the Delta Sigma Nus do Demolition Day with sledgehammers to beat up an old car and old computers."

"That sounds kind of violent," Roni said.

"It's supposed to be, Boston," Lora-Leigh said. "These are guys we're talking about. No candles or singing here."

"It's more like testosterone-induced insanity," Tiger said with a laugh. "I won't deny it. And we have to set up all the functions and entertaining along the way."

"Of course, some of the entertaining isn't all that bad," Chris said, smiling at Roni. "It all depends on who the guests are."

As everyone kept talking, Jenna could already guess how the pairings were going to go. It turned out that Corey was from outside Houston, and since Danika was a Texan, too, the two of them immediately started swapping stories about their home state. Chris only had eyes for Roni, but she didn't seem to mind. Roni was smiling coyly as she played with her hair, a tactic Chris seemed mesmerized by. And Sandy was deep in conversation with a cute blond Rushee on the nearby couch.

"Uh-oh," Jenna said, realizing she knew that Rushee,

"Sandy seems to be getting close to Brent Gleason."

"You know him?" Tiger asked.

Jenna nodded. "He's a bass drummer for the Marching Raiders. And he's dating the second clarinet, Lisa Stratford."

"Oh," Tiger said.

"I'll go give her the red light," Lora-Leigh volunteered. "I want to check out the rest of the scene here anyway."

Lora-Leigh headed in Sandy's direction, but not before smiling at Jenna and giving her the "he's all yours now" signal with her eyes. Jenna's heart fluttered as she turned back to Tiger.

"So how do you know who plays in the Marching Raiders band?" Tiger asked.

"Um, you're looking at the third trumpet," Jenna said. She cringed slightly as she said it, hoping that Tiger didn't have any preconceived notions about band geeks. That was always such a buzz kill at the start of any getting-to-know-you confab.

But Tiger just smiled. "That's cool. I heard brass players have great lips."

Jenna's heart stopped in her throat. Great lips for . . . kissing? Just the thought of kissing Tiger made her cheeks ignite.

"That's the theory," she said, trying to keep it light even though she was having a hard time finding her breath. "No one's ever told me if I live up to it, though."

"You'll have to test it out sometime, then," Tiger said with a laugh.

Omigod. Test it out with who? Him? "Right" was all she could manage to say.

"Well, what about dancing?" Tiger asked as the music cranked up a notch. "Are brass players good dancers?"

13

Jenna met his sparkling blue eyes and smiled. "Now that's a proven fact," she said.

"Then let's go," he said, leading her onto the dance floor.

Her skin nearly sizzled as Tiger's hand made contact with her shoulder. With her hip pressed to his, she worried that he might be able to feel her insulin pump, so she adjusted to put some space between them. But not too much. It didn't take her long (oh, maybe about five seconds) to decide that she could do this all night long and be totally and completely happy.

Roni felt the vibration of her BlackBerry in the front pocket of her jeans. She was only half-listening to Chris Stevens brag to a Rushee that they'd won the intramural football trophy last year and the two years before that. She'd enjoyed the harmless flirt session with Chris, but they'd run out of things to talk about after the first fifteen minutes, and now it was getting the teeny-tiniest bit awkward. Unfortunately, her parents had only taught her the fine art of schmoozing with people, not anything about the fine art of ditching them. (Where was Lora-Leigh when you needed her?) So when her BlackBerry buzzed, she took the opportunity to make a polite exit, excusing herself to duck onto the front terrace.

She glanced at her BlackBerry to see an e-mail from Kiersten, her best friend from back home. Roni scrolled down and read:

> Roni! I got your message about ZZT! So incredibly happy for you. Enjoy yourself and when you come down off your cloud, call me with the details. Can't wait to hear all about it!
> XOXO, Kiersten

Roni sat down in one of the rocking chairs that lined the Phi Omicron Chi porch and reread Kiersten's message. Roni had called Kiersten yesterday after the new member ceremony, but she'd missed her. Kiersten was the one who had encouraged her to go through sorority recruitment, since she, herself, had been a sorority girl during her time at Emerson University in Boston. Kiersten had been Roni's au pair growing up, but now she was her staunchest, most loyal supporter. More so than her parents, who hadn't even bothered to call and see which sorority she'd joined. Roni's choosing Latimer University—a state college, God forbid!—over her mother's Wellesley and her father's Harvard was unforgivable, apparently.

Roni had to get updates on her parents from their housekeeper. The latest Van Gelderen headlines were that her father, a prominent Boston attorney, was planning to run for an open state legislature seat, and her mother had been nominated for Wellesley Alumna of the Year. Surprise, surprise. She just wanted them to tell her the news themselves. No matter how hard she tried not to set herself up for disappointment, she couldn't help wishing that there was more of a connection between her and her parents. Like, maybe, familial love and affection?

Kiersten cared, though. She'd cared enough to e-mail and call Roni throughout the sorority recruitment process and give her advice on how to choose the right house. Roni would give her a buzz tomorrow afternoon, when she knew Kiersten would be home.

"I never would've figured you for a social pariah, Boston," a familiar voice said, and Roni looked up to see Lora-Leigh.

"Didn't hobnobbing with New England's A-list teach you anything?"

"Yeah." Roni smiled. "It taught me to wish I *was* a social pariah."

Lora-Leigh laughed. "You're not getting your wish tonight. In case it's escaped your attention, there's a room full of gorgeous guys in there."

"I was just checking a message," she said, standing up and smoothing out her top.

"Messages can wait," Lora-Leigh said. "The party can't."

Roni let Lora-Leigh lead her back into the room; then they scanned the crowd. A lot of the Rushees were starting to leave, but there were about a dozen or so left in the room talking to the actives. Her heart nearly came to a complete halt when she saw . . . him.

It was the guy from the natatorium.

Earlier in the week, she'd swum in the lane next to him at the LU indoor swimming pool. They'd barely spoken, but they'd struck up a friendly race and had shared a smile before they went their separate ways. There had definitely been a brief flash of chemistry.

And now, here he was—across the room, standing with a Dr Pepper in one hand and the other tucked into the pocket of his jeans. Was he a Phi Omicron Chi? No, he wasn't wearing their letters. Definitely a Rushee. He was talking with a couple of the Foxes.

But as Roni was looking, he raised his eyes to hers and smiled in a flash of recognition, then motioned her to come over.

She smiled and turned to Lora-Leigh. "I'll catch up with you in a few, okay?"

"Sure," Lora-Leigh said. "I'll go see if I can track down Jenna and Lion."

"Tiger," Roni said with a giggle, then headed toward the mystery man.

When she reached him, he stepped away from the rest of his group and smiled. Roni swallowed down her hammering heart. What was wrong with her? She normally didn't have a problem talking to guys. In fact, in Boston, Roni'd had her fair share of "suitors," as her mom had called them. But the guys she'd dated had been boarding school preps stamped for Ivy League. They were mostly matches encouraged or (even worse!) arranged by her parents. Even though she'd never been without an escort for dances and dinner parties, she'd never connected with any of those guys. Playing the dating game without her parents' looming shadows was a different experience entirely. Here, Roni didn't have her impeccable family name to pave the way for conversation. Here, she was just like everyone else, and she was suddenly at a complete loss for words.

"I've been waiting for my rematch," he said.

"Are you sure you really want one?" Roni teased, finally finding her voice. "Most people don't like losing."

He laughed. "I was hoping I'd have a chance to redeem myself. You know, heal my wounded male ego, that sort of thing."

"I'm ready whenever you are," Roni challenged, tossing her hair over her shoulder and putting on a killer smile. The tactic had always worked to reel in the Boston preps, and she hoped it would have the same effect on this guy.

"Good," he said, extending a hand. "Lance McManus."

She felt a thrill as she took his hand and introduced herself.

He cocked his head to the side. "I assume from the accent that you're not from 'round here?"

"No, I'm from Boston."

"LU's a long way from home."

"Thankfully," she said with a twist of sarcasm. "What I mean is, it's nice to be somewhere different. Now I'm just trying to fit in and get used to the South."

"Oh, Florida's not really the South. It's . . . Florida."

"Are you from Florida?"

"I am now. My family has moved around a lot over the years. I was an army brat." He squinted at her closely. "Hey, aren't you taking Geography 101?"

She rolled her eyes. "Yeah, I have Dr. Sylvester. I can barely stay awake in his class."

His smile widened. "I *thought* I saw you in class! I have the Tuesday lab with you."

"You do?" Her pulse skittered. "But I haven't seen you. . . ." How could she *not* have seen him?

"You sit up front, but I sit way in the back." He peered down at her with his thick bangs falling nearly into his eyes. "Personally, I think I have the best view from the back row." He smiled at her, and her heart jumped to her throat.

"So I'm guessing if you're bored in Dr. Sylvester's class that you're not a Geography major."

"No way," Roni said emphatically. "I'm undeclared right now. I figured I'd get the core curriculum classes over with first and then see what interests me so I can start focusing junior year.

But I think I can safely say Geography is out of the running." And she was *not* going to automatically do pre-law, either, just because that was what her father wanted . . . expected. "What about you?" she asked Lance.

"I'm thinking about going pre-med," Lance said. "Believe it or not, Anatomy 101 sounds way more interesting than Geography."

Roni laughed. "I think I'd choose studying earthquakes over cadavers, even if it means putting up with Dr. Sylvester. But the idea of helping to cure people of disease. That's an amazing thing."

"Plus, the doctors in *Grey's Anatomy* get all the cute girls," Lance said with a laugh. "Since I've always had bad luck in that area, I figured pre-med was worth it to see if I could improve my odds." He grinned at her.

"Are—are you having fun rushing?" she asked, having a mental fight with the blush she could feel creeping across her cheeks.

"I guess," he said. "My folks thought it would be a good way to get more involved here at Latimer, but I already have a full course load, and I'm on the LU swim team, too. I don't know if I'll have enough time to dedicate to a fraternity. But it's nice meeting everyone. Either way, I'll get some friends out of it, so it's all good."

"I just joined ZZT, and so far, Greek life is amazing. I've already met so many awesome people."

He leaned down to her—he had to be at least six-six—and said in a stage whisper, "Maybe I should join ZZT, too."

She smiled, glad that she seemed to be making some progress

on the flirt front with him. Talking to Lance was easy. No mandatory polite inquiries about his family's health, no small talk about summering in the Hamptons. No, just a getting-to-know-you chat without the WASPy niceties. It was actually— what was the word?—fun!

Roni had no idea how much time had passed until Danika tapped her on the shoulder. "Here you are! Lora-Leigh and Jenna are waiting outside. We're heading over to the athletic dorm for their party. They've got a band and everything." Danika looked at Lance and back at Roni. "You coming?"

Reluctantly, Roni nodded. She didn't want to leave Lance, but she wasn't ready to stick it out solo at the party without the other girls. "I've got to go," she said to him. "It was great talking to you, Lance."

"Finally," he said.

She took two steps, stopped, and turned back to face him. "Maybe I'll see you at the pool again?"

"Definitely," Lance said. "I'll be waiting for that rematch."

His hazel eyes connected with hers, and he smiled one last time. As she stepped onto the front porch to catch up with the other girls, she couldn't stop smiling herself. Oh, yes. There'd be a rematch. She'd make sure of that.

Lora-Leigh could hear the pounding of the bass in the band long before the girls reached the athletic dorm, and her adrenaline picked up the pace as soon as she did. She'd been waiting all night for this party, biding her time while Roni, Jenna, and the other girls flirted with the frat boys. She could take or leave the frat guys she'd met so far, but she couldn't say the same for Jenna, who had been on a guy-high ever since she'd seen Tiger tonight.

"You keep smiling like that and you're going to pull a muscle," Lora-Leigh joked as they walked toward the end of Frat Row.

"I can't help it," Jenna said blissfully. "Tiger asked me to come to his next golf tournament. Did I tell you that?"

"About five hundred times," she said with a laugh.

"Sorry. I just can't believe he asked me to go."

"That's all right," Roni said. "It's your first date with an older college man. You *should* be excited."

"I sense a sordid, scandalous love affair in the works," Lora-Leigh teased.

"Sordid and scandalous?" Jenna laughed. "I'll settle for sweet with a little bit of sappy thrown in for good measure."

Lora-Leigh shrugged. "To each her own."

Personally, she thought scandalous might be fun, but Jenna was too softhearted for that. Lora-Leigh, on the other hand, had always had tons of guys as best friends, or even friends she dated casually like her bud Brian from high school. A big, long-term BF had always eluded her, and that was fine by her. But DeShawn Pritchard was different. He was a walking enigma—a die-hard jock with a serious art talent.

She and DeShawn had Western Civ and Art classes together. He spent most of his time in Western Civ snoozing behind his Ray-Ban sunglasses. But in Art, he came to life, so intensely absorbed in sketching and painting that half the time he didn't even stir from his seat until ten minutes after class ended. She'd snuck a few peeks at his canvases, and they were incredible.

He turned the brainless muscleman stereotype on its head, and she found that downright sexy.

"Well, ladies," Lora-Leigh said as the dorm courtyard came into view. "I think we've found the hot spot of the night."

There was no question about it. This party was hopping. The band was pushing the amps to the max, and the courtyard was packed with people. The football players in the crowd were obvious, towering over everyone. The dorm sat at the end of Frat Row next to the Omega Phi house, so there were several dozen frat guys who had spilled over into the courtyard during the post-Rush party.

"I think I liked our odds at the Phi Omicron house better," Sandy said. "Look at all the girls here."

It was true. Unlike the girl/guy ratio at the frat parties, here the girls clearly outnumbered the guys.

"They're cleat chasers," Lora-Leigh said, rolling her eyes. "They know LU has a great athletics program with pro potential, so they come here to nab a future proball player. NFL, NBA, or MLB, doesn't matter. They're not picky, and they're all the same—a bunch of miniskirted, stiletto-wearing carbon copies."

"But you're here chasing one of LU's star athletes, too," Jenna pointed out with a good-natured, teasing smile.

"I never chase," Lora-Leigh said emphatically. "That's the act of only the truly desperate. *I'm* in a league of my own, girlfriend!"

"Is that so, Curly?" a rumbling voice said behind her.

Lora-Leigh froze. Oh, no. It couldn't be. There was no way that *he* had heard her say that. But he had. Because standing behind her was DeShawn Pritchard, grinning down at her, clearly enjoying the fact that he'd caught her off guard. Well, she wasn't going to let him revel in self-satisfaction for too long.

"You know it," Lora-Leigh said, recovering in time to throw him a chill smile. "But do you think you can handle it?"

"Not even a question," DeShawn said with a wink.

Lora-Leigh avoided Roni's and Jenna's eyes, wondering if Jenna's jaw had dropped yet. She was pretty sure neither of them was used to talking like that to guys, but Lora-Leigh relished it. Especially with someone like DeShawn, who could match her head-on in conversation without being intimidated by her.

"I see you've got your posse with you," DeShawn said, smiling at Jenna, Roni, and the other girls.

"Yeah, my sorority sisters." Lora-Leigh ran through the introductions she felt like she'd already made a hundred times tonight.

"Y'all help yourselves to some drinks and get out there and dance," DeShawn ordered. "We have the band until midnight."

"Great!" Roni said, clearly picking up on the subtle hint. "Come on, Jenna, I'm parched."

Jenna and Roni headed for the drink table, with Sandy and Danika following.

Lora-Leigh smiled at DeShawn, grateful to have a few minutes to talk to him alone. There were times when her sisters were absolute essentials, but when she had the perfect opportunity to talk to DeShawn mano a mano, essentials they were not. "So . . . are you ready for the game against Georgia Tech next week?"

"I better be," he said. "Coach Meyers has had us running the Gauntlet six times a week to prep."

"Brutal," Lora-Leigh said. Since she'd grown up going to LU games with her mom and dad, she knew all about the Gauntlet. A training ground that involved a timed workout with agility ladders, swinging hundred-pound sandbags, knee-high trainers, parachute resistance trainers, and hurdles, it wasn't so much an obstacle course as it was a deranged torture chamber.

"He's hoping we'll make it to the Gator Bowl this year," DeShawn said. "If we survive till then."

"No wonder you've been snoring in Western Civ," Lora-Leigh teased.

DeShawn shrugged. "I have to save up my reserves for Art and Architecture class. That's my soul food."

"I know what you mean," Lora-Leigh said. "My core classes are completely yawn-worthy. But Art is different. I'm just biding my time until I can take all design classes and nothing else."

"What type of design?" DeShawn asked.

"I'm wearing it," Lora-Leigh said, motioning to her top. "Fashion design is *my* soul food. Can't live without it."

"So you made that?" DeShawn asked, then whistled in appreciation. "Nice, Curly. *Very* nice."

Lora-Leigh's temp rose about twenty degrees with DeShawn's approval, but she willed her cheeks to stay cool. "Thanks," she said. "It's just too bad you're not in the market to buy a clothing line."

"With taste like that, you'll get there," he said. He finished his can of Red Bull in one swift gulp and leaned toward her.

"Hey, you want to come upstairs with me for a sec? There's something I want to show you."

"Oh, I don't know," Lora-Leigh said teasingly. "Us southern ladies should always be accompanied by a chaperone when in the company of a gentleman."

DeShawn laughed. "Come on," he said, taking her hand to lead her away from the crowds of gyrating dancers.

She followed him into the dorm, a veritable ghost town with the party going on outside, and upstairs to his room, all the while wondering where this was going.

He walked into his room, then propped the door open, explaining, "House rules. In the presence of a lady." Lora-Leigh stepped across the threshold and looked around in surprise. Instead of the football paraphernalia she'd assumed would be gracing the walls, she found Salvador Dalí posters and even a few Picassos.

"Definitely not the locker room I was expecting," she said.

"I think I'm supposed to take that as a compliment?" DeShawn said with a laugh.

"You are."

He led her to a white drafting table in the corner, littered with charcoal, sketch pads, and blueprints. DeShawn pulled a large portfolio from underneath the table and laid it across his bed.

"I haven't shown these to anyone yet," he said, with a slight hint at shyness that seemed in complete opposition to his massive build. "My Architecture prof hasn't even seen them. I did them over the summer at home. But you have a great eye, and I thought you'd give me an honest opinion."

He opened the portfolio, and Lora-Leigh bit back a gasp as she looked at the first sketch—a simple but beautiful ranch-style house with clean lines and floor-to-ceiling windows that seemed to hint at a little bit of Frank Lloyd Wright. The next sketch was a two-story mountain cabin that had a rotunda in the center with a domed ceiling made completely of glass. On and on the sketches went—at least a dozen, each more incredible than the last.

"These are amazing," Lora-Leigh finally managed to say when she'd found her voice.

"You really think so?" DeShawn said, looking relieved. "I'm trying to break the mold, you know."

"I'd say you broke it wide open."

"Thanks, Curly," DeShawn said. "That means something, coming from you." He slipped his arm around her in a half-hug, but he didn't let go right away, and a wave of electricity bolted through her.

"Hey, DeShawwwwwwwwn," a singsongy voice suddenly called out, and DeShawn's arm quickly slid off Lora-Leigh's shoulders.

She looked up to see a girl leaning against the doorway in skintight, low-rise jeans and a cropped top. Her teardrop belly chain hung from her navel and just brushed the top of the dragonfly tattoo across her left hip. A classic cleat chaser.

"Here you are," the girl said, walking into the room hips first. "I was looking for you, so your bud Mike let me come up to see if you were in your room."

DeShawn smiled. "Hey there, Kimberly. Whatcha up to?"

Kimberly slinked up to DeShawn's side. "Same old, same old. You're looking cute as ever."

Oh, please. If Lora-Leigh had to hear much more of this, she was going to gag. Was DeShawn really buying into this girl's calculated giggles, eyelash batting, and ego stroking? He was above that, wasn't he?

"So," Kimberly continued, linking her arm through his, "when am I going to get that dance you promised?"

"Um" was all DeShawn could say, looking uncertainly from Kimberly to Lora-Leigh. Meanwhile, Kimberly shifted her mascara-heavy lashes toward Lora-Leigh and smiled pointedly, as if to imply that Lora-Leigh wasn't needed here anymore and should move along.

Lora-Leigh counted to three, waiting for DeShawn to make a move...any move. But he just stood there. And suddenly, the silence spelled out a-w-k-w-a-r-d in a big way. *Got it.* Message received, loud and clear. So DeShawn *was* just another sucker for the cleat chasers. So much for giving him the benefit of the doubt. Now she knew better. And she was not going to play the part of the naive, rejected girl left on the sidelines. She'd never give Kimberly the satisfaction. Or DeShawn the ego boost, for that matter.

"You know what?" Lora-Leigh said. "You two go dance. I've gotta get going."

Just as she turned, DeShawn captured her hand in his, stepping away from Kimberly. "Wait, Lora-Leigh, stay—"

"Nah." She shrugged his hand off as playfully as she could manage. "You have plenty of company already, and my sisters are probably looking for me. I'll see you in class later."

Kimberly smiled smugly as Lora-Leigh walked past, and Lora-Leigh resisted the urge to ask if J.Lo was missing her jeans.

Lora-Leigh caught up with the other girls outside and, after hearing the story, they decided it was time to walk to the twenty-four-hour Albertsons for some Ben & Jerry's pints. An hour later, as she was taking her last bite of Chunky Monkey ice cream, Lora-Leigh made her decision. If DeShawn was just another jock, fine by her. She wasn't going to waste time mourning over a walking cliché. She was holding out for an original. Besides, she had plenty of classes to keep her busy this semester and, more importantly, plenty of sisters to bond with, plenty of outfits to make, and plenty of ice cream to eat.

CHAPTER
2

Lora-Leigh had never been a fan of sitting still, especially for a call-to-order type of meeting with motions, voting, blah, blah, blah. But when the new members and actives gathered Sunday evening in the ZZT living room for the first official house meeting, she felt a bubble of excitement tickling her chest. The actives were going to give the new members an introduction to ZZT tonight and then hold their own chapter meeting. New members weren't allowed to attend chapter meetings—where they voted and made house-affecting decisions—which was fine by Lora-Leigh. She figured the overview of ZZT was more than enough. But she still couldn't wait to see what ZZT had in store for them. She'd gone from anti-Greek to pro-ZZT, and once she'd made that decision, she knew she'd throw herself into ZZT as passionately as she threw herself into her sewing.

As she squeezed her way onto the already crowded couch with Roni and Jenna, she looked around at the girls filling nearly every corner of the large room.

"It's like one big lovefest in here," she said, watching girls laughing and chatting about classes and boyfriends.

"Isn't this just fabulous?" Jenna cried excitedly, perched on the edge of the couch with pen and paper ready for note taking. "All of us here. Together. Sisters."

"I don't know if I can handle all the emo," Lora-Leigh said.

"Of course you can," someone said behind Lora-Leigh, wrapping friendly arms around her shoulders.

Lora-Leigh looked up and saw Camille Crawford, who had hosted her at every recruitment event and convinced her ZZT was where she belonged.

"I see you came back," Camille said.

"Thought I'd ditch you once I was out the door on Bid Day?" Lora-Leigh teased.

Camille's smile grew huge. "Admit it; we had you at 'hello.'"

"Oh, she'll never admit that," Roni piped in. "Be glad she's here. And wearing a new member pin, no less."

"Hey, the pin just happens to go with my other hardware," Lora-Leigh said, revealing the dangly rose earrings she'd chosen to wear tonight. Of course, she loved her white rose pin more than she ever thought she would, but admitting that wasn't her style.

"Nice try, but I know you're jacked up to be here," Camille said, nudging Lora-Leigh. "And I'm happy you're all here!" she said to Jenna, Roni, and the other new members sitting around them.

The room quieted down, and Camille waved to Lora-Leigh, then took her place among the other actives as the president of the sorority called the meeting to order. "Hi, I'm Marissa. I just want to say how awesome it is to have such a great group of new members. Over the next few weeks, you'll be going through your new member education period, learning things about the organization as a whole and about our chapter here at Latimer. We're all one big family, and we welcome you."

Everyone clapped, and Marissa went on with her introduction, explaining all the fun stuff that ZZT would be involved in— football games, Homecoming, fraternity swaps and mixers, and philanthropy projects, too.

"We have full house meetings every Sunday night before the actives' official chapter meeting," Marissa said. "New member meetings will be every Wednesday night after dinner here at the house for the next eight weeks until your initiation ceremony. At that time, you will be ready to accept the rituals and oaths of our great sorority and become full-fledged, initiated members."

Lora-Leigh was surprised that her heart did a ridiculous dip. Initiation would be such an amazing experience, and she couldn't wait for that day to come. She exchanged smiles with Roni and Jenna.

"There'll be more info about each activity as the semester goes on," she said, "but I wanted y'all to start brainstorming about Homecoming, since that's one of our biggest events just before the Thanksgiving holiday. The theme this year is Latimer Memories. ZZT will be building a theme-inspired float for the Homecoming parade. Start thinking of some possibilities now; we'll have to have the float design chosen at least a month before Homecoming so we have time to build it. In just a couple weeks, you'll be voting for a New Member

President, and she will be instrumental in the planning and organizing of your part of Homecoming."

Lora-Leigh's ears perked up. She remembered that her mom had been the New Member President during her first semester as a Tri-Omega. She didn't know much about the role the president played, but maybe she could ask her mom about it later. She usually loved talking about her Tri-O days, and if she thought Lora-Leigh was interested in running for president, it might help smooth things over between them. Or at least give them something—anything—to talk about. Lora-Leigh twirled an earring as she thought about it.

"Hey," Jenna whispered, nudging Lora-Leigh. "Aren't you going to take notes?"

Lora-Leigh laughed and tapped her head. "I've got a steel trap right up here, baby. Who needs notes?"

Lora-Leigh tried her best to listen as Marissa finished and went on to introduce Mrs. Walsh, the housemother, and some other important actives, but it was getting tough to stay focused. So many names, events, meetings—it was all a bit overwhelming.

The other girls seemed a little lost in the nonstop stream of info, too, so it was a great relief when Camille shouted, "Hey, Marissa. What about the parties and the boys?"

Everyone laughed, and suddenly the whole room came to life again.

Marissa snickered and did a weak "shame on you" with her eyes. "All right, all right, I hear you. Heather, do you want to come up and give these girls what they want?"

Heather Bourke, the Social Chair, stepped to the front with a smile, and Lora-Leigh immediately recognized the short-haired blonde from sorority recruitment. She'd been the head Rho Gamma and was loads of fun, so Lora-Leigh'd been glad to learn she was a ZZT.

"Did somebody say party?" Heather said, and a cheer rose up from the girls. "Well, that's my specialty. I'm no matchmaker. Y'all are on your own in that department. But it's my job to organize swaps and mixers with the fraternities so you can get to know more people—*especially* guys."

Another collective hoot sounded out, and Lora-Leigh held back a smirk. Please. Some of these girls were starting to sound as desperate as the cleat chasers.

Heather handed out the calendar of social events.

"Lora-Leigh," Jenna whispered, looking more than a little concerned. "What's a swap?"

"Well, it involves a lot of lurid, naked dancing around a bonfire," Lora-Leigh said, deadpanning. "Everyone does it."

Jenna visibly paled. "What?" she practically shrieked.

"Relax." Lora-Leigh laughed. "I was just kidding. A swap's a party where new members from one fraternity and one sorority get matched up on a sort-of group blind date. A mixer's a party, too, but it's just everyone hanging out without the pairing up. Got it?"

"I think so," Jenna said.

"Consider them your chance to score dates for the football games," Lora-Leigh said. Most of the student body at LU had dates for the games. It was an unofficial university tradition. And even if frat guys weren't her first choice, Lora-Leigh was sure she could have fun with them at a game.

"I can't have dates for the games," Jenna said forlornly. "I'll be playing with the band."

"That's all right, Jenna," Roni whispered with a smile. "There's only one guy you'd want to go with to the games anyway, right?"

Jenna blushed, and Lora-Leigh knew she was thinking of Tiger.

"I'll give updates every week if there are any changes," Heather continued. "And it just so happens that I got a call from the Kappa Omega fraternity today. They want to have a swap with our new members Friday night. The theme will be Graffiti Night, so you'll graffiti your own T-shirts to wear to the party. It should be fun!"

"Oh, no," Jenna moaned. "I'm going to Tiger's golf tournament on Friday."

"The swap won't start until at least eight or nine," Roni said. "You'll be able to make it back in time."

"Tiger's playing in the afternoon, so it'll be tight," Jenna said worriedly. "But I'll try."

"There is no trying; there is only doing," Lora-Leigh teased. "I'll handle your shirt for the swap; you just take care of getting there. Deal?"

Jenna laughed. "I'm a little scared about the shirt, but . . . deal."

"The swap on Friday will be at the KO house," Heather went on, "but some of the mixers later will be off-campus at people's houses or apartments."

"Ahhh . . . a way around the administration sniffing out alcohol," Lora-Leigh said with a snicker. She was glad to hear it, especially since her dad—LU's dean of students—happened to be the number one authority she didn't want spying on her "extracurricular activities."

"Now that we've gotten that really important matter out of the way," Marissa said with a teasing smile, "let's move on."

Marissa wrapped up the rest of her spiel quickly and then led the actives upstairs for the chapter meeting while Beverly, the New Member Educator, took over.

Roni whispered to Lora-Leigh, "Beverly was my escort during recruitment! She's such a sweetie!"

Lora-Leigh looked at Beverly in her sleek capris and knit tank, her wavy brown hair pulled back, and understood right away why Roni and Beverly hit it off. They both had the same sophisti-chic style and a certain grace about their movements.

"Once y'all get to know each other and then pick a New Member President," Beverly said, "I'll work very closely with her to teach you everything you'll need to know about Zeta Zeta Tau. I'm here to be your teacher, your coach, your guide, and hopefully your friend. It's my job to provide you with the most positive new member experience, encouraging friendship, character development, and relationship building."

Beverly passed out the new member binders, and Lora-Leigh gawked at all of the pages. The binder, which was full of handouts about all the new member activities and events on top of the rest of the ZZT social activities scheduled for the next eight weeks, almost put her mom's notebook to shame!

"Look at this calendar," Jenna said meekly. "There's an activity planned for almost every day."

"So what's the prob?" Lora-Leigh asked.

"Nothing," Jenna mumbled. "I mean, I just have tons going on already. I have band practice every afternoon, and I can't miss too many rehearsals or they'll kick me out." She sighed. "I was hoping to move up to second trumpet at the end of this semester, too."

"You can do it all," Roni said. "I can help you plan out your schedule, if you want."

"Thanks," Jenna said. "I'm sure I can juggle everything. I did it at home with my family, and I can do it here, too."

"It's all a state of mind, girlfriend," Lora-Leigh said, trying to be encouraging. But even though Jenna was smiling, her smile was strained with worry.

And the truth was, Lora-Leigh was having a tough time keeping track of everything herself, as the paper bombardment kept coming. Beverly passed around a pamphlet from the national ZZT office called *We Are Family in ZZT.*" It was chock-full of information about the founding sisters and what they did to establish the tradition of Zeta Zeta Tau. Opening the pamphlet, she saw a picture of the ZZT crest. It had two crossed silver swords over a globe of the world with a white rose (their official flower) crowning the top, but the meanings of these things wouldn't be revealed to them until the initiation ceremony.

And as if all that wasn't enough, also in the binder were contact numbers and e-mails for the chapter officers; a sheet of financial information about slush funds for T-shirts, parties, and other ZZT odds and ends; lists of dues, fees, and meal plans.

"Okay, enough paperwork," Beverly said. "Let's move on to the fun stuff! After tonight's meeting, you'll receive your first

Rose Bud. This is a sister to welcome you to ZZT, to make you feel at home. You'll get a new Rose Bud each week of your new member time up until you choose your Big Sister."

"It sounds like a Rose Bud is sort of like a Big Sister?" Jenna asked.

"A little bit. A Rose Bud is a friend to help you through your new member education period. A Big Sister . . ." Beverly trailed off for a second. "Well, a big sister is that special someone who takes you under her wing and becomes the one person you can go to no matter what. When the time comes for the selection process, you'll be able to request who you'd like for your Big Sister, and she you."

"Sounds amazing," Roni whispered to Lora-Leigh. "But I don't know how I'll ever choose one. All the actives seem so great."

"I always wanted a real big sister," Jenna said. "Someone to go to for advice, you know? It'll be nice to finally have one. Who do you want as a Big Sis, Lora-Leigh?"

"I don't know, but I hope Camille's my first Rose Bud," Lora-Leigh admitted.

"Hey . . . pizzas are here," Danika announced from the back of the room, and soon everyone was scarfing down slices and talking all at once about Rose Buds and Big Sisters and Homecoming and everything they'd learned so far tonight. Beverly handed out Getting to Know You questionnaires for each of the girls to fill out and then collected them to put into a folder that all the new members could look at to learn more about one another. Then, following a reading of the chapter history and founding in Macon, Georgia, Beverly had them all stand in a circle around the room, holding hands.

"We want each and every one of you to take pride in being a part of ZZT," Beverly said. "You were chosen to be here, and you chose to be with us. Remember that, and put your best foot forward. Get to meetings on time, and try to come to all house events. Always bring your enthusiasm to everything you do."

"Now, if you'll indulge me . . . " Beverly put a CD into the sound system and pressed "play." The familiar eighties song "We Are Family" rang out, and Beverly led them in singing. Instead of singing, "I've got all my sisters with me," they inserted a sister's name in place of the lyrics. Each girl took a turn dancing and grooving inside the circle so everyone could put a name to a face. Normally, Lora-Leigh would've been the first to scoff at something so campy. But as everyone sang, laughing and clapping along, Lora-Leigh couldn't help but join in. Because here, in the company of new friends, campy suddenly seemed doable, and even fun.

Roni took a sip of her mocha latte and scanned the list of dues in her ZZT info packet one more time.

"Memorizing the Greek alphabet?" a voice said above her, and she looked up to see Lora-Leigh and Jenna smiling down at her. They'd agreed to meet for A.M. coffees at The Funky Bean café on the Strip before their Monday morning classes started.

"Memorizing the speech I'm going to give to my parents about my dues," Roni said as Lora-Leigh and Jenna sat down with their drinks. At the meeting last night, Stacy Fagen, the sorority's VP of Finance, had explained the list of fees. For them there was a new member fee, badge fee, initiation fee, and chapter fee. Then the fees would go up once the girls were initiated, with money going to house maintenance, dues, and meal plans. Even the initial new member fees were a little daunting.

"The ZZT dues aren't anywhere near as bad as the Tri-Omegas'. Thus, the Ethan Allen furniture filling their house. At least our dues aren't that scary." Lora-Leigh took a sip of her coffee. "Four hundred bucks is nothing to your 'rents, right?"

"Sort of," Roni admitted, trying not to feel awkward that her friends knew her parents were well off. "But that doesn't matter. They weren't happy about footing the bill for my tuition to come here. I don't know what they'll say to this."

"I know. My parents weren't counting on these fees on top of all my other expenses," Jenna said. "So I told my mom I'd contribute to the dues out of the money my grandparents gave me for graduation. That helped."

"What about you, Lora-Leigh?" Roni asked. "You think your mother will be okay with paying dues to ZZT instead of Tri-Omega?"

Lora-Leigh ran her fingers through her hair, setting the curls away from her face. "I called her last night, but I didn't even get the chance to ask. When Mom heard my voice on the line, she just handed the phone to my dad. The Ice Queen continues her reign." Lora-Leigh rolled her eyes. "My dad said he'd pay the dues, but I could hear Mom in the background banging pots and pans and slamming kitchen cabinet doors. That's her version of staging a protest. If I'd joined Tri-Omega, Mom would have sold a body part if that's what it took to cover all of the expenses. But ZZT is a different story."

"So what will your dad do?" Jenna asked.

"Oh, he already paid," Lora-Leigh said. "He stopped by Tuthill this morning to bring me my mail from home and drop off a check for the dues. He always finds ways around Mom's tirades." Lora-Leigh smirked. "In the meantime, I'm making my own version of a peace offering for her. Check it out." Lora-Leigh pulled her sketchbook from her bag and opened it to a drawing of a crimson silk shrug with a silver-and-pearl clasp in the center.

"Ooh la la. Very Marc Jacobs," Roni complimented.

"You think so?" Lora-Leigh said with a pleased smile. "My mom bought this fab Donna Karan dress for the big faculty banquet in November. She showed it to me before the family feud started. It has spaghetti straps, and I knew she was looking for a wrap or jacket to cover her shoulders at the dinner, so I thought I'd make her something. If clothing isn't an acceptable olive branch, I don't know what is."

"She'll love it," Jenna said. "How could she not when you're making it for her?"

"That's exactly why she might hate it," Lora-Leigh said.

"Jenna's right; it'll be perfect." Roni stood up. "Well, I have half an hour before my class, and I should call home. I'm going to head back to Tuthill for a few. I'll catch up with you guys later?"

The girls nodded. "Good luck," Jenna said.

"Thanks. I'll need it."

Ten minutes later, in the comfort of her own room, Roni dialed her parents' number.

"Van Gelderen residence. How may I help you?"

Roni cringed at the voice. So official. So fake. Her parents had obviously parted ways with Olivia, their former housekeeper, and hired someone new to answer the phone and tend to their every whim.

"Hi, this is Veronica. May I speak to my mother, please?"

"Just a moment, Miss Veronica."

Roni smirked at the "Miss." How pretentious could her parents get?

A few moments later, Roni heard the extension click on. "What is it, dear? I'm meeting Martha Ducett for drinks at the Ritz in fifteen minutes."

The familiar throat-tightening endangered Roni's breathing. Why did her mother always have to make her feel like everything she said and did was an imposition? The Ritz was only a few blocks from the Van Gelderen town house anyway. And it wasn't like she'd drive herself.

"It's nice to hear your voice, too, Mother," Roni said drily.

Cathryn Minson Van Gelderen scoffed. "I see that hick school is teaching you to disrespect your elders."

"I'm not disrespecting anyone. Latimer's a great school," Roni started. "I'm having a fabulous time, and I'm getting a great education."

"*That* remains to be seen," her mother said.

Roni bit her lip, forcing herself to swallow down a cutting retort. She wanted just one conversation with her mother to go smoothly. A brief vision of a *Gilmore Girl*–style mother–daughter chat over cappuccinos flickered before her eyes. But it was quickly dimmed by a looming silence, and Roni wondered if her mother was even still there.

"I really do have to run, Veronic'er. Was there a reason you called?"

Because I kind of miss you? Because I hoped you missed me, too?

"I have to pay my sorority dues this week."

"And?"

"I need money for it, please." Roni told her the amount and listened to the near moan in response. It wasn't an exorbitant amount. Four hundred dollars was chump change to a Van Gelderen, less than the price of just one of the dozens of pairs of Jimmy Choo shoes gracing her mom's closet.

But her mother sighed as if this request would be like parting with a vital organ *and* her fortune. "Honestly, Veronic'er," her mother said, "call your father and let him deal with this. He's at the office, of course. I have to go. I'm late."

Click.

Roni stared at the phone for a moment and staved back the hot tears that threatened to fall from her eyes. Fine, she'd call her father. His executive assistant would answer—poor woman had no life of her own. She'd make excuses for him, Roni would hold, and then her father would be as terse and impatient with her as her mother had been. Story of her life.

With growing dread, she dialed his office number anyway, just as a knock sounded on her door.

"I'm so glad you're here, Roni!" Beverly Chang said when Roni opened her door. "I tried to catch you after—oh! You're on the phone . . . sorry!"

"That's okay. I'm on hold."

Beverly held out a large blue-and-white gift bag with something that resembled a feathery boa around the top of it. "I just wanted to give this to you. I'm your Rose Bud this week. I know you like to swim, and so do I. I thought we could go work out together one day this week and then go to the Fast Break Café for burgers and fries. What do you say?"

Roni's threatening tears dried away. In one short minute, Beverly Chang had paid closer, more detailed attention to Roni than her parents had in years. She took the bag—heavy with ZZT trinkets and Power Bars—and smiled gratefully.

"I'd love to, Beverly." She held up one finger when her father's assistant came on. "Hi, yes, this is Veronica. I'm holding for my father." She covered up the phone and said to Beverly, "Thanks for being my Rose Bud."

"No prob. I'm looking forward to it!" Beverly winked and waved, already heading toward the elevator. "I'll chat with you later."

Roni nodded, just as her dad's assistant came back on the phone. "Veronica, your father's on a conference call right now," she said. "He asked me to find out what you need."

Roni rolled her eyes and tightened her grip on the phone. "I need to know how to pay my sorority dues."

"One minute."

A massive sigh escaped Roni's chest as the assistant put her on hold again. She tapped her foot impatiently as the elevator music repeated in the earpiece.

What seemed like an eon later, the assistant came back on the line. "Veronica, he said for you to use your American Express for anything you need."

Translation: Don't call and bother him.

"Thanks," Roni said quietly, and clicked her phone off.

Why couldn't she have a normal home life? Like Jenna.

Jenna's mom and three sisters had called her at least three times already, not counting the daily e-mails and huge care package in the mail. Roni supposed there were just some people who weren't meant to have that perfect childhood.

Well, her biological family might not care about her, but she was finding that her sisters did—Beverly included. So Roni was ready to be the best new member they had, to make them her new family.

Catching up with Beverly in the foyer, Roni called out to her.

"Beverly, I *really* want to get involved with ZZT. Anything you need me to do, just let me know. I'm your girl."

Drenched from marching double time in the ninety-degree heat at Tuesday morning's band practice, Jenna quickly showered, threw on shorts and a T-shirt, and then splayed out on her bed. She knew she should be studying, but she pushed aside her textbooks and the class syllabuses that she'd been trying to decipher earlier and focused on the shopping bag full of paraphernalia she'd just picked up from the campus drugstore. She emptied the bag onto the bed and surveyed its contents: Blow Pops, Kleenex, dental floss, Altoids, Tylenol, breath strips, Q-tips, AA batteries, toothpicks, tampons, *condoms* (!), and a bumper sticker with the Latimer University crest on it. None of it made any sense to her, but she slowly placed the items in one of her empty makeup bags, ticking them off in her head as she did to make sure, for the tenth time, she wasn't forgetting anything.

"What *are* you doing?" Amber scoffed, eyeing the pile of

items with annoyance. "If you think that kind of emergency kit is going to get you through hurricane season, you need to double-check your insulin levels."

"Ha." Jenna laughed, even though she knew Amber was definitely *not* being funny. "No, it's just, um"—she paused, not wanting to fess up to the truth. "It's my ZZT preparedness kit. I have to carry it with me all the time, just in case."

Amber snorted and rolled her eyes. "How stupid is that? What is it for, some kind of ridiculous joke?"

"I don't know exactly," Jenna admitted. "It's part of this bonding thing we're doing with the senior actives. They want to get to know us better, and it's to show them that they can depend on us for anything, I guess."

The preparedness kit had been the idea of the masterminds behind the Seniors Love the New Members ad hoc committee, Nava Holmes and Chandra Kearney. Camille had explained that they lived off-campus and didn't come to too many of the house meetings, but they'd formed the committee so that the seniors could bond with the new girls. Jenna wasn't entirely sure if it was bonding or teasing Nava and Chandra would be doing, but Camille had assured her that it was good-natured.

Jenna slipped the preparedness kit into her bag, trying to avoid Amber's ridiculing gaze.

"What a waste of time," Amber muttered, laughing under her breath. "I'm glad I don't have to worry about brownnosing with sorority snobs."

Jenna sighed. "It's not brownnosing. I just have so much else to do for school, and I wanted to put the kit together now so I could focus on studying. It's only the third week of school, and already I have a test coming up in Western Civ. Can you believe that? I've got new member education classes at the ZZT house, a swap with the Kappa Omegas, two lab quizzes in Biology, a paper due in English, and the football game on Saturday. When will I fit everything in?"

"Woe is you." Amber stared at Jenna and let out a long sigh. She banged away on her computer, no doubt IMing with her high school friends about her loser roommate. (Jenna knew because she'd seen the screen a couple of days ago when one friend IM'd Amber with "Can you chat or is SHE around?") "No one said college was one big party, Jenna," she snapped.

A wave of nerves rumbled in her stomach, but Jenna didn't dare ask what she'd done to deserve this constant barrage of insults from Amber. She knew: *I got a bid. . . . She got dropped.*

"I don't expect college to be a party," Jenna said, "but there's just so much to do. Especially with band." Before ZZT, Jenna thought the marching band would be her biggest extracurricular activity. Now it almost seemed like too much to juggle. "They've got us practicing some mornings and late in the afternoon. I just don't want to miss out on any new member activities." She tacked on, "Or, you know . . . hanging out with you."

"Right." Amber snorted. She turned her back to Jenna, slipped in her earbuds, and cranked up her iPod until Jenna could clearly hear the words to "Hate Me Today" blaring out. Jenna stifled a nervous giggle as she listened to the lyrics. Oh, how appropriate they were right now.

Nausea suddenly surged over Jenna, and she quickly grabbed a Diet Coke from the minifridge, hoping that it was just her nerves and not her 'betes acting up. How was she going to study in here? There was no way she could concentrate with Amber sending venomous glances her way every few seconds. She'd have to head to the library.

She was just packing up her books when Roni popped her head in, her smile breaking through the stony tension. "Hey, Amber! Can I steal Jenna away?"

Amber didn't even acknowledge Roni's presence, and Jenna just shrugged at Roni to signal that the effort was futile.

"You want to walk over to the house with me and check out what we're having for dinner later?" Roni asked.

"Definitely," Jenna said gratefully, glad to escape Amber for a few hours. As new members, the girls were allowed to have a meal plan at ZZT, and Jenna'd been trying to squeeze it in as often as she could so she'd have time to hang with the other girls. Even though she'd had a meal plan on campus to begin with, she'd talked to the school, and they'd been able to give her a credit, since she wouldn't be using it. "I'm starving."

Roni laughed. "Jenna, dinner's not until six. I just thought we could check out the menu in case we needed a plan B. Did you eat lunch?"

"Um." Jenna thought for a sec. "No, I guess I forgot."

"But it's almost two!" Roni cried. "We'll have to pick up something on the way to ZZT."

"That'd be great," Jenna said. So that was why her stomach was rebelling! Come to think of it, had she even eaten breakfast? Oh, right, she'd overslept after staying up late studying, and she'd had to scarf a donut on her way to band practice. "I wonder what concoction Miss Merry's going to cook up tonight."

"Probably something you're not allowed to eat," Amber piped up from her corner.

Jenna leveled her eyes into a "don't go there" stare. She didn't want Amber to blurt out the news about her 'betes. Jenna hadn't told any of her friends yet, and Amber only knew because Jenna's mom had told her on move-in day. Her 'betes was something she wanted to keep a secret, at least for now.

Not seeming to pick up on the hidden meaning of Amber's words, Roni laughed over both of them. "None of us can eat the food at the house. Half the time, we can't even figure out what it is we're eating. Not with Miss Merry cooking."

Jenna laughed. She'd already learned that ZZT dinners—served promptly at six P.M.—were an adventure. Their chef (that was using the word loosely), Miss Merry, posted her menu every day at one o'clock. The sorority sisters had until two P.M. to "sign out" if the food sounded questionable. And with bizarre creations like escargot gumbo—the food was almost *always* questionable.

Even when there were the occasional appetizing entrées, they certainly weren't the well-balanced, low-carb meals Jenna was used to at home (of course, neither was a donut!). But she wanted to be there, so she simply adjusted her insulin accordingly and went with the flow.

"I hope tonight is better than last night," Roni said as they worked their way out of the dorm and across the street to Sorority Row. The sun shone brightly above, warming the September day with summery heat. Sorority girls strolled up and down the walkways, many returning from class, others leaving for the gym or getting ready for evening activities.

"Shoot!" Jenna cried as they climbed up the steps of the ZZT house a few minutes later. "I forgot to grab something to eat."

"Maybe we can find you something inside," Roni said. "If not, we'll check the dinner menu and then head over to the student center."

"Hey, y'all," Lora-Leigh called from where she was hanging out in one of the rocking chairs, looking through some shopping bags from The Sewing Bee. Danika, Juliana, and some other girls were on the porch, too, studying and chatting. "Don't bother checking the menu. Been there, done that."

"Is it that bad?" Roni asked, playing with her hair.

"Worse than bad," Lora-Leigh said. "Carrot raisin salad and Mexican meat loaf, which apparently involves ground tortilla chips and salsa."

Roni turned to Jenna. "You definitely better get something to eat now. Dinner sounds inedible."

"What, you missed lunch?" Lora-Leigh asked. "I ate at Fast Break after I went to The Sewing Bee to get the fabric for my mom's shrug." She nodded to the bags at her feet. "I've got half a dozen buffalo wings and fries in the fridge left over. Help yourself."

"Um, thanks," Jenna said, trying to sound grateful. Why, oh why hadn't she made herself a sandwich from the stash of healthy food she kept in her minifridge? Too late now, and she was so hungry that if she didn't eat something soon, her levels were going to get totally screwed up. She sighed. It was chicken wings or nothing.

"No prob," Lora-Leigh said. "As for dinner, I say we sign out."

Roni's brows creased. "But we're only allowed so many

signouts per month and we *just* joined. It might look bad if we don't go. Like we're being antisocial or something."

"Boston, you crack me up," Lora-Leigh said with a laugh. "We got in. You don't have to keep selling yourself."

"I'm not! But we've got to learn everyone's names—full names—and their hometowns by tomorrow's new member meeting. How are we going to do that if we don't meet everyone?"

"Omigod," Jenna groaned, flopping into the chair next to Lora-Leigh. "I forgot all about that."

"You're looking at the master," Lora-Leigh said, taking a bow. "Ask me anything. I know shoe sizes, birth dates, *and* nicknames. I'll quiz you both between now and dinner."

"Hey, newbies," a voice behind them said. Jenna turned and saw Nava Holmes and Chandra Kearney standing there. Nava was dressed in black combat boots, black pants, and an LU sweatshirt. Her hair was wild-curly, and a stud sparkled on the right side of her nose. Jenna hated to admit it, but she was the teeny-tiniest bit scared of Nava.

"Anyone got a Blow Pop for me?" Nava asked.

"And I could use a Band-Aid for this paper cut I got today." Chandra held up her hand.

Immediately, Jenna, Roni, and Lora-Leigh all reached into their purses and bags for their preparedness kits. Jenna dug past her books and pens to try to find the cosmetic bag she'd put all her ZZT trinkets in. She had the cutest colorful Band-Aids ... if she could just get to them.

"Here you go," Lora-Leigh said, getting to the Blow Pop first. "Hope you like grape."

Nava smiled at Lora-Leigh. "You get an A for speediness, newbie."

"And for you," Roni said, smiling from ear to ear. She handed over a Band-Aid to Chandra.

Jenna finally felt her hand close around her kit, but it was too late now. *Crud . . . they both beat me.*

Nava linked her eyes with Jenna's. "Well . . . you were the last to the punch. That means you get to do a task to show your sisters how much you care about them."

"I do?" This did not sound good.

"Phone duty would be really nice," Chandra said.

"Excellent idea." Nava nodded. "There's a house phone in the front alcove where everyone's mailboxes are. For the next two hours, you've got phone duty."

Jenna's heart sank, thinking of wasting two hours sitting in that tiny room answering a phone. "Don't we have voice mail?"

"Sure, but it's a nice touch to have a newbie answer the main line every now and then," Chandra explained. "It's just more personal. You'll do a great job—"

"Jenna. I'm Jenna," she said when she saw they were seeking her name.

"Have fun!" Nava and Chandra called, waving and laughing as they headed down the front steps.

Jenna sighed and looked at her friends. "I guess I'll see you later. Save me a seat at dinner."

"I'll go heat up your wings for you," Roni said. "At least you can eat while you answer the phone."

Two hours and a serious case of heartburn later (thank you, buffalo wings!), Jenna found herself running across the fifty-yard line of Daniel Stadium to catch up with the band. They were already in formation, and Jenna was hoping she could slide into her spot on the field unnoticed.

"You're late," Papa Skank, the trumpet section leader, hissed at her when she stepped into place.

So much for going unnoticed.

She blushed as she felt the other trumpets in her section swivel their heads in her direction when Papa Skank walked over. He was the strongest trumpet in the band, but also the scariest section leader. Before practices had even started, she'd heard rumors that he'd made at least a dozen band members walk off the field crying during his two years as section leader. And now, after meeting him, she didn't doubt it.

"Driscoll, you already told me you have to miss practice this Friday for a doctor's appointment, correct?"

"Yes," Jenna mumbled, hoping that if she spoke softly the lie wouldn't be as bad. She was actually going to Tiger's golf tournament on Friday. But there was no way she would've been able to skip band practice with a boy as an excuse. So she'd lied, something she'd done only a handful of times in her entire life. It didn't feel good, but there weren't any other options.

"Occasional doctor's appointments, hernias, deaths in the immediate family are fine," Papa Skank said, his sarcasm biting into her. "But don't think I'll excuse you if you make a regular habit of being late, too."

"It won't happen again," Jenna whispered.

"Good," he said. "Now give me two laps around the field, warm up, and then get in formation."

Jenna set her trumpet down and took off running. What a day this had been so far. And it was only Tuesday. She still had to get through the rest of the week, not to mention tonight. Once this practice was over (if she survived the rest of practice), she'd have to race back to ZZT to make it in time for dinner (a dinner that she probably wouldn't be able to eat), then hit the books during study hall—time set aside for the new members to study together at the house—and then memorize the names of all the new girls and finish reading the new member binder. And maybe, if she was lucky, there'd be some sleep involved in there somewhere. But that was a big maybe.

Her stomach roiled at the thought of how she was going to get everything done. But she would. She was Jenna Driscoll—type A overachiever. She'd never been anything less. She'd make it all work . . . somehow.

CHAPTER
3

Jenna gripped her lukewarm beer and laughed enthusiastically at the not-even-remotely-funny band camp joke that Kelly, the second trumpet, had just told. Then she tried, ever so discreetly, to check her watch: 7:30 P.M. She sighed. The Wednesday-night new member meeting at ZZT was already halfway through, and she was missing it. But band practice had run late, and then, in a sudden, earth-shattering gesture of goodwill, Papa Skank had invited their section out to The Brass Billiards for drinks. Jenna was still trying to figure out if Papa Skank had undergone a frontal lobotomy—that was pretty much the only fathomable explanation she had for his good mood. But, hey, she'd take it. She was just relieved that he hadn't made her run more laps at today's practice. She knew she should've gone to the new member meeting, but she figured it was far better to skip the meeting and make nice with Papa Skank than it was to risk pissing him off again. She felt honored he'd invited her to tag along to the bar at all, being that she was only a lowly freshman.

She swirled the liquid in her full glass and stared at the foamy bubbles gathering on the sides. She'd barely taken two or three sips of the beer. She couldn't even afford the smallest buzz tonight. She was already drawing on emergency reserves, stifling yawns every few minutes and feeling the heaviness in her eyelids. But she still needed to work on the English paper due in class tomorrow (which she hadn't even started yet, sigh). And who knew how long that would take? Visions of an all-nighter were already dancing in her head. But maybe if she left right now, she could still squeeze in an hour or two of sleep at some point.

Jenna stood up reluctantly. "Y'all, this has been a blast, but I need to get going."

"Hot date?" Papa Skank teased.

"I wish," she said with a grin, not quite believing she was actually sharing a laugh with him. And she did wish she had a date tonight instead of piles of homework. But she'd have to hold out until Friday, when she'd see Tiger. And that was well worth waiting for, she figured.

She waved and turned to go, but Papa Skank grabbed her arm. "Gotta down that beer first, Driscoll. No one leaves a beer on the table. No man gets left behind in the brass section of the Marching Raiders."

Jenna laughed but stared at her mug hesitantly for a few seconds. This was the last thing she needed—the last thing her body needed. She'd been dizzy on and off since she finished band practice, and she'd run out of the juice boxes she'd put in her backpack earlier today. She hadn't had time to go to the store to restock, so she'd have to suffer until she got back to

Tuthill. The occasional dizziness was something she was used to, anyway, but she still hated when it crept up on her like this. It was as if she had no control over her own body.

But she couldn't explain her dizziness or her 'betes to the band. As she looked around at the expectant faces of her section, she knew this was more than a joke. This was a test—an initiation into their world. So she lifted her glass and took a deep breath before diving in. As she gulped down the remains of the warm, bitter ale, she heard her fellow brass players shouting, "Drink, drink, drink!"

Somehow she got it all down and wiped her mouth with the back of her hand. Then she flashed a victory grin at her fellow trumpet players.

"Now may I be excused, sir?" she asked Papa Skank.

"You may." Papa Skank raised his glass and saluted her. "Way to hang with the big boys, fresh meat."

Jenna said good night and left the bar, then slowly headed toward the lights of campus, feeling a fuzziness settling over her. Her feet felt as heavy as anvils from all the marching she'd done today, and even though Tuthill wasn't a horrendous hike from here, it seemed like it would take forever. It would be so nice to just crawl into bed right now. She sighed.

"Jenna? Is that you?" she heard someone call out.

Jenna turned toward Bash Riprock's restaurant on the corner and caught sight of Darcy, the ZZT active who'd been Jenna's Rho Gamma during recruitment. Jenna'd wanted more than anything to be in the same sorority as Darcy, and she'd gotten her wish. "Hey, Darcy! What are you doing here?"

"I just got off work." Darcy pulled a name tag out of her bag and held it up to Jenna. "I waitress at the caf at the Strumann Student Union. But I can't handle their food, so . . ." Darcy grinned and held up a Bash Riprock's bag. "Stuffed baked potato to go."

"That smells great." Jenna's stomach lurched at the thought of food. All she'd had to eat was the day-old popcorn at The Brass Billiards that she'd washed down with the beer.

Darcy looked at her watch. "Why aren't you at the new member meeting? It's not over yet, is it?"

"I don't think so." Jenna blushed, not wanting to look bad in front of Darcy. "I couldn't make it tonight. I just wrapped up things at marching band, and now I have a twenty-page paper to write."

"Ouch," Darcy said. "That's gonna hurt around midnight."

"Tell me about it," Jenna said. She looked through the glass front of Bash Riprock's and saw the tables full this Wednesday night. The aroma of fresh grilled hamburgers, steak-and-cheese sandwiches, and greasy fries penetrated the air, making Jenna's mouth water.

"Hey, do you want to walk through campus together?" Darcy asked. "I'm heading back to ZZT, but I think your dorm is on the way."

"That'd be great," Jenna said. "I just want to grab something to eat first, if that's okay with you. I haven't had dinner yet."

"I don't mind. I was just going to ask if you were okay," Darcy said as they went into Bash's and took seats at the bar. "You look pretty wiped."

Jenna nodded. "I left the dorm at seven this morning and haven't been back yet." She turned to the bartender, not even needing to look at the menu to know what would settle her hunger. "Can I get the chicken souvlaki with extra yogurt sauce and a side of fries to go?"

"You got it," he said.

"It sounds like you're pretty swamped, huh?" Darcy said to Jenna. "Anything I can help with?"

Jenna steadied herself against the counter as the room spun slightly.

"Not unless you want to write my paper for me," she joked weakly, rubbing her temples to try to make the dizziness go away. "I'm just freaking a little about my schedule this semester. I need to do well in band to keep my scholarship, but I want to spend time with everyone at ZZT and get to know all the girls, too. I'm just worried I'm not going to have time for everything."

Darcy nodded in understanding. "I remember feeling that way at the start of freshman year when I joined ZZT. I was already working at Strumann to help my parents out with tuition, and I didn't know how to deal with ZZT, my job, and my classes."

"So what did you do?" Jenna asked.

"I just tried to take it one day at a time and to be really careful with how I managed my schedule."

"I guess I need to start doing that, too," Jenna said, just as the bartender came over with her order. He handed Jenna a slightly greasy bag.

She quickly paid, and then she and Darcy walked out the door and into the humid night air, heading toward Tuthill.

"What if I get you a Day Planner so you can map out your schedule, day by day?" Darcy suggested. "Then you can work out a study plan alongside your social calendar."

"Maybe that would help," Jenna said. "I don't know...." She lost her voice as the pavement underneath her feet buckled, and the streetlights danced in front of her eyes.

Just as Jenna felt herself tipping forward, Darcy grabbed her by the shoulders and steered her over to the steps in front of Billado Hall to sit down. "Jenna, you're white as a sheet and your cheeks are fiery red. Are you okay? I can drive you over to the Student Health Center if you're feeling sick."

Jenna shook her head, wanting the sidewalk to turn into quicksand and swallow her whole. Talk about embarrassing. Why couldn't her body behave itself when she needed it to? "I'm fine," she lied. "I'm just ... tired. And I didn't eat much today."

Darcy watched her for a few seconds before saying sternly, "You know, you're a horrible liar. So, are you going to spill it, or do I have to drag you to the Health Center to have one of those doctors tell me instead?"

Jenna hung her head, avoiding Darcy's eyes.

"Honestly, you can tell me anything, Jenna, and it won't go any further," Darcy assured her.

Jenna's dizziness and clamminess increased, and she knew she had no choice. She'd have to dial up her insulin in front of Darcy. Now there was no way around it.... She'd have to tell her the truth. She just hoped Darcy would keep it to herself, since the last thing she wanted was the whole ZZT house to know about her 'betes and pity her for it.

59

"Promise you won't treat me any differently . . . once you know," Jenna said in a quivering voice. "Or tell anyone else, even the other ZZTs."

"I swear," Darcy said with dead honesty in her voice.

Taking a deep breath, Jenna lifted the left corner of her shirt, revealing the small, beeperlike device on her hip with the tiny tube attached to her stomach. She didn't dare raise her eyes to see Darcy's reaction as she dialed in the right dose of insulin. Only when she'd moved her shirt back into place did she venture a peek at Darcy.

Instead of the pitiful glances she usually got, all she saw in Darcy's eyes was compassion . . . and understanding.

"You know," Darcy said matter-of-factly, as if none of this were a surprise in the least, "I've been trying to get my dad to get one of those pumps instead of constantly giving himself shots. But he's just too stubborn to listen."

Jenna's eyes grew wide. "Your dad's a diabetic?"

"Yeah, since he was in his thirties. He never ate right traveling like he did for work, and it finally took a toll on his body. He especially hates the finger prick tests."

"Me, too." Jenna's dizziness fled, and wonderful relief took its place as she smiled at Darcy. "'Course, I don't even feel the finger prick anymore when I test my blood. I'm so used to it. My mom used to cry every time she gave me my shots when I first started taking them. She always thought she was hurting me."

"Parents. What are you gonna do with them? My dad *still* doesn't eat like he should, no matter how much I nag him about it. His big weakness is Reese's Peanut Butter Cups."

Jenna giggled. "Mine is Lindt chocolates." She stood up, testing her legs out. "I think I'm better now."

Darcy smiled and hugged her. "Good. You know, there's no reason to be embarrassed about diabetes. Everyone at ZZT would understand."

As they walked, Jenna thought about that. "You're probably right," she finally said, "but I'm just not ready to tell anyone else yet. I need to learn to deal with my 'betes on my own first."

Darcy nodded. "I can understand that. But in the meantime, the ZZT sisters are here for you, no matter what, whenever you need us."

"Thanks," Jenna said.

As they reached Tuthill, Jenna stopped in the doorway. Even though she was still exhausted, she suddenly felt happier than she had all day. "You know, I think I can make it all work— band, classes, and ZZT."

Darcy smiled. "You can. And tomorrow, first thing, we'll swing by the Supe Store and get you a planner to map out your schedule."

"You don't have to do that, Darcy," Jenna said. "You're not even my Rose Bud this week."

Darcy gave her a sly look. "But I'm your friend and your sister. I can't think of a better reason than that."

As she smiled and walked into Tuthill, Jenna couldn't think of a better reason either.

"Where's Jenna?" Lora-Leigh whispered to Roni as she stretched out on her stomach on the dark blue carpet of the ZZT living room. The new member meeting only had about fifteen minutes left, and her fellow sisters were scattered about in the Victorian lords' and ladies' chairs and couches, but there was still no sign of Jenna.

"I don't know," Roni whispered. "She missed out on dinner, too."

"That's no tragic loss," Lora-Leigh said. "But I thought she'd at least be here later on. She doesn't have to be the busiest girl at LU."

"I'm sure she had a good reason," Roni said, and Lora-Leigh nodded.

She knew that had to be true, because Jenna was too responsible to miss the first new member meeting unless something important came up. Especially since tonight was the night of nominations for the New Member President. Beverly had mentioned it at the house meeting last Sunday, and Lora-Leigh'd already made up her mind: she was going to run.

She waited, a little impatiently, as Beverly took care of some final pieces of business and then introduced Betsy Bickford, the ZZT Philanthropy Chair, to talk about the semester's philanthropy activities. There would be a fund-raiser for a nonprofit education center called Crank It Up for Kids and a toy drive for Toys for Tots.

"Our biggest event will be during Homecoming, though," Betsy explained. "In addition to building a float for the parade, we'll also be doing a book drive for the Latimer Public Library. They had a fire over the summer, so we're going to help them restock their shelves."

Betsy spoke for a few more minutes, and then Beverly jumped into the ZZT history lesson for the night, a talk about Estelle

Orval Cornett, the founder and a former president of ZZT. Lora-Leigh fiddled with the jagged hem of her jeans while Beverly talked. It wasn't that Lora-Leigh wasn't interested, but she'd already read up on all of the founders, and, to be honest, there were other things on her mind tonight. First, the New Member Presidency, and second, her run-in with DeShawn.

She'd seen him this morning for the first time since the party last weekend. He'd plopped down right next to her in Western Civ with a nonchalant, "Hey, Curly," as if nothing completely awkward had happened on Saturday night.

"So I'm going to miss Friday's class to go to Atlanta for the game," DeShawn said. "Mind if I copy your notes later?"

Lora-Leigh scoffed. "First you ditch me for that Kimber-brat on Saturday night, and now you want to copy my notes? There're two things you should learn about me quick. Number one: I don't like being used. Number two: I especially don't like being used by two-faced jocks who think they can mack on every girl in a hundred-mile radius. Got it?"

DeShawn stared at her in disbelief for a few seconds, and then a lightning flash of anger lit up his face. "Okay, time for you to learn some things about *me*. Number one: I don't like being stereotyped. Number two: I especially don't like being stereotyped by someone who doesn't have the first clue what they're talking about and never bothered to ask. Number three: That Kimber-brat happens to be my best friend Garrett's little sis. I've known her since she was five, and if I ever messed around with her, Garrett would kick my ass so bad I'd have to crawl back onto the football field. Got it?"

After eating a megadose of humble pie, Lora-Leigh agreed

to let him copy her notes whenever he had an away game, and they'd swapped numbers so he could get them from her outside of class. On his way out of class, he'd called after her, "Hey, Curly, just FYI, I'd never go for a girl like Kimberly anyway." He'd smirked and added, "I love a challenge."

Since then, every time she'd thought about their run-in, she'd wanted to crawl into a pair of cheap polyester plaid pants and stay there for eternity. It was a fate worse than death, and she deserved it. She couldn't believe she'd misjudged him so completely. She'd always thought she was pretty good at nailing people's MOs. And now she blushed all over again thinking about his last words to her. Because the thing was, she loved a challenge, too. And she thought that maybe she had one on her hands.

"Earth to Lora-Leigh." An elbow nudged her. "If you start dozing off, you're on your own," Danika said.

Lora-Leigh blinked and refocused on the meeting, pushing away thoughts of DeShawn.

And it was a good thing she did, because Beverly had finished the lesson and was finally bringing up the New Member Presidency.

"You'll vote for your president at Sunday's meeting," Beverly said, "but tonight we'll be accepting nominations after the meeting ends. The president is the voice of the new member class to the house board. She'll be helping quite a bit with our Homecoming preparations and with our house meetings. But most importantly, she will help me with the New Member Education Program, and she will be your leader."

Murmurs broke out across the room as the girls chatted about potential candidates.

Lora-Leigh's heart pounded as she thought about the presidency. She'd been instrumental in the Theater Guild in high school and had organized several youth Seders at the temple, but could she lead her sorority new member class? Then she thought of her mom. If her mom had been able to do it, so could she. Her dad was always saying how much alike she and her mom were (thus, the constant head-butting), so it made sense that she could take on this role, too. And if she got the presidency, it wouldn't be possible for her mom to stay angry at her. She'd be proud of her instead. It was a shot in the dark, but at this point, Lora-Leigh was running out of options.

"I think I'm going to nominate myself," she said to Sandy. "What do you think, do I have that presidential look?" She waggled her ZZT-colored earrings back and forth for emphasis.

Sandy laughed. "You certainly dress better than most of them."

"So true," Lora-Leigh said.

Feeling great about the decision she'd made, she smiled to herself as the meeting finally wrapped up, and her smile got even bigger when Beverly announced one last activity—a Name Your Sisters quiz. Lora-Leigh knew before she even saw the quiz that she'd ace it. While the other sisters struggled to remember names and hometowns, Lora-Leigh whizzed through them and turned her quiz in first.

After checking over all the quizzes, Beverly lifted a gift basket from underneath the table. The basket was filled with goodies that sported the Latimer University crest. Eyes shining, Beverly announced, "Our quiz winner tonight is Lora-Leigh Sorenstein. One hundred percent right! Way to go, Lora-Leigh!"

Lora-Leigh took the heavy gift basket and gave a dramatic bow for good measure. If she was going to run for New Member President, this was a great way to jump-start her campaign.

Later that night, before Lora-Leigh could even think about studying, she did the one thing she'd been thinking about doing since the meeting. She sat down at her computer and e-mailed her mom:

> From: lora-leigh.sorenstein@latimer.edu
> To: hannah.sorenstein@email.com
>
> Hey Mom,
> Your prodigal daughter here, just checking in to make sure you're still breathing. I don't remember you ever being this quiet, with the possible exception of when I was in your womb. But I'm not even sure about that (I have a vague recollection of you lecturing me about kicking too much during Seder . . . ha ha). Anyway, just wanted to give you the latest headline: Lora-Leigh Sorenstein to run for New Member President at ZZT! That's right, even though I'm doing it with ZZT instead of Tri-O, I'm following in your footsteps (scary thought, I know). So if you have any advice for me, I'm all ears!
> LL

She reread the e-mail, then clicked "send." There had been countless times in her life when Lora-Leigh would've given anything to get her mom to be quiet, to stop with the lecturing and the endless Tri-O stories. But right now, all she wanted was to break the silence, once and for all. Maybe, just maybe, this e-mail might do the trick.

❖

In Jenna's opinion, there were three essential things needed to make golf an interesting spectator sport: an occasional shank into the trees; a close competition; and—the most exciting—a sandy-haired, drop-dead-gorgeous guy who really knew how to swing a club and looked seriously hot in a polo (yes, it was possible) and aforementioned hot guy smiling in your direction after every swing. On Friday afternoon, Jenna had all of those things, and she couldn't have been happier. Of course, she was especially glad that Tiger was the one sinking his putts instead of shanking them, as opposed to the poor guy from Baylor who was still stuck in a sand trap on hole 13. Even with as little as Jenna knew about golf, she could see that Tiger was a great player. He'd birdied three out of the eighteen holes, and he'd even had one eagle. She wasn't entirely sure what either of those were, exactly, but she could tell from the overwhelming applause of the crowd that they were good.

It was a beautiful day, and even though she couldn't talk to Tiger while he was playing, she was enjoying just being outside on the lush green course. The fresh air and bright sunshine were taking her mind off her schoolwork for once, and she was almost forgetting how awful she still felt about the English paper she'd turned in yesterday. It was her worst work to date . . . no doubt about it. But at four A.M. yesterday when her computer screen started blurring before her eyes, she knew it was time to throw in the towel; print out what she'd done, which was at best a rough draft; and go to bed. Watching Tiger play today was the best distraction from the worries she'd had all week.

As he sank the putt on the eighteenth hole to cheers from the crowd, he didn't even wait to see the leader board for his final score. He just handed his clubs to the LU team caddy and headed straight for Jenna.

"So you're not too bored, are you?" he asked, giving her hand a quick squeeze.

"Are you kidding? I'm having a great time."

"It's way more exciting when you're playing." He smiled.

"I just have one question. What's the fascination with feathered friends? Birdies and eagles . . . I don't get it."

"That's going to take some explaining." Tiger laughed. "Let's go grab something to eat at the clubhouse, and I'll talk you through it."

While they ate hot dogs (the best option on the clubhouse menu), Tiger explained all the golf terms and what the rankings at the end of the tournament would mean. Jenna was just about to ask what a mulligan was when her cell rang.

"It's my little sister," Jenna said, glancing at the screen. "Hopefully this will only take a sec."

"No prob," Tiger said.

"What's wrong?" Jenna asked Jayne, the middle Little J, who was sniffling into the phone.

"Mom's making me write a book report on a book I hate," she said. "I don't want to, and she sent me to my room."

Jenna smiled into the phone. She'd gotten at least a dozen phone calls like this since she'd started the semester. Because her parents worked a lot, Jenna had babysat her sisters all the time, so she was the one who had to neutralize fights and handle homework situations. Now her mom was back to doing homework duty, and Jenna could tell it wasn't going well.

"Why don't you do the book report on the book Mom wants

this time," Jenna said, trying to sound as serious as possible so that Jayne wouldn't detect her smile, "and then maybe you can pick the book you do your next report on. How does that sound?"

"Okay," Jayne mumbled through her sniffles. There was a muffled voice in the background, and then Jayne said, "Mom just came into my room and told me to stop bothering you at school."

Jenna laughed, and, after a string of "I love yous" and "I miss yous," hung up.

"Sorry," Jenna said, turning to a grinning Tiger. "A small family crisis averted."

"I heard," Tiger said. "It's the never-ending plight of the oldest sibling. Maybe that's why I want to become a lawyer. I'm already an expert negotiator."

"You want to go to law school because you're the oldest in your family?"

"In a roundabout way, I guess so," Tiger said, brushing his hair out of his face. "I have two younger brothers, and I feel like the constant peacemaker when I'm home. Not to mention the family chauffeur."

"You, too!" Jenna exclaimed with a laugh. "I'm also the family chef. But, actually, I love to cook. I'm pretty good at it, too. I cooked a lot for my sisters when my parents worked late, and I just started experimenting here and there with spices. My sister Janice even nicknamed our kitchen Jenna's Café." Of course, what she didn't say was that she'd learned a lot about food—carbs, calories, sugar, etc.—when she got diagnosed with the 'betes.

"You know, LU has a great cooking school."

Jenna shifted her eyes to where Tiger's hand rested on the back of her chair. The tips of his fingers were just inches from her shoulder. It was a rush being so close to him. "I know; my mom suggested I look into some cooking classes here. I'll think about it for the spring."

"Maybe you should consider that for your major," Tiger suggested.

"Not exactly law school, now is it?" she quipped.

"Hey, lawyers have to eat, you know." He smiled. "You'll have to whip something up for me next time."

Next time? That meant Tiger wanted to see her again.

"I don't know," Jenna said. "I've never cooked for anyone outside my family before."

"Then I volunteer to do the taste-testing free of charge," Tiger said. "You can show off your culinary talents after we work up an appetite playing eighteen holes together. I want to get you out on a course. It'd be fun."

"Oh, no," Jenna said, shaking her head adamantly. "There's a reason why I joined band. Ever heard of athletically impaired? That's me. If you want me to come with you, I'll drive the golf cart. That's much safer than letting me swing a club."

"I'm not giving up that easily," Tiger said. "Maybe we'll start out at the driving range and then ease you onto a course."

"We'll see," Jenna said reluctantly, but she secretly knew she'd already given in. She'd make a fool of herself on a golf course, especially if it meant spending one-on-one time with him for an entire eighteen holes.

They kept talking, and before Jenna knew it, two hours had

gone by, and it was time for her to meet up with Lora-Leigh and Roni for the Kappa Omega swap. She couldn't believe how much she and Tiger had talked about in such a little time: their similar family backgrounds (Tiger had stepparents, too), their classes, their friends. Up until now, she'd been drawn to his looks, but getting to know him better made him even more attractive. And she could only hope he felt the same way.

As he dropped her off in front of the ZZT house, he said, "So be careful tonight. The Kappa Omegas are some of the meanest, most obnoxious guys on campus."

"Really?"

Tiger hesitated for a sec and then shrugged. "Nah, not really. They're great guys. I just said that so you wouldn't talk to any of them." He smiled. "Hey, you can't fault me for wanting to keep a good thing to myself, can you?"

Jenna laughed and blushed, and before she could get out of the car, Tiger leaned over and gave her a millisecond peck on the cheek. She ran into the house smiling. She was "in like" with Tiger. And now there was no question about it; he felt the same way.

"I don't know if I can do this," Jenna whispered to Lora-Leigh and Roni as they stood in front of the Kappa Omega house with the other ZZT girls. She pulled at the front of the extra-extra large men's T-shirt she was wearing to make sure it was still covering her knees. "I feel like I'm naked."

Lora-Leigh laughed and elbowed her playfully. "Like I told you fifteen times on the way here, you look fab. I made sure I cut your T-shirt so you'd be comfy in it. Stop stressing."

"You really do look great," Roni said. "Lora-Leigh did an amazing job on the T-shirts."

Lora-Leigh grinned. "Thanks, Boston. A little bit of spray paint goes a long, long way."

When Lora-Leigh had volunteered (er, more like begged) to make Jenna's and Roni's shirts for the Kappa Omega Graffiti Swap, Jenna hadn't really thought about the potential consequences.

"I was inspired," Lora-Leigh had said when she'd pulled out their shirts for tonight's swap. But inspired was an understatement. Each was an oversized T-shirt that Lora-Leigh had altered into a makeshift dress. But the spray painting was where Lora-Leigh had really gotten creative. Roni's T-shirt was painted to look like a sleek Gucci-esque halter dress in metallic golds and silvers, and around the bottom hem was written "I SPEAK CHIC" in shimmery copper letters. Lora-Leigh had turned her tee into a wearable version of Picasso's *Tête de Femme*, with one-half of the woman's face on the front and the other half on the back. But Jenna's was brighter and bolder than both of theirs. Lora-Leigh had painted a huge butterfly on it in brilliant turquoise, emerald, and violet hues. Flutter sleeves at Jenna's shoulders and a scalloped hem completed the look. The dress accented Jenna's petite figure, and the colors brought out the blue in her eyes and made her hair look almost platinum.

Jenna smiled at her friends, trying to get into the spirit of the night. She had to admit that the dress looked great on her. But still, she felt self-conscious knowing that she was wearing only a T-shirt (even if it was long enough to pass for a dress). Every time she looked down at her outfit, she could think of only one thing: her insulin pump. It was tucked away under the T-dress, but she still worried there was a visible lump on one side of her hip.

She pulled at the T-dress one last time, but Lora-Leigh grabbed her hand.

"If you don't stop fidgeting with my masterpiece, I'm going to get insulted," Lora-Leigh said half-teasingly.

"Okay, okay," Jenna said, reluctantly letting her hands fall to her side. She'd just have to make sure she kept a safe distance between herself and her "date" for tonight. That way, her pump would stay undiscovered.

"I just wish Tiger was going to be here," Jenna said. "I had so much fun with him today. I'm kind of all flirted out." She felt comfortable around Tiger, too—more comfortable than she had around any guy since her 'betes diagnosis. And she couldn't help wishing she was getting set up with him tonight instead of with some stranger.

"There is no such thing as 'all flirted out,'" Lora-Leigh said. "So quit with the mope-age and live up to your outfit. Think social butterfly and you will *be* social butterfly."

Jenna nodded, but she had a feeling her inner social butterfly was more like a caterpillar, building a very large, very safe cocoon right at this very second.

"All right," Heather, their Social Chair, said as she knocked on the door to the KΩ house. "Y'all look great! We're gonna have a fantastic time. If anyone has too much to drink, remember who your Rose Bud is and stick together."

A guy with short blond hair and a deep tan in a T-shirt that was painted to look like a shirt and tie opened it and welcomed everyone inside. As she walked in, Jenna took a deep breath to steady her nerves and caught the scent of men's deodorant mixed with musty beer. The living room had a white-and-tan cowhide couch and end tables made from antlers. A huge wagon wheel coffee table sat in front of the fireplace, and the walls of the room were covered in photos of the Kappa Omega guys on fishing trips, camping trips, and at rodeos.

"This is a little…rustic," Roni said, smothering a giggle in her sleeve.

"The word is *redneck*, girlfriend," Lora-Leigh said.

"All they need is a few deer heads mounted on the wall to complete the picture," Sandy whispered.

"Oh, those are in the dining room," Lora-Leigh said.

"What?" Roni shrieked, blanching.

"Just kidding." Lora-Leigh chuckled.

"They're our good ol' boys," Camille said. "Boots, big belt buckles, and Stetsons. They might look a little rough around the edges, but they're really great."

A guy wearing a T-shirt with "Yippee KΩ, Ki Yay" painted onto it like a brand led the girls into the dining room, which had been cleared of furniture. "Howdy, y'all," he said with a friendly smile. "I'm Cody Fitzsimons, and on behalf of the brothers of Kappa Omega, we're honored to have you here tonight. Let's pair the newbies up and let the party begin."

"Maybe we should've worn checkered skirts instead. I feel a hoedown coming on," Lora-Leigh whispered, and Jenna tried not to giggle.

The ZZT new members lined up, and each of them pulled a name out of the cowboy hat Cody held out to them.

"I'm with Joe Wentworth," Roni announced, and Jenna watched as a tall, gorgeous guy with jet black hair stepped forward and took Roni's hand.

"Of course she gets the Ben Affleck look-alike," Jenna whispered to Lora-Leigh as she reached into the hat. "I have Rhett McFadden."

She tried not to laugh at Lora-Leigh's dramatic whistling of the *Gone With the Wind* theme when Rhett, a blond-haired cutie with chocolate eyes, stepped up to take her hand. Jenna didn't hear the rest of the pairings because Rhett was already leading her toward the refreshment table.

"Hey, there," he said. "I'm Rhett."

"Jenna," she said. "Nice to meet you." Her eyes quickly flitted to his outfit, jeans and a T-shirt with a yellow smiley-face on it that read I'D LIKE TO CHECK YOU FOR TICKS. Okay, well, that was definitely unique. A brief picture of Tiger flashed in front of her eyes, and she felt heat rise to her cheeks as she remembered the quick kiss he'd given her this afternoon. It had only been a few short hours ago, and now she was with a smiley-face-laden stranger. Granted, he was cute, but he was no Tiger.

"Do you want some punch?" he asked.

She glanced at the punch, then weighed her other drink options. She saw several kegs and coolers full of fruity malt drinks. But there were no sodas in sight. "Is the punch really sweet?" she asked, wondering how much it would mess with her 'betes.

"Nah, the alcohol kills the sugar," he said with a laugh.

He ladled a cupful and passed it over. It tasted like Kool-Aid, but the slight burn she felt as it slid down her throat gave away the alcohol in it. She figured she could have one of these and then switch to water. She'd just sip this slowly, and adjust her pump if she started to feel iffy.

"So where are you from?" she asked, starting with the standard who, what, where questions.

"Gaffney, South Carolina. You know, home of The Big Peach."

She pulled the cup away from her mouth. "The big what?"

Rhett smiled. "The Big Peach is a huge, famous water tower that can be seen from the interstate, and it looks like . . . you know, a gigantic peach."

She smiled politely and took another sip, trying not to think about how much she'd rather be with Tiger right now than with Rhett. It wasn't fair to him, she knew, but it was true. "Tell me more about yourself."

He told her he was planning on majoring in agricultural engineering and that he ran track for Latimer. Jenna tried to keep the conversation going, but her heart just wasn't in it. Rhett drained his punch and poured himself another, and halfway through the second glass stopped asking her questions about herself. Instead, he droned on and on about his plans to buy a farm someday, as his words started to slur slightly. Jenna nodded and "hmmm-mmm'd" and "uh-huh'd" at all the right places in the conversation. Tuning out Rhett's monologue for a second, she surveyed the rest of the room. Danika had been paired up with a lanky guy who was showing her pictures of his dad's cattle ranch in Texas, and she looked bored out of her mind. Minnie Montiero was about a foot taller than her date, so she was sitting down so they could see eye to eye.

But Jenna didn't have a chance to spot Lora-Leigh or Roni

in the crowd, because Rhett (who was on his third cup of punch already) was playfully tugging her out onto the dance floor. The music was blaring now, and more and more couples were starting to dance. The overhead lights were off and were replaced by several black lights, which made everyone's graffiti tees glow eerily. Rhett pulled her toward him, spinning her around the floor so fast that everything around them blurred. He pulled her tighter against his chest, and the smell of the stale liquor on his breath wafted over her. And suddenly that felt way too close.

"So," she yelled above the music as she tried to keep her footing, "I'm from the Atlanta area and I just need to know . . . are you named after Rhett Butler?" It was the stupidest question ever, but she hoped it might slow him down a little, give her time to catch her breath, and put some space between them all at the same time.

"No." Rhett shook his head, laughing in a hard way that hinted of ridicule and made Jenna even more uncomfortable. "Hey, you're so stiff. Just relax and dance."

He wrapped his arms around her waist and stepped closer, but she kept her arms firmly planted on his shoulders, pushing back slightly so he'd get the message. Sweat was breaking out on her forehead, and the constant pounding of the music and the flickering black light were making her dizzy. At least, she hoped that was what was making her dizzy.

"I'd like to sit down for a sec, if that's okay," she said, feeling the room spinning slightly, along with her stomach.

"Oh, come on," he said as she unsteadily headed for the couch. "We just got out there."

Jenna tried to smile through her nausea. "I need a little break."

"I know what you need," Rhett said. "Punch . . . and lots of it. I'll go get you some."

"Actually, could you get me some water?" Jenna asked. "Or some Diet Coke, if you have it?"

Rhett laughed. "You're kidding, right?"

Jenna leaned her head back on the couch, wishing that the music, the ghoulish purple lighting, and Rhett would all just disappear. "Just some water," she said, giving Rhett her best attempt at a don't-mess-with-me look. "Please."

Rhett's smile dropped off his face, and irritation replaced it. "Whatever," he muttered, then stumbled off in the direction of the kitchen.

Jenna closed her eyes for a second to try to bring the room back into focus and then slowly made her way to the bathroom. She dabbed some cold water on her face and checked her insulin pump. Sure enough, an alarm was going off, indicating she'd forgotten her last insulin dose. She quickly gave herself a stronger dose than usual to make up for missing the last dose and to account for the punch she'd had to drink. She'd known that drink was a bad idea to begin with, especially on an empty stomach. But she'd been hoping that maybe her body would regulate itself. Stupid, stupid, stupid. She couldn't believe she'd forgotten to check her readout. But she'd been in such a rush getting ready for the swap, and now she was woozy from the punch, so it was no wonder she'd forgotten.

She waited a few minutes until her head cleared and then stepped out of the bathroom. It didn't take her long to spot

Rhett, downing another cup of punch with some other Kappa Omega.

She started to walk over but froze when she heard Rhett say, "What a downer I'm stuck with tonight. She's barely touched her punch, barely touched me all night, and now she's asking for water."

"Sorry, bud," one of his friends said with a snort. "I didn't think the ZZTs initiated prudes."

The two of them bent over laughing while Jenna quickly backpedaled toward the couch, her face on fire with embarrassment and fury.

She searched the room for Roni and Lora-Leigh, wanting to tell them everything about how horribly this night was turning out. Jenna saw Roni and her date, Joe, sitting over in a dark corner with their heads bent together, laughing. Lora-Leigh and her date, Rob Cowen, were happily dancing. She headed toward them, but then she remembered . . . they didn't know about her 'betes, and she didn't want to tell them. She didn't want to tell anyone, especially after what happened tonight. It was too humiliating.

Feeling tears threatening in the corners of her eyes, she made her way over to Darcy instead.

"Hey, Jenna," Darcy said cheerfully, patting the seat on the couch next to her. "Having fun?"

"Um, actually, I think I need to head back to Tuthill," Jenna said, hoping Darcy couldn't hear her voice trembling. "I have a headache, and I'm just not feeling like myself."

Darcy's smile faded, concern creasing her forehead. "Did something happen that upset you?"

"No, no," Jenna said quickly. After all, Rhett only wanted to have a good time, like everyone else. And she'd ruined it for him. "It's just been such a long week. I'm worn out. And tomorrow I have to get up really early for the bus ride to Atlanta for the away game, and I won't even get to see my family while I'm there. Do you think you could walk with me back to Tuthill?"

Wrapping her arm around Jenna, Darcy said, "Sure thing. Maybe we can grab something to eat on the way back? That might make you feel better."

"Yeah, that sounds great." Jenna smiled gratefully. Getting some food in her system would help stabilize her insulin level.

Jenna quickly waved to Roni and Lora-Leigh, signaling to them that she'd explain her early exit later. Then she stepped out into the cool night air with Darcy, relief sweeping over her now that Rhett was out of sight. But even as she made small talk with Darcy, the heaviness that had settled over her at the party wouldn't subside. The truth was, she was sick of her 'betes. Sick of getting sick and sick of altering her life to accommodate a damn disease. Rhett was right. She was a downer, and the worst part of it was, she didn't have a clue what to do to change that.

CHAPTER
4

Roni sat down on her bed and booted up her laptop when she returned to her dorm room late Saturday night. She'd gone with Beverly, Camille, and Sandy to the L&M Train Depot, an old railroad station on the west end of Latimer that had been converted into a restaurant and club. The cover band that played was great, and Roni'd loved every second of her time with her Rose Bud, Beverly. Beverly was an only child, and her dad was the president of Techtonic Oil and Gas in Houston, so she knew all about being raised by nannies. She'd given Roni some helpful info about the New Member Presidency, too, answering all of Roni's questions about the president's duties at ZZT. Roni'd been nominated by Danika at the meeting on Wednesday, and ever since then, she hadn't been able to stop thinking about it. The job sounded perfect for her, but there was something holding her back. She needed some advice, and she knew that Kiersten was the person she needed it from. So she'd left her friends at the bar at ten and headed back to Tuthill. She was exhausted from all the week's new member activities anyway, and she knew she wouldn't be able to sleep until she got this figured out.

Now she kicked off her heels, not caring where they landed in her room, but knowing someone else wouldn't pick them up for her either. Just as she liked it. Scooting back on her bed, Roni tucked her feet up underneath her and pulled the computer onto her lap. She IM'd Kiersten, hoping she might still be awake.

k_douglas: Look who's up!

veronica.van.gelderen: Hey Kiersten!!!!

k_douglas: What r u doing home on a Sat nite?

veronica.van.gelderen: I just got in. Went to hear a band with some ZZT sisters.

k_douglas: Sounds like fun. Any hotties?

veronica.van.gelderen: ALL hotties. :)

k_douglas: Perfect! So, u need guy advice?

veronica.van.gelderen: Not yet. (I'll keep u posted.) But I do need some advice. I'm running for New Member President at ZZT.

k_douglas: That's gr8t! My roommate was our New Member President, and she loved it. Ur so überresponsible, it'll be prfct 4 u.

veronica.van.gelderen: Thing is, my bf Lora-Leigh is running, too.

k_douglas: Ahhhh . . .

veronica.van.gelderen: I don't know what to do. I don't want LL mad at me.

k_douglas: It's about you, Roni. No one else. Will your friend really be angry at having some competition?

veronica.van.gelderen: I don't think so. I just don't want it to affect our friendship.

k_douglas: It won't. Not if she's a true bff.

veronica.van.gelderen: You're right.

k_douglas: Oh, I hate to do this, but I need to run. Phillip just got here.

veronica.van.gelderen: <giggle>. . . a little booty-call?

k_douglas: U know it. :)

veronica.van.gelderen: Tell him I said hi!

k_douglas: K. Talk to u soon.

veronica.van.gelderen: Luv ya!

k_douglas: U too, sweetie. XOXO

Roni stared at her laptop for a few seconds before clicking it shut. Kiersten was right. This was about her, and only her. She'd always been the model daughter, listening dutifully to her parents. But she'd come to LU to find out who she was minus the Van Gelderen family crest, and this was her chance. The New Member Presidency was something she wanted. It wasn't expected of her or demanded of her, and her parents had nothing to do with it. She knew she'd be great at it, and she suddenly realized that there was no question of what she was going to do.

There was just one more person she had to talk to first.

Roni quietly knocked on the door to Lora-Leigh's room. It was close to midnight, but it was Saturday. If Lora-Leigh was actually in her room and not out (and that was a big if), she'd be sketching out a design or reading the latest copy of *Vogue*.

The door jerked open. "What?"

"Oh, sorry, Virginia," Roni said, trying not to stare at the girl's ghoulishly white face — mouth outlined with black lipstick and eyes with purple shadow. Roni had seen Lora-Leigh's roommate a dozen times, but her whole vampress look still freaked her out a little. "I was looking for Lora-Leigh."

Virginia ran a hand through her black hair. "She's out with her Flower Petal, Betsy Bickford."

"Oh, you mean her Rose Bud." Roni nodded, stifling a giggle. "Okay, sorry I bothered you. I'll catch up with her tomorrow morning, then."

"No prob," she said. "I was just meditating."

There was a pungent odor emanating from the far corner of the room, where Roni saw a Tibetan rug set up on the floor surrounded by tea lights. Wow. She was glad she didn't have to live with that smell . . . whatever it was.

"Just tell Lora-Leigh I stopped by," Roni said, already turning away. But Virginia didn't need to, because there was Lora-Leigh, walking up the hallway.

"Hey, Boston, what's up?" Then she put her hand over her nose. "Virginia, what is that smell?"

Virginia stepped back into the room and moved toward a black curtain that cordoned off her desk space. "Patchouli incense. It's meant to cleanse and purify."

"Yeah, well, it's cleansing my nasal cavity right now," Lora-Leigh said. "I don't mean to disrupt your chakra, but can you kill the incense while we're in here? And crack the window so everything I own won't smell like a burning boot!"

Virginia smirked. "Fine. No one appreciates an Emo these days."

"Not true," Lora-Leigh said, blowing her a kiss. "I love ya, babe, spiderweb stockings and all."

Virginia rolled her eyes but smiled as she disappeared behind the black curtain.

"So, Lora-Leigh, it's not too late, is it?" Roni asked.

Lora-Leigh laughed. "We're in college. No such thing."

"Good," Roni said, taking a deep breath. "I was hoping we could talk." She wrinkled her nose. "Maybe we could head to the lounge."

"Sure," Lora-Leigh said, grabbing her flip-flops and a shopping bag from under her bed. "I want to air out my mom's shrug anyway. She'll never wear it if it smells like a spice shop."

"You finished it already?" Roni asked as they made their way to the lounge.

Lora-Leigh nodded. "She still hasn't answered any of my e-mails or phone calls. So I figured the sooner I finished it, the better. When in doubt, clothes make a fab apology." She plopped down on the sofa and pulled the shrug out of the bag. "What do you think?"

"Omigod." Roni gasped. The shrug was raw silk in a brilliant shade of scarlet, with tiny beading detail around the edges. "Lora-Leigh, this is completely gorgeous. My mom would pay hundreds for something like this on Newbury Street. Your mom's going to love it."

"I hope so," Lora-Leigh said. "If she doesn't, I'm out of ammo. Except if I get picked for the New Member President. Then I might have another shot with her. My mom had that job at Tri-O. I thought she might come around if she saw I was following her lead."

Roni swallowed painfully as guilt washed over her. She'd had no idea why Lora-Leigh would even be interested in the presidency until now. Knowing that it had to do with her mom only made her feel worse. But she had to be honest with Lora-Leigh. It was now or never.

"The New Member Presidency is what I wanted to talk to you about." Roni sighed. "I'm running for it, too."

The hint of a smile flickered across Lora-Leigh's face as she slipped her mom's shrug back into the bag. "I heard."

"You did?" Roni gaped.

"Sure." Lora-Leigh shrugged. "So now we have our own ZZT minidram. You think we could pitch it as a possible episode of *Greek*?"

Roni tried to laugh, but the knot in her stomach was almost choking her, and she suddenly couldn't find her voice at all.

"Breathe, Roni, breathe," Lora-Leigh said, shaking her. "I know it was a bad joke, but I didn't think you'd go AWOL over it. Does being New Member President mean that much to you?"

"Yes . . . no . . . yes," Roni started, then threw up her hands. "Yes, I want to be New Member President, but not if it means losing our friendship over it."

Lora-Leigh stared at Roni for a full minute, then finally said, "Okay, time to leave the parallel universe you're in and come back to the mother ship. You're not going to lose my friendship. If there was any danger of that happening, it was when I saw your designer closet. Crimes of passion have been committed over lesser wardrobes. But I've accepted your aristocratic upbringing and made peace with your clothes, so you're safe."

Roni laughed, and some of her tension eased. "Yeah, well, my aristocratic upbringing may have gotten me some great clothes, but other than that it was a pain in the ass."

Lora-Leigh broke into applause. "Did I just hear Roni Van Gelderen curse? Love it!"

Roni gnawed on her bottom lip. "Well, it's true. My mother has time to chair every committee in Boston, and my father has time to represent every corporation in New England, but when it comes to being Mom and Dad to me, that's a secondary job."

Lora-Leigh nodded. "Welcome to the Estranged Daughters Club."

"You know your mom will come around sooner or later," Roni said. "My mom is different." There was no hope that Cathryn Minson Van Gelderen would ever change her designer spots.

Roni told Lora-Leigh about being raised by au pairs and her parents' indifference to her except when it came to her choice of colleges. She explained her friendship with Kiersten and how she felt she was the only family she had . . . until she joined Zeta Zeta Tau.

"I feel like if I get elected New Member President," she said, "it'll prove there's more to me than just being the daughter of wealthy Beacon Hill parents. That they couldn't buy this for me, and I did it all on my own. My parents are so disappointed I didn't choose Wellesley or Harvard. I want them to be proud of something I've done on my own, you know?"

"Do I," Lora-Leigh said with a smile. "You want to talk about disappointment? Google the word, and my mother's name comes up first. If anyone can relate, it's me."

"I know." Roni lifted her eyes to her friend's. "So what are we going to do?"

"Simple. We both run. We let the sisters decide."

"I'll totally vote for you," Roni said.

"I'll vote for you, too."

Roni flung herself forward and hugged Lora-Leigh, smiling with relief. "No matter what, we're going to have a *great* president."

Lora-Leigh flipped through her latest *Cosmo* while she waited for the Sunday night meeting to start, but it was no use. Not even Versace's new winter line could keep her attention. All she could think about was that tonight—in just a few minutes, in fact—the New Member President would be announced. There had been no campaigning or speeches. Simple ballots had been passed out earlier tonight with all of the nominees' names on it, including hers. Once the results were announced tonight, she'd either be in…or (gulp) out. She'd scolded herself a thousand times for being nervous, but it didn't matter. She didn't just have butterflies in her stomach; she had swarms of stinging bees in there, too.

She sighed, throwing her magazine on the floor in frustration just as her cell phone rang, making her jump. She did a double take when she saw the number on the screen. It was her mother! Lora-Leigh gripped the phone, feeling happiness sweep through her. Maybe her mom was calling to wish her luck tonight. Maybe she was calling with some last-minute advice. Maybe she was calling just to say hi. Lora-Leigh would take A, B, C, or all of the above.

"Hey, Mom, what's up?" Lora-Leigh said cheerfully, deciding it was best to act like this was an everyday, hey-how-are-you type of confab.

"Hello, Lora." A heavy sigh sounded on the other end of the line. "I've been trying to get your father, and I can't seem to reach him."

Lora-Leigh's heart fell. Her mother seemed as cold and distant as the last time she had talked to her. No mention of the e-mails she'd sent or the messages she'd left. Nothing but the stony voice on the other end of the line. "I haven't heard from Dad today," Lora-Leigh said, trying to keep her voice even.

"Well, he was supposed to drop off your mail."

Lora-Leigh frowned into the phone. "Where? Here at the sorority house?"

"Yes."

"Mom, I could have come home and picked it up. I actually have something for—"

"That's all right," her mother said quickly. "He had some errands to run on campus anyway. And I'm sure you're busy with that sorority of yours. If you see your father, please tell him I need him to stop at the Riches' house and pick up my chafing dish. The Tri-Omega officers are coming over this evening for dinner."

"Are you making your knishes?" Lora-Leigh said, her mouth watering at the thought. "I miss those. Maybe I could bring some of my friends over for one of your awesome dinners? Maybe for a Shabbat sometime?"

There was a long pause, and then Hannah Sorenstein said, "We'll see, dear. I must run." She hung up.

Lora-Leigh returned her phone to her pocket and tried to tamp down the ache in her stomach. Shaking it off, she ventured to the foyer of the ZZT house and poked her head into the front room, where the house phone and the mailboxes were. Her mailbox was full, so her father must have already stopped by.

She picked up the stack and thumbed through it. A "Where Are They Now" from Latimer High School, two solicitations for credit cards, and . . . a letter from her friend Brian Gregory. He was on Parris Island in training for the Marines right now, and she hadn't heard from him since before the semester started. Now she eagerly ripped the envelope open, hoping the letter would take her mind off her mom for a few minutes. But all it did was get her started worrying about her mom *and* Brian. As it turned out, Brian was miserable. He hated boot camp, hated his commanding officers, and hated mess hall food. There was nothing in his letter that sounded like the fun, easygoing Brian she used to know.

"What's with the frown?" Roni asked as Lora-Leigh walked back into the formal living room. The two of them sat on the sofa together, and Lora-Leigh let Roni read Brian's letter.

"Poor guy," Roni said.

"Tell me about it," Lora-Leigh said. "I can't just let him

wallow like this. I've got to do something for him." She thought for a second, then smiled as an idea hit her. "Hey, do you think Beverly would let us put together a care package for him? You know, from the ZZT girls? He'd love that."

"I bet she would," Roni said. "You can talk to her about it after the meeting. And you know, if you get elected New Member President, you can probably orchestrate the whole thing."

"Here's to hoping," Lora-Leigh said. Her mind was already spinning with ideas for the care package, but just then Marissa stood up to call the meeting to order, and she had to refocus.

"First, we have some news to share about Homecoming," Marissa said. "Camille submitted an idea for a float design, and I want everyone to take a look. I think she did an amazing job."

Marissa asked Camille to come up, and together they unrolled a large piece of poster board to reveal a sketch of a ZZT float that was set up like a colorful collage of huge seven- to eight-foot picture frames. In each frame were photos from the past 159 years of Latimer history.

"I'm not the artist Lora-Leigh is, but this should give you the idea. I thought we could go to the LU historical society and see if we could transfer some photos onto huge posters, or we could even paint versions of them to put in these frames," Camille explained. "We could have some of the past ZZT sisters, the old football stadium, some of the old mascots, whatever we want to put in the frames to show LU history."

Applause broke out around the room, and girls were already shouting out ideas for the photo frames.

Marissa laughed. "Okay, I think that's resounding approval. So Camille will put together a list of materials for the float. Then if each of you can find a historical photo you like, we'll look all of them over and choose five or six to use on the float. Now we'll have a quick update about our Homecoming book drive."

But just as Betsy Bickford, the Philanthropy Chair, stepped forward, the double doors of the living room opened, and everyone turned to see who it was.

"Sorry I'm late," Jenna said, blushing furiously. "The band bus broke down and then got stuck in traffic on the way back from Atlanta."

"You okay?" Lora-Leigh whispered as Jenna flopped down onto the couch. She knew Jenna'd left the Kappa Omega swap early on Friday, but she didn't know why, and now she saw dark circles under Jenna's eyes.

"Fine." Jenna nodded, stifling a yawn. "Just tired beyond belief."

Betsy nodded to Jenna and then brought everyone's attention back to the front of the room. "I'm going to pass around a participation sign-up sheet for the Homecoming book drive," she said. "The booth will have hourly shifts, so we'd love to have as many sisters participate as possible."

"We're signing up for Homecoming activities already?" Jenna mumbled, looking dismayed.

"Homecoming's only four weeks away," Roni said, jotting her name down as the sign-up sheet came her way. "We have a lot to do to get ready."

Lora-Leigh took the sheet from Roni. There was no question

she wanted to be involved, especially since her father was known to visit all of the sorority and fraternity philanthropy booths and get his picture taken with them. And, surely, her mother would have to be proud of what she was doing for the Latimer Library. Wouldn't she?

She wrote her name next to Roni's and passed the paper to Jenna. "Want to man the booth with us?"

Jenna bit her lip. "There's already the parade and the pep rally *and* the game."

"So?" Lora-Leigh asked.

"The band's involved in all of that."

"You'd only have to work the ZZT booth for an hour," Roni said.

"Come on, Jenna," Lora-Leigh said. "We've barely seen you all week. Your whole life can't revolve around band." She snorted. "Well, it *could*, but we're putting a stop to that before you enter the realm of Band Geekdom, got it?"

Jenna laughed, and Lora-Leigh took that as an affirmative answer. She scribbled Jenna's name next to hers and Roni's.

Marissa stepped back up. "If anyone has more questions about Homecoming, please e-mail Betsy or Beverly. Beverly will be helping the New Member President with her Homecoming duties in the next few weeks." Marissa smiled. "And speaking of the president, I have the results of the vote right here."

"I hope it's a tie between both of you," Jenna whispered.

Lora-Leigh smiled at Jenna. She was such a sweetie, of course she would wish that. Too bad it couldn't happen.

Lora-Leigh's pulse sped up, and she tried to tell herself that no matter what happened, it would all be copacetic. Of course, telling herself that and believing it were two entirely different things. She slid her gaze to Roni and crossed her fingers.

Marissa opened the sealed envelope and smiled hugely. "Let's give a big hand to our New Member President, Veronica Van Gelderen. Roni! Stand up and take a bow!"

The room erupted in applause, and Roni stood, blushing and graciously nodding to everyone. "Thanks so much!" she said.

Disappointment poured over Lora-Leigh, and her heartbeat threatened her hearing. She knew nabbing the presidency had been a long shot. Roni was much more the Queen Bee type anyway. But still, Lora-Leigh had really wanted this. Not so much for her own sake, but for her mother's. Now she'd have to tell her mom that she hadn't made the cut. And she was pretty sure that wouldn't help salvage their relationship. Lora-Leigh sighed. Well, she'd deal with that later. For now, she had to swallow down her own disappointment and be there for her friend.

She glanced up, and her eyes locked with Roni's. Roni's smile tightened with concern.

"Oh, Lora-Leigh," Roni whispered. "I'm sorry. I know you wanted this, too."

"No biggie." Lora-Leigh smiled, not wanting to dampen Roni's excitement. She hugged her and then playfully mussed with her perfectly coiffed hair. "Congrats, Boston! You're going to make a kick-ass president."

"Thanks," Roni said, returning her hug.

Even though the heaviness of disappointment still weighed on her, Lora-Leigh knew Roni Van Gelderen would be the best New Member President in the history of Zeta Zeta Tau.

And she'd be there right by her side to help.

CHAPTER
5

Jenna hated waking up for an eight A.M. class. Particularly on Monday morning, and particularly for an English Comp class. Dr. Ned Whipple was already returning their English papers from last week with all the enthusiasm of the Grim Reaper, and Jenna had a growing dread that she was headed straight into a Shakespearean tragedy. And sure enough, when her paper landed with an ominous *thunk* on her desk, her worst fear came true. An F. A big, fat, ugly, Sharpie-made F on the top of her paper. Her stomach went into a free fall as she stared at Dr. Whipple's comment:

You're not in high school anymore, Ms. Driscoll. Don't write like you are.

Ouch. She'd never failed a paper in her life! In fact, come to think of it, she'd never gotten a grade less than a C (and the one C she'd gotten in AP Bio last year she'd cried about for two days).

She bit her lip to keep tears from crowding her eyes as she slid her paper into her bag before anyone else could see it. She just didn't understand. She'd always procrastinated on her assignments in high school, and it hadn't mattered. She quickly got next week's assignment and left. She was so deep in thought as she walked down the stairs of Billado Hall, she didn't hear someone calling her until a tap on her shoulder snapped her out of her trance.

"Hey, Jenna!"

She looked up into a pair of amazing blue eyes. "Tiger! Hey, sorry. I was zoning."

"I noticed," he said, his smile warming her all the way to her toes. "Tough class?"

"Yeah." Jenna sighed. "I just got my first English paper back."

"Not good, huh?"

"Abysmal. And I have another one due this week, but you don't want to hear the sob story. Trust me." She smiled, trying to shake off her gloominess. "So, I didn't know you had a class in this building."

Tiger's face turned three shades pinker, and he smiled in an adorably bashful way. "Um, actually, I don't. I stopped by Tuthill this morning to see you, but you weren't there. I ran into your friend Roni, and she told me where your class was."

"Oh." Now it was Jenna's turn to blush. Tiger had walked all the way here from Tuthill just to wait for her to get out of class. That was so sweet.

He walked with her as they made their way out of Billado Hall and into the sunshine. "I thought if you had a break between classes or something, we could grab a coffee at Strumann. I want to hear how your trip to Atlanta was, and…" He blushed slightly again. "I have something I wanted to give you, too."

Jenna's heart fluttered, and she momentarily forgot about her crappy morning. "I don't have band practice until eleven," she said, "and coffee sounds great!"

"I was hoping you'd say that," Tiger said, leading the way toward Strumann. As they crossed the street near the art building, he reached for her backpack and added it onto his shoulder. Jenna grinned at the gentlemanly act. Either Tiger was trying really hard, or he was, in fact, the picture of hottie perfection, chivalry and all. Whatever the case was, she'd take it.

Once they got to Strumann, Tiger ordered a double espresso for Jenna and a black coffee for himself. Jenna knew the caffeine jolt wasn't great for her 'betes, but at this point, she just didn't care. She'd been humiliated by her illness enough on Friday. She wasn't going to let it rule every decision she made in her life anymore.

After Tiger sat down with the drinks, he pulled a plastic bag out of his backpack. "So this is what I wanted to give you," he said. "It made me think of you."

He reached into the bag and pulled out a fat cookbook titled *The Southern Gourmet*. "I figured if you're going to cook dinner for me sometime, you better start practicing," he joked.

"Ha ha," Jenna said. "Scared I might give you botulism, huh?"

Tiger grinned. "Not really. Seriously, I thought you might enjoy trying some of these recipes. Especially if you're thinking about taking cooking courses here."

Jenna thumbed through the book, already seeing a few recipes that looked fun. "This is so nice of you. I love it."

"I'm glad," Tiger said. "So is your day improving?"

"Definitely."

They talked for another hour, until Jenna reluctantly said she needed to go prep for band and her next class, and then he offered to drive her back to her dorm.

"Well... thanks for the ride... and the coffee," she said when they pulled up in front of Tuthill. She didn't want to get out of the car and back to reality. She wished she could hang out with him for the rest of the day and forget about her classes, band, everything.

"Wait, Jenna," Tiger said softly. He stretched his hand out, threaded his fingers through hers. A soft flutter spread up her arm, teasing her heart to beat faster. "When can I see you again?"

"Soon" was all she could manage to say. She thought about all the activities she had going on this week between band and ZZT, but suddenly none of that seemed to matter as much as making the time to see Tiger.

"I hope so," Tiger said. "I'll call you later this week?"

In a fleeting moment of bravery, Jenna smiled and said, "You better."

He squeezed her hand just before she got out of the car, and she walked—no—she floated through the doors of Tuthill. Forget Dr. Whipple's F. This was turning out to be one of the best Mondays she'd had this semester.

When DeShawn sat down next to her on Monday afternoon

in Western Civ, Lora-Leigh was ready and waiting. She slid a copy of her notes over to him before he even had a chance to ask. She'd never been the best at apologizing, but this was her way of trying to make up for the whole Kimberly fiasco.

"Hey, Curly," he said, tousling her hair. "Thanks for the notes."

"No prob," she said. "I photocopied them for you already so you can keep that set."

"Nice," DeShawn said.

He took off his jacket and plopped down next to her, and as soon as he did, she gasped. "Omigod, what happened to your arm?"

"This?" He motioned to a bruise that stretched the whole length of his forearm, crisscrossed with brush-burn scratches. "It's nuthin.' Number ninety-four from Georgia Tech. Big bastard gave me turf burn when he tackled me Saturday. I got a slight concussion, too, but don't worry." He grinned. "All I need is this class to sleep that off."

"You're crazy," Lora-Leigh said, shuddering at his arm again. "I mean, don't get me wrong. I'm a die-hard Red Raiders fan. But I'm not sure I'll ever understand what possesses you to get tackled by guys twice your size over a little stupid pigskin. Why do you do it?"

"Come on, you know you love it." He chuckled low. "You're cute when you're all riled up."

"Don't change the subject," she said, even though she was smiling inwardly at the "cute" comment. "I'm serious."

He shook his head, looking out at the auditorium, which was still filling with students.

"I do it for my family," he said. "I mean, I know I'm a walking cliché. . . . Black boy with athletic talent wants to make it big so he can get an NFL contract and take care of his family. But my dad works long hours, and my mom takes care of everything else. I want to give them back something for all they've sacrificed for me. If I can catch the eye of a pro scout and get into the NFL for even a few years, I'll make some decent money, and my whole family would be set for life."

"That makes sense," she said, "as long as you don't get yourself killed in the process."

DeShawn leaned toward her and whispered mischievously, "You'd miss me; admit it."

"Never." Lora-Leigh playfully slapped him on his good arm. "But what about becoming an architect?"

"I still want that," he said, "*after* my NFL career. I can't play football forever. I mean a guy like Earl Campbell, who played back in the seventies, can barely walk from all the hits he took over the years. I'll play for as long as my body can take it, and then I'll hit the drafting table."

"Just remember that Frank Lloyd Wright wouldn't have been able to design Falling Water with a broken arm," Lora-Leigh said. "Get some rest later today. You look like hell."

"Thanks," DeShawn said with a laugh. "But there's not a chance of R and R today. I've got a model due in Advanced Architecture Design tomorrow. I'll be pulling an all-nighter at my drafting table at Ferguson Hall tonight, and I've got two hours of practice before I can even get there."

He laughed. "Don't look so worried, Curly, or people might think you actually like me."

"Not a chance," Lora-Leigh quipped.

She smiled, trying to play chill, but she *was* worried. And when she saw him wince as he painted during Art later, she worried even more. As much as she hated to admit it, she was getting more and more attracted to him. But losing sleep over a bruised and battered football player was not exactly her idea of a good time. And if DeShawn wasn't going to take better care of himself on the field, then maybe she could do something for him off the field. She just had to figure out what.

"This was the perfect idea," Lora-Leigh said to Jenna as they tucked the rest of the picnic dinner into Lora-Leigh's bag. "And it smells delish. If I'd known you could cook like this, Jenna, I would've boycotted Miss Merry's cooking days ago."

Jenna smiled. "Yeah, well, cooking a picnic dinner for you and DeShawn is one thing; cooking for an entire sorority is another." Jenna checked one more time to make sure everything was in the bag. "I hope he likes it."

"Are you kidding?" Lora-Leigh said. "Grilled chicken, corn bread, sweet potato soufflé, and peach cobbler. What's not to like?" Just smelling all the food made her mouth water. After her class with DeShawn this morning, she'd told Jenna and Roni all about the whole walking wounded sitch, and Jenna'd come up with the brill idea of bringing DeShawn a picnic dinner at Ferguson tonight. Jenna'd desperately needed to take her mind off the F she'd gotten on her English paper, and she said cooking was the best way to do that. So they'd gotten permission to use the ZZT kitchen after Miss Merry was done cooking the house dinner, and the two of them had gone right to work. It had taken them until almost ten o'clock to cook everything, but it had all turned out perfectly, and now Lora-Leigh couldn't wait to surprise DeShawn with the meal.

"I so owe you for this," she said to Jenna.

"Forget about it," Jenna said. "It was just nice to be in a kitchen. I've missed cooking since I came here, and this cookbook Tiger gave me came at just the right time."

Lora-Leigh smiled. "You better not tell him you've been cooking for another man. He'll be jealous."

"I doubt it," Jenna said shyly.

"I don't," Lora-Leigh said, hoisting her heavy bag onto her shoulder and heading for the backdoor. "I'll see you later."

"I want all the details," Jenna said. "Second helpings, third helpings, and what he liked the best."

"Those aren't exactly the kind of details I'm hoping to have," Lora-Leigh said, laughing at Jenna's blushing cheeks as she walked out the door.

Ten minutes later, Lora-Leigh stepped off the elevator onto the fourth floor of Ferguson Hall, the LU architecture building, and headed for the sea of drafting tables set up under the dreary fluorescent lights. She saw a handful of architecture students bent wearily over their tables, constructing their models with tiny pieces of wood and corrugated cardboard. And there was DeShawn, towering over everyone else, carefully cutting windows out of his model with an X-Acto knife.

Lora-Leigh's adrenaline picked up as she cleared her throat and said, "Delivery for Mr. DeShawn Pritchard."

DeShawn looked up with tired eyes, but the second he

recognized Lora-Leigh, a smile spread across his face. "Curly, what are you doing here?"

Lora-Leigh opened her bag to reveal the Tupperware containers full of food. "If you're going to be here all night, you need some brain food, so here I am."

"That smells amazing," DeShawn said. "Did you cook this?"

"Not really," Lora-Leigh admitted. "The last time I cooked at home, the fire department had to come. It wasn't pretty. But I did help my friend Jenna cook it. So can you take a break?"

"For you?" DeShawn said. "And there's food involved, too? You don't even need to ask. Come with me."

She followed him through the hallways of the building until they came to a quiet alcove full of couches. There was one lone student snoozing on the couch in the far corner, but as soon as he saw them intruding on his nap time, he wearily trudged back to his workstation. Lora-Leigh laid out the food on the coffee table, and they both dug in. She hadn't even been able to touch Miss Merry's liver and onions tonight, so she was starving.

"Wow," DeShawn said, going for a second piece of chicken. "This is amazing. I haven't had a meal this good since the last time I was home."

"I'll let the chef know," Lora-Leigh said. "How's your model going?"

"Oh, I'm guessing I'll be done around sunrise." DeShawn grinned, gingerly stretching his arms and neck, but avoiding bumping his turf burn.

"It's a model of one of the sketches you showed me before,

right?" Lora-Leigh asked. "The cabin?" She'd had a brief glimpse of it on DeShawn's drafting table.

DeShawn nodded. "After I showed those sketches to you, I finally went to my prof with them. He loved them. In fact, he thinks that I might be ready for an internship this summer at an architectural firm if I work on my portfolio between now and then."

"Kewl," Lora-Leigh said. "Will you do it?"

DeShawn shrugged. "I want to, but we start Red Raiders training camp in early August. I don't know if I'll be able to take a job for the full summer."

"But you've got to do what you love," Lora-Leigh said, hating the idea that he'd give up the internship opportunity for football. "I'd sell my soul for a fashion internship."

DeShawn grinned. "I hope not, but I wouldn't put it past you. 'Course, the devil might want one of your Lora-Leigh outfits instead."

"Now *that* I can definitely do," Lora-Leigh said.

"I'm sure it won't come down to that. I bet you'll be selling your designs to Juicy Couture before you even graduate. They'll know an original when they see one."

"Thanks," Lora-Leigh said as she dished out the last of the peach cobbler onto DeShawn's plate. "You know, if I didn't know better, I'd say you were laying it on thick in hopes of getting lucky tonight," she teased.

DeShawn laughed. "And I'd say that was wishful thinking on *your* part."

"Don't bet on it," Lora-Leigh shot back, but she kept her face turned toward the food so he wouldn't see her blushing.

Just the thought of what it might be like to kiss him made her breath short.

She didn't even know how much time passed as they kept talking until she heard the campus bell tower toll two A.M. Unfortunately for her, DeShawn heard it, too, and he was up off the couch and packing the leftovers into her bag before she had time to protest.

"I hate to ditch you for my model," DeShawn said, "but if I don't finish, my prof is going to kick my already sore butt."

"And that's the last thing you need after the beating you took this weekend," Lora-Leigh said, lifting her bag onto her shoulder. "I guess I'll see you later this week?"

"Yup." DeShawn seemed to debate with himself for a few seconds before leaning forward and pulling her into a soft hug. "Thanks for tonight, Curly," he whispered.

"Hey, anytime you get the midnight munchies, I'm your girl," she joked.

But he caught her eyes and held them, saying, "I wasn't thanking you for the food."

"Oh," Lora-Leigh whispered, leaning into his chest and breathing in his spicy cologne. She was just inches from his face now, and if she turned her head a little, then maybe . . .

But DeShawn pulled back at the last second and gave her a kiss on the forehead that smacked of brotherly love. It took Lora-Leigh a minute to get her bearings and realize that she had, in fact, just been rejected. It was a nice, sweet rejection, but still, rejection all the same.

"Okay, then," she said, breaking free of his hug and shifting into platonic mode. "See ya."

She gave him a quick, no-harm-no-foul smile and made her exit while she still had a semblance of self-esteem left intact. But during the ride down in the elevator, she stood in a daze, wondering what had just happened. And more importantly, what had gone wrong?

Roni took a deep breath as she climbed the front steps to the ZZT house on Wednesday night. Tonight was her first meeting as New Member President, and even though she'd been looking forward to this all week, she was still nervous. She wanted to do everything right. But she knew that it wasn't the presidency that was making her so nervous; it was Lora-Leigh. Sure, Lora-Leigh hadn't even flinched when Roni'd gotten elected, and she'd sworn she was okay with it. But Roni still worried that things would get awkward once she started doing her presidential duties. When she stood beside Beverly tonight, she just hoped Lora-Leigh would still look at her the same way she always had, as a friend.

"Hey, Roni!" Chandra Kearney called out, pulling Roni out of her thoughts and nearly knocking her down, too, as she bolted out the front door. "Say, I could really use a breath mint."

"Oh, sure," Roni said, diving into her preparedness kit and removing the tin of Altoids. "Aren't you staying for dinner?"

"Nah. Got stuff to do tonight." Chandra popped the Altoid between her teeth and smiled. "Just remember, the seniors love the new members! We'll be showing you *how much* soon."

Chandra moved down the walk and slipped into her car, and Roni stared after her, wondering what exactly she was plotting. Whatever it was, she hoped it wouldn't be during the meeting tonight.

She made her way into the house and grabbed a seat next to Lora-Leigh for dinner. There was no sign of Jenna, and Roni guessed, with a sinking heart, that she was going to be MIA for the meeting again tonight. Jenna'd mentioned earlier that she had a big Western Civ quiz tomorrow, so, after band practice, she'd probably be cooped up in her room, trying to ignore Amber's diabolical mood swings long enough to study. Poor Jenna. She was stretching herself so thin with all her activities, and it was starting to show on her stressed-out face. And Lora-Leigh's face tonight during dinner didn't look much better.

"What's wrong, Lora-Leigh?" Roni asked, holding her breath and hoping that the issue wasn't what she thought it was.

"Men are what's wrong," Lora-Leigh said. "I'm busy wishing they were lower down on the evolutionary ladder. Like, possibly on the last rung with amoebas."

"Is this about your dinner last night with DeShawn?" Roni asked.

"I don't want to talk about it."

"Okay," Roni said. "Any progress on the Mom front?"

Lora-Leigh pushed her food around her plate. "I don't want to talk about that either."

"Got it," Roni said. "I just want to make sure you're all right . . . with everything. We really haven't talked much since Sunday, and I was worried that—" She broke off, afraid to say it out loud.

"You're worried that I'm plotting to assassinate the New Member President?" Lora-Leigh laughed. "Come on, Boston, I'm not that delusional. I know the best person for the job won. Don't doubt it for a second. And to be honest, it was really more for my mom than me. I'm over it."

"Really?" Roni said, smiling with relief.

"Yup. I'm just licking my wounds from last night. I make it a point never to brood over guys for long, so I'll be fine by tomorrow. But thanks for worrying."

"You're welcome," Roni said, giving her a quick hug. Still, she wasn't sure she bought Lora-Leigh's blasé attitude about losing the presidency. She knew what a big deal it had been to her, and it was just like Lora-Leigh to act as though everything were okay when it wasn't. But Roni knew one thing she could definitely do for her friend to try to set things right and get past the awkwardness. "So," she said, "I was thinking about your friend Brian, and I talked to Beverly about putting together a care package for him tonight."

"You did?" Lora-Leigh said, visibly brightening. "That would be great!"

Roni smiled. "I'm glad you think so, 'cause I'm going to need your help orchestrating the whole thing. You think you're up for it?"

"Who do you think you're talking to?" Lora-Leigh grinned. "Of course I am."

"Good," Roni said, standing up. "Well, I better go help Beverly get ready. I'll see you at the meeting in a few."

Lora-Leigh tried to tune out the images of DeShawn running through her head and tune in as the meeting got under way with announcements about the ZZT new member activities for the week. She wished she wasn't still thinking about the way he'd dissed her last night. She'd been rejected by guys before, but it had never gotten to her the way this had. She knew there was something between her and DeShawn; she felt the chemistry every time she was around him. But she didn't understand why—or how—he could ignore it. Feeling herself dangerously close to becoming a whining, semi-obsessed rejectee, she put the brakes on her Poor-Me attitude and refocused her attention on Megan Gleason, who was thumbing through the new member manual.

Megan said, "It says this week's lesson is 'We strive for academic excellence, cultural growth, and moral strength.'"

Sandy's brows creased. "What does 'moral strength' mean?"

"It means don't be like my roommate, Goth Virginia, who's been sleeping over at Manning Hall for the past three nights." Lora-Leigh snickered.

"Isn't Manning the boys' dorm?" Bonni Ruiz asked, her mouth hanging open.

"Case in point," Lora-Leigh said emphatically to a smattering of muffled giggles.

"Okay, ladies, let's settle down," Beverly said. "Roni's going to be leading tonight's sisterly task, so she has the floor."

Roni placed her long black hair back behind her ears and cleared her throat uneasily. Lora-Leigh thought it was adorable that she was still nervous, even though everyone loved her to death.

"Heather and I have talked to several fraternities, and they're anxious to set up swaps and mixers with us over the next few weeks. Thursday night, we're having a Bowling Swap with the Pi Theta Epsilons. The swap has a fifties theme, so wear sweater sets, poodle skirts, pedal pushers, bobby socks, the works."

Lora-Leigh raised her hand. "I can help people with costumes."

"Definitely!" Roni said. "Our resident fashion goddess can come to anyone's rescue."

Feeling a blush creep up her cheeks, Lora-Leigh played it off with a mocking eye roll.

"I'll let everyone know when Heather and I set up other swaps," Roni continued, then paused and broke into a wide smile. "Now, for tonight, we have a very special project to do. A friend of Lora-Leigh's is away in the United States Marine Corps and is homesick. His name's Brian Gregory. Lora-Leigh came up with the fab idea of putting together a care package for him, and I thought we could all write him letters, too."

Roni asked Lora-Leigh to join her up front to share a few things about Brian. Lora-Leigh told the girls about Brian's family and about him running track in high school and all of his favorite foods, movies, etc. Then she and Roni passed out stationery to all the girls for the letters. The girls spread out around the room and worked on their projects; some even teamed up to take some pictures with digital cameras to include in their letters. After an hour, Lora-Leigh and Roni collected the letters.

"Looks like Brian's going to be the envy of all the guys on Parris Island," Lora-Leigh said with a smile, looking at the huge pile of letters. She added her own letter to the pile and then turned to her sisters. "Thanks, y'all. He's going to love this."

Then she pulled Roni aside, hugging her. "And thank you, Boston. You made my day." She knew Roni had offered to help orchestrate this more for her than for Brian. It was her way of making sure that everything was okay between them. And just like that, the tiny bit of lingering disappointment Lora-Leigh still felt about losing the election disappeared. She knew beyond any doubt that Roni really was the right choice.

"So does that mean you're over your funk?" Roni asked her.

Lora-Leigh grinned. "Well on the way."

Before she could say anything else, loud music suddenly rang out from the TV room's speakers, the double doors to the living room opened, and in burst a bunch of shouting and clapping seniors wearing ZZT sweatshirts and led by Nava Holmes and Chandra Kearney.

"Sorry to bust up your meeting, Bev," Nava yelled. "But the Seniors Love the New Members committee is here to kidnap them. Newbies, I hope you brought your preparedness kits, 'cause you're going to need them tonight. We're all headed to a party at our apartment!"

"Yes!" Lora-Leigh shouted, grabbing Roni and dragging her toward the door to join the rest of their sisters, all squealing with excitement. "This is just what I needed tonight." Her funk was officially finito. It was time to bring on the party.

Roni stared at the drinks lined up in front of her, wondering what she had gotten herself into. There was no way she could do this.

"Come on, Boston," Lora-Leigh said, shaking the box of matches in her face. "You volunteered for this. You said, and I quote, 'As New Member President, it's my duty.'"

"Show us some ZZT spirit," Danika kidded.

"All right," Roni said with a nervous giggle, and Sandy,

Danika, Darius, and Lora-Leigh burst into cheers as they crowded around to watch. They'd been at Chandra and Nava's apartment now for two hours, and they'd been two hours of nonstop fun. Minnie and Lindsey were doing karaoke to a Madonna CD, and Danika and Sandy and Darius were playing quarters and laughing hysterically. Molly Ballard, Emma Cox, and Amy Tubbs were doing some sort of line dance they'd learned out at Morgan's, the dance club on the Strip. Hollis Hendricks and Margo Pratt were out on the front porch with a couple of the seniors talking to Melody about the upcoming Homecoming election.

Of course, Roni already had a light buzz. She was just hoping that she could get through the Greek alphabet without bursting out laughing. If she didn't, she'd be drinking all of the cups of beer lined up in front of her.

"Here's the deal," Lora-Leigh said. "You recite the entire Greek alphabet three times before the match burns out. Or you drink for every letter you miss."

"Got it," Roni said. At least Nava'd ordered pizza, and it was on its way. Her stomach grumbled.

As the rest of the girls cheered, Lora-Leigh lit a match. "Go, girlfriend!"

Roni took a deep breath. "Alpha, Beta, Gamma, Delta, Epsilon, Zeta, Eta, Theta, Iota, Kappa, Lambda, Mu, Nu, Xi, Omicron, Pi, Rho, Sigma, Tau, Upsilon, Phi, Chi, Psi, Omega!"

"Again!" Lora-Leigh cried, still holding the match.

Roni raced through the alphabet a second time, barely taking a breath before she finished.

"And one more time!" Chandra shouted.

"Alpha, Beta, Gamma, Delta, Epsilon, Zeta, Eta, Theta, Iota, Kappa, Lambda, Mu, Nu, Xi, Omicron, Pi, Rho, Sigma, Tau, Upsilon, Phi, Chi—"

"Stop! It almost burned me." Lora-Leigh flicked out the match. "Almost three times, Roni. Not bad. But you've still got to drink." She slid two cups to Roni.

Roni groaned dramatically, but she downed the two cups as fast as she could. When she finally came up for air, a monstrous burp burst out of her before she could stop it. She slapped a hand over her mouth, giggling and blushing furiously.

"Omigod, that was disgusting," she said, hiccuping. "I'm so sorry. My parents would probably disown me if they saw me now."

Lora-Leigh elbowed her. "Oh, what's a little belching among friends?"

"Damn straight," Roni said, stumbling over the curse word that sounded foreign on her tongue. And just to prove that she could, she burped again, making Lora-Leigh bend over laughing. It was a relief to forget about all the Bostonian niceties she'd been raised with and just let down her guard for once. And if there was anyone she could do that with, it was her sisters.

"Come on, newbies, pizza's here," Nava called from the kitchen at the front of the apartment.

"Yeah, food!" Keesha exclaimed, and then wobbled a little to the left.

"I'm *stahhhhhvin*," Roni said, her New England accent as thick as a Kennedy's now.

Just then the doorbell rang, and Nava yelled, "Hey, Johnson, get the door, will ya?"

Keesha saluted. When she opened the door, it was Heather Bourke, Nicole Gentry, and Betsy Bickford. Heather held up a half case of Coors Light and a brown paper sack. "We brought reinforcements."

"Come on in," Chandra shouted.

As the seniors made their way into the kitchen, Roni struggled to her feet with Lora-Leigh's help, and then they helped Darius up, too. The girls stumbled into the kitchen, where Minnie, Lindsey, and Sue-Marie all held each other up, giggling.

Taking notice, Nava said, "Okay, more pizza and less drinking." She opened the pizza boxes, and all the girls took a slice. "Y'all are totally wasted. Except for you, Sorenstein. Cast-iron constitution or something?"

Lora-Leigh shrugged. "Something like that."

Nava snapped her fingers. "Bring it in," she instructed to Heather.

Heather went to the fridge and withdrew the paper bag she'd brought. "As requested, O great one." She bent low in front of Nava in mock reverence as she handed over the sack.

Chandra peeked into the bag. "Oh, you didn't!"

"Did," Heather said.

"Did what?" Roni asked.

Roni watched as Nava pulled out two forty-ounce cans of—*ewww!*—Milwaukee's Best. Roni gagged just thinking about it. She'd only tasted it once at the party at the athletic dorm a few weeks ago, and just the thought of it made her stomach turn.

"Lora-Leigh, you're not going to drink that, are you?" Roni shrieked.

"She sure is," Nava said as she placed a forty-ounce can in each of Lora-Leigh's hands.

"Don't worry," Chandra said. "None of you are going anywhere tonight on our watch. It's a lock-in, and we have enough pillows and blankets for everybody. You don't have an eight o'clock, do you, Lora-Leigh?"

Lora-Leigh smirked. "An eleven."

Heather winked. "You'll make it."

"Now drink up, Sorenstein!" Chandra said.

Lora-Leigh looked at one can and then the other. With a shrug and a grin, she said, "Bottoms up."

"Oh, I can't watch," Roni said, clinging to Sandy and giggling. Roni *did* have an eight o'clock, but maybe, for the first time in her life, she'd break the rules and ditch. After all, her parents weren't around to disapprove. And for once, being out of sight, out of mind to them might not be a bad thing. In fact, it might just be a lot of fun.

CHAPTER
6

Jenna took a halfhearted nibble of her pizza and tried to focus on something—anything—other than Megan Gleason's nonstop chatter about the Seniors Love the New Members Party. She'd agreed to meet the girls for dinner at "Say Cheese!" Pizza before heading to the fifties swap with the Pi Theta Eps. But for the last half an hour, since Jenna sat down at the table, last night's party was all that anyone could talk about. It was Nava-this, Chandra-that, and wasn't-it-hilarious-when from Lora-Leigh, Roni, and the other girls. Not only had Jenna missed out on all the fun, but now she was missing out on all the inside jokes, too. It was like her friends had experienced this secret induction into the inner workings of ZZT, and Jenna'd been left out in the cold.

"Omigod, Jenna," Megan was saying now. "You should have seen Roni. Lora-Leigh convinced her to put on these pleather bell-bottoms from Nava's closet, and Lora-Leigh wore Chandra's Tina Turner wig from last Halloween and they sang the most hilarious rendition of 'Dancing Queen.'"

"I was wearing *pleather?*" Roni shrieked. "So that's where the rash on my legs came from."

Lora-Leigh smirked. "An allergic reaction to your first brush with synthetics, huh?"

Roni shot her a dirty look, then dropped her head to the table. "I can't believe you did that to me!"

"It took very little convincing." Lora-Leigh laughed. "You were an immovable force. It was like watching Sanjaya on *American Idol.* Painful but enthralling. I think someone recorded the whole performance on their cell phone, too."

"If it takes the rest of the semester, I will hunt that recording down and burn it," Roni said, only half-jokingly. "I'm never drinking again."

"Sorry I missed it," Jenna muttered, not even trying to hide the sarcasm in her voice. This was the last straw. She couldn't take it anymore.

A look of surprise crossed Roni's face, and then she put her hand over her mouth. "Oh, we're awful. I can't believe we've been sitting here going on and on about the party without thinking of you. Shame on us." She wrapped her arms around Jenna. "I'm not going to let you miss another thing. Like tonight's swap. Period. End of sentence."

"Thanks," Jenna said, feeling a little bit better. "I want to be there for everything moving forward." And she meant it. She'd do all she could to make sure nothing got in the way of her new member semester. Darcy had bought her that Day Planner, as promised, and since Jenna'd gotten her F in English, she'd been trying to be diligent about scheduling her weeks. She'd realized that she had been wasting a lot of time, but it was still tough to plan out everything from classes and papers to band practice to new member education and frat parties. But if she just stuck with her planner, she could do it. And so what if she'd skipped out on the last half of band practice tonight to make it to the swap? The notes she played on her horn weren't that vital. And Papa Skank had been too busy riding Becca, another poor frosh, to notice Jenna's escape.

"So," Lora-Leigh said. "Let's iksnay on the arty-pay. And talk about something really important. Like scoring dates to Saturday's football game against Mississippi River College."

"Wait a sec. You said guys were basically amoebas, and now you want a date?" Roni asked.

Lora-Leigh shrugged. "Last night in a moment of lucidity after the event-which-shall-not-be-named, I made my peace with amoebas, with one exception. The jury's still out on him."

"And we all know who that is," Roni said. "Well, maybe we'll meet some Pi Theta Eps with date potential tonight."

"Maybe," Lora-Leigh said. "Just remember who we're dealing with. I told you the Pi Thetas were the craziest frat on campus. I heard two PTEs got picked up by campus police last Friday for streaking through Strumann. Where there's disorderly conduct, there's usually a Pi Theta."

"Maybe we should be having a swap with the Tau Delts instead," Sandy said. "Most of them are lacrosse and basketball players." She giggled. "I would totally go to a game with one of them. I have a thing for lacrosse players. They're so neo-preppy."

"I'll see if I can set up a swap with them some other time.

Tonight it's the Pi Thetas, streaks or no." Roni froze, then added, "I can't believe I just said that. Anyway, tonight will be fun, and not all the Pi Thetas can be that crazy, can they?"

Jenna caught Lora-Leigh's snort of laughter, but Roni pretended to ignore it.

"I already have a date with Daniel Cervantes from Sigma Sigma," Bonni singsonged.

"That's awesome," Sandy said. "What are you going to wear?"

Jenna knew that fraternity guys and sorority girls all dressed up for the games, so Bonni's clothing choice was a big deal. As Bonni described the outfit she'd already picked out for the game, Jenna felt herself sinking back into her funk again.

"Now what, Miss Debbie Downer?" Lora-Leigh asked, elbowing her. "Are we not allowed to talk about dates either?"

"Of course you are," Jenna said sadly. "It's just that while you all are sitting in the fraternity section at the game, looking cute in your outfits, I'll be stuck sitting by myself with the Marching Raiders wearing scratchy polyester and a Shaker hat that makes me look like a boy."

"Come on, Jenna," Lora-Leigh said. "You get to play along with all of the cheers and perform for thousands of people in the stadium and on TV."

"Right!" Roni said enthusiastically. "And we're all going to cheer you and Shauna on."

Shauna Burke, a junior ZZT, was one of the Latimer University High Steppers—known throughout the conference for their perfectly polished white boots. 'Course, Shauna got to wear a sexy red mini and sequined halter, and everyone knew who she was. Jenna seamlessly blended into the brass section. Just another one of the plume heads with a gold horn.

Jenna shrugged. "It won't be as much fun as sitting with y'all in one of the frat sections."

"You mean sitting with the *Fox* section." Roni gave Jenna a teasing smile.

"No," Jenna protested, but she knew her red cheeks were a dead giveaway.

"Okay, attitude adjustment time," Lora-Leigh said, standing up and pulling Jenna to her feet. "Let's get you out of here before you sink into a despair that can only be brought on by really nasty 'Say Cheese' pizza."

"It's time to head to the swap anyway," Roni said. "Even if you can't get a date for the game, you'll still have fun."

"I know," Jenna said, trying to sound more upbeat.

She followed everyone out of the restaurant and through campus, finally crossing over to Sorority Row. Just before they reached the ZZT house, Jenna's cell buzzed with a text message. She checked the screen, and her heart flip-flopped when she saw the text was from Tiger.

> Caddyshackman: Hey u. What r u up to?
> ChezJen: Heading to a swap with PTE.
> Caddyshackman: Make sure they keep their clothes on. :)
> ChezJen: They better!
> Caddyshackman: I know u have to sit w/band on Sat. But I'll be thinking of u. Can I see u after the game?

Jenna gasped, and her fingers froze on her cell keys. She

grabbed Lora-Leigh and Roni. "Tiger wants to meet me after the game, y'all," she said breathlessly. "What should I say?"

"Um, yes would be a good start." Roni grinned.

"Tell him you'll meet him at Morgan's," Bonni suggested. "Heather told me that's where all the ZZTs go after the games and the football players, too."

"But how do we get in?" Jenna asked.

Sandy smiled. "Our older sisters have connections."

"And I have a fake ID," Roni sang out, flashing her ID for everyone to see. "Julie Elizabeth Stephens from Mountain Brook, Alabama."

"Where did you get that?" Lora-Leigh said with a hint of envy.

"From Nicole Gentry," Roni said proudly. "She's my Rose Bud this week. She said it was a freshman essential."

"Well, Julie Elizabeth," Lora-Leigh said. "I suggest you work on that southern accent of yours." Then Lora-Leigh turned to Jenna. "Did you text him back?"

"I'm doing it right now," Jenna answered, her thumbs flying over her cell.

"And?" Roni asked.

Jenna grinned and held up her cell for the girls to see.

Caddyshackman: See u at Morgan's. Can't wait!

"And you were worried about a date for the game," Lora-Leigh scoffed. "Please. You've caught the eye of the Tiger, girl."

Jenna rolled her eyes, laughing. "That was a horrible pun."

"I know, I know." Lora-Leigh smirked. "Sometimes I just can't help myself. So are you better now?"

"Much," Jenna said. Now she couldn't stop smiling as she left with her sisters for the swap. Things were looking up. She had her planner, her schedule, her ZZT activities, and a postgame date! And nothing was going to keep her from having fun with her sisters tonight.

Jenna Driscoll was back in action!

Roni crossed Williams Drive Monday afternoon after speed-walking from her last class to meet up with Beverly Chang at the natatorium for an afternoon swim.

Waiting for the DON'T WALK sign to change, Roni adjusted her Gucci sunglasses. The pavement was hot beneath her feet, even though it was October in Florida. A warm breeze blew her along the sidewalk toward the natatorium. At the door, she showed her student ID and slipped into the girls' locker room. There, she changed into her black Speedo tanksuit, pulled her long hair up into a ponytail, and stashed her things in a locker.

Beverly wouldn't mind if she started without her. Besides, Roni could completely outswim Beverly, so if she got the intense workout done first, she and Beverly could have a more leisurely pace together.

When she stepped into the natatorium, the smell of chlorine scratched at her nose. The pool was busier than usual, full of people doing laps, with a section blocked off for diving practice. She dove into the water, feeling refreshed as she cut through the surface, kicking a steady pace and stretching out to pull herself along.

On her eighth lap, she stopped to catch her breath. Her eyes were drawn to a lean, long figure with shaggy dark hair atop the high dive. Her breath caught in her throat when she realized it was Lance. He seemed oblivious to everything around him, focused intently on the water below him. His legs were muscular and flexed, poised, and balanced backward on the high dive. His arms spread wide, he bounced on the balls of his feet twice and then launched into the air, twisting one ... two ... three times before sluicing into the water with only the smallest sprinkle of a splash.

"That was amazing," she said, swimming over to him as he climbed out of the pool.

"Hey, Roni!" He smiled, and she relished the fact that he remembered her name. They'd exchanged smiles and brief waves in Geography, but it was tough to talk in class and lab, and because their awful T.A. loved to keep them late, Roni usually had to rush to her next class right afterward.

"I knew you were a good swimmer, but I didn't know you could dive like that," Roni said.

Lance just shrugged. "I've always been a stronger swimmer, but I love to dive, too. That dive wasn't great, though. I overextended on my last twist."

"A perfectionist, huh?" Roni teased.

"Definitely," Lance said with a smile as he used his shammy towel to dry off. "It's something in the genes, I think. On my dad's side. He was a swimmer, too. He actually made it to the finals for the nineteen seventy-six Olympics."

"What happened?" Roni asked.

"He made a bad entry from the starting block and tore a ligament in his shoulder," Lance said. "He had to drop out. But as soon as I was old enough to swim, Dad started grooming me for the water, too."

"But you enjoy it, right?" Roni asked. "I mean, you don't just swim for your dad, do you?"

"No way," Lance said. "I wouldn't do it if I didn't love it. I just put a lot of pressure on myself to perform. You know, for his sake."

"Yeah, I know what you mean," Roni said. "My parents have all these expectations for me. But no matter how hard I try to live up to them, I never quite make the cut."

Lance leaned over the side of the pool and smiled intently at her. "Somehow, I have a hard time believing that. You strike me as the model-daughter type. How could your parents not love that?"

"You don't know my parents." Roni laughed. She thought about how just last week she'd e-mailed them to tell them about winning the New Member Presidency. All she'd gotten back was a short note from her mother saying, "Congratulations, dear. I can't say I'm surprised you won. At a mediocre school, you can't expect a lot of top-caliber competition." So, even if she was a model daughter, Roni wasn't exceeding expectations. As usual.

"So did you end up joining a fraternity?" she asked Lance. "I thought maybe I'd see you at some of the mixers coming up."

Lance shook his head. "I dropped out of Rush," he said. "I've got enough going on with the swim team, and I have to keep my grades up for my athletic scholarship. Greek life was just too much on top of that."

"Oh," Roni said. "Sorry."

"No biggie," Lance said. "Swimming is what I really want to spend most of my time doing anyway. Especially with someone like you to race with." He grinned. "You promised a rematch, remember?"

Roni smiled, tilting her head to the side in the slightly girlish way she'd learned most guys had a tough time resisting. "I'm ready whenever you are," she said. "Just say when."

"How about now?" he said, dropping his shammy on the bench by the pool.

"Sure," Roni said. But just then a splash a few feet away startled her, and Beverly sprang up from the water.

"Hey!" Beverly said, looking from Roni to Lance and back again. "Sorry I'm late. Couldn't find anywhere to park."

"Don't worry about it," Roni said with a smile. But she secretly wished that Beverly had been even later so she and Lance could have had a chance to race. Now she turned back to him, but he already had his sports duffel in hand.

"I guess we'll have to try it another time," he said.

"I guess so," Roni agreed, "but I'll see you later. Either here or in Dr. Sylvester's snore fest."

"I hope so." Lance waved and retreated to the guys' locker room.

"I didn't interrupt anything, did I?" Beverly asked.

"Nope," Roni said, trying to sound nonchalant.

But it didn't work, because Beverly smiled knowingly. "Whatever you say," she singsonged. Then she got into position, holding on to the side of the pool. "Ready to work out?"

Roni shook off images of Lance and focused on the water. "Let's go!"

An hour later, Beverly hung on to the side of the pool, trying to catch her breath. "I'm completely exhausted. I don't know how you do this every day."

Dabbing her face with a towel, Roni said, "Well, I haven't been coming every day like I should, but I need to get back in the habit." Especially if it meant seeing Lance in action on a daily basis.

Quickly, Roni re-dressed in her jeans and long-sleeved T-shirt in the locker room, then checked her BlackBerry. While she was waiting for Beverly to finish changing, she noticed two new e-mails had come through, one from her Rose Bud, Nicole, and the other from her friend Kiersten Douglas. Roni clicked on Kiersten's message first:

> I tried calling your phone, but I guess you're in class. I just wanted you to know that Phillip and I got engaged last night! We think the wedding will be sometime around New Year's, but I'll let you know when we set the official date. And I'll want you in the wedding, of course. I'll call later. . . . I promise.
>
> Hugs,
>
> Kiersten

Her hand flew to her mouth. "Oh my God!"

Beverly burst out of the stall. "What's wrong?"

Roni handed over her BlackBerry. "My friend Kiersten is getting married! She got engaged last night."

Reaching out, Beverly hugged Roni, and they celebrated together.

"You should call her," Beverly said when they pulled apart.

Without hesitation, Roni dialed Kiersten's number, but it went straight to voice mail. "Kiersten!!! I'm standing here with my sorority sister Beverly—"

"Hey! Congratulations!" Beverly chimed in.

"—and I'm sooooooooooo happy for you and Phillip. You know I would be honored to be in your wedding. I'll do anything to help. Give me a call or e-mail me more details. Love ya!"

Clicking the phone off, she thought of all the things to come with Kiersten. The wedding would probably be in Boston, so that would mean helping her with preparations over the holidays. Trying on bridesmaid's dresses. Going to a shower. It would all be so much fun and would give her plenty of excuses to get out of her parents' holiday soirées. Between her running into Lance and the great news from Kiersten, Roni's day couldn't get much better. Now if she could just cross Lance's path more often, and maybe even score a date with him, her semester would be well on its way to perfect.

"Are you sure this looks okay?" Lora-Leigh whispered to Roni for the third time as they made their way to the roped-off Phi Theta Ep section in Daniel Stadium. She was wearing a funky asymmetrical petal skirt with a linen halter in a filmy baby blue—something she'd copied from an old episode of *America's Next Top Model*.

"You look fabulous," Roni insisted.

"Well, it's not Max Azria," Lora-Leigh said, eyeing Roni's ultra chic black mineral silk knit tank and chai-colored rayon jersey skirt.

"No," Roni said. "It's better."

Chris Segalini, Roni's date, leaned toward her and smiled approvingly. "Ben, I do believe we're sitting with the hottest girls here."

"No doubt about it," Ben Bowden, Lora-Leigh's date, said, taking her hand.

"Thanks." Lora-Leigh smiled. "Y'all aren't too shabby yourselves." She and Roni had met Ben and Chris at the bowling swap, and they seemed like nice enough guys. Not to mention they were both pretty cute. Even though Lora-Leigh wasn't as much of a frat groupie as some of the other ZZT girls, it was fun to be on the arm of a great-looking guy for the afternoon.

Of course, she kept trying to tell herself that she'd dressed in her newest creation for the sake of Ben, but who was she kidding? Even though she still blushed with embarrassment and frustration whenever she thought about DeShawn's hands-off attitude after their picnic, she knew there was something between them. And she'd picked this outfit hoping that maybe she'd catch DeShawn's attention at some point tonight.

"Think we'll win today?" Roni asked as other guys and their dates began filling the section.

"No doubt," Chris said. "I never even think about the *L*-word before a game. Bad luck."

"In fact, I think we should start celebrating our soon-to-be win now," Ben said. "Lora-Leigh, would you do the honors?"

"My pleasure," Lora-Leigh said, slipping the flask of Jack Daniel's Ben had given her earlier out of her purse. Ben and Chris popped the lids off the Diet Cokes they'd gotten from the concession stand, and Lora-Leigh poured a swig of whiskey into each of the guys' cups.

"Keep it coming," Chris said, tipping the flask until at least a third of it emptied into the soda.

"Isn't that a lot?" Roni asked.

Chris laughed. "That's the whole point, sweetie."

Lora-Leigh glanced at Roni and shrugged, trying to let her know it was just the way the Pi Thetas worked the games. And, luckily, just then the LU fight song erupted from below to distract Roni as the Marching Raiders came into the stadium for the kickoff. The brass instruments shone in the afternoon sunshine, and the dark red plumes of the band hats stood out against the bleachers like a beacon of LU spirit. Everyone jumped to their feet and began screaming, and Lora-Leigh craned her neck to try to pick out Jenna in the band section.

"Do you see her?" Roni asked.

"Who?" asked Chris.

"Another ZZT new member, Jenna. There she is!" Lora-Leigh screamed out. "Horn section. Third row, second person."

"She looks so cute in her uniform," Roni said, clapping her hands to the drum cadence.

Lora-Leigh yelled out to Jenna and waved, but she was sure Jenna couldn't hear anything over the blaring of the horns around her.

"Man, check out Pritchard," Ben said to Chris. "He got bigger over the summer."

"He's gonna take us all the way this year," Chris said.

Lora-Leigh swiveled her eyes to the field at the mention of DeShawn. It was easy to pick him out among the players running onto the field, and when she did, her heart beat faster against her will.

The Red Raiders kicked off deep, and Lora-Leigh jumped to her feet to cheer on the defense. "Come on, guys! Stay tough!" she shouted.

"You're really into this, huh?" Ben asked.

"Well, I do love football—come on, ref! He was out of bounds!"

Roni frowned at her. "That wasn't good, was it?"

"No. The ref called it a fair catch, and Mississippi got a first down."

Ben wrapped his arm around her and squeezed. "I like a girl who knows about sports."

"Thanks," Lora-Leigh said absently, but she kept her eyes on the field as Mississippi fumbled, and Latimer finally came out on offense. This was what she'd been waiting for, a chance to see DeShawn in action. From the second he stepped onto the turf, he was all over the ball, cutting upfield, executing the draw play up the middle, and shoving aside defenders as he powered down the field.

"DeShawn's amazing," Roni noted.

"He's the best player we've got," Chris said. "He'll go pro before he graduates, sure thing."

Lora-Leigh stayed quiet, afraid of what she might give away if she opened her mouth. DeShawn was a force on the field, and she couldn't take her eyes off him. By halftime, the score was 21–0 with Latimer in full control of the game. While the guys went to get more sodas, Lora-Leigh and Roni watched the Marching Raiders give the halftime show, cheering Jenna on as she marched double time to the LU fight song.

Chris and Ben returned with stadium cups for everyone.

"Here y'all go. Drink up. We've got two more quarters to go."

However, when the third quarter began, Chris and Ben started going downhill. Roni was battling Chris's roaming hands with polite attempts at ladylike rejection. Ben's eyes had descended to half-mast, and he was catnapping on Lora-Leigh's shoulder.

When Chris stumbled off to the bathroom, Roni scooted next to Lora-Leigh, frowning. "Okay, when I said I wanted a date to the game, I didn't mean I wanted a *wasted* date."

"They're both tanked," Lora-Leigh said. "But the game's almost over. It can't get much worse."

But when Chris came back, it did. He took off his blazer, twirling it over his head like a lasso.

"Yo, Segs!" someone shouted behind them. "Take it all off."

"Okay, this is getting embarrassing," Roni muttered. "We're supposed to go back to the Pi Theta Ep house with them after the game before we go to Morgan's."

Ben chose that moment to fall forward one row into the Zeta Theta Mu brothers and their dates. The ZΘMs caught him and let him bodysurf down at least ten more rows.

"Yeah, I don't see that happening," Lora-Leigh noted as the last five minutes of the game ticked by. "I say we ditch them, go to Heavenly BBQ for dinner, and then head straight to Morgan's."

Roni gaped at her, horrified by the idea. "Ditch them? That's so rude."

"You think they'd care?" Lora-Leigh motioned to Ben and Chris, who were leading the way out of the stadium, tripping over each other as they slurred the words to the LU fight song. "Or even notice?"

Roni looked uncertain until Chris and Ben stumbled and fell into a mud puddle on the lawn in front of Daniel Stadium.

"Okay, I vote for plan B," she muttered to Lora-Leigh as they watched Chris and Ben stagger off toward Frat Row. "So, BBQ and Morgan's. Are you ready?"

"Bring on the dancing, girlfriend," Lora-Leigh said.

Three hours, two flaming Dr Peppers, and a whole lot of dancing later, Lora-Leigh couldn't wipe the smile from her face. This beat hanging out with drunken Phi Theta Eps any day. She and Roni had been tearing up the dance floor with Sandy, Minnie, Bonni, and the other ZZTs who'd shown up at Morgan's for the after-game party. Jenna'd met them after the game, too, and had been dancing with everyone. But the second Tiger showed up, she'd disappeared into a quiet corner with him, where they were chatting and holding hands. It was about the time Jenna'd made a beeline for Tiger that Roni'd pulled out her platinum Amex and announced, "Drinks on me all night!"

Now, as the set of fast songs came to an end and an R&B ballad started playing, Lora-Leigh left the dance floor and headed for the bar. She was parched and in serious need of some water.

She'd just ordered a bottled water when a voice said behind her, "Can I get that for you?"

She spun around and met a wall of chest. Looking up, she saw shining green eyes glinting down at her. She'd been hoping DeShawn would make an appearance here tonight, but at the same time, she'd been dreading it. She wanted to be mad at him for blowing her off earlier, but she was afraid, if she saw him, that'd be impossible. And of course, it was. But she'd keep her distance this time. She had to, for her own good.

"Well, if it isn't Latimer's star running back," she said, trying for a blasé attitude.

DeShawn tugged one of her loose curls. "If it isn't my biggest fan," he teased.

Swatting his hand away, she swallowed the cooling water and said, "You read too much of your own press, DeShawn."

"Wait'll you see what they say about me tomorrow." He graced her with a brilliant smile that made her resolve weaken.

"You're very sure of yourself, aren't you?"

He winked, then reached for her hand. "Come dance with me," he said in a near-whispered invitation.

Lora-Leigh looked at him doubtfully. Well, this was a change. The other night he'd dismissed her without a second glance, and tonight he was asking her to move in closer. She knew this was the danger zone, but danger or not, she liked him.

"One dance," she said. "That's it."

"We'll see," DeShawn said simply, leading her out onto the dance floor.

DeShawn slipped his hands to her waist, tugging her toward him as they moved to the music. She wrapped her arms around his neck, nestling her face into his shirt and smiling. Now, *this* she could do all night. For a moment, she felt she might have a chance with him after all . . . that she'd broken through the wall he'd put up the other night.

But as the song ended, DeShawn stepped away. "Well," he said, suddenly awkward and distant, "thanks for the dance, Curly."

"No prob," Lora-Leigh muttered with a sigh. She watched DeShawn rejoin his friends with a sinking heart, then turned to track down Roni and the other girls. Being ditched by Chris and Ben she could handle. She'd had enough of laying herself on the line with DeShawn, and as of tonight, that was over. But she still had two hours until the last call and the last dance, and she promised herself that for the next two hours, it was all about her, her sisters, and the dance floor.

Right before Sunday evening's house meeting, Jenna burst through the front door of ZZT, only to be met by Darcy, Roni, and one of the Nicoles.

"Sorry I'm late. Am I late?" Jenna looked at her watch. Yup, she was definitely late. So much for sticking to the schedule in her Day Planner. But she'd been in a daze ever since she'd seen Tiger last night at Morgan's, and she'd forgotten all about her planner.

"Don't worry; the meeting didn't start yet," Roni said, but *she* looked worried. "I thought you said you were trying to schedule your time better."

"I did. I am," Jenna said, throwing up her hands in frustration. "I was just trying to be social with Amber, so we went to Sonic for burgers and slushes. Big mistake. She barely said two words to me, and when I told her I had to go for the meeting, she said she didn't have time to drive me back for it. So I had to walk from Fifteenth Street."

"That's over two miles!" Roni's mouth dropped. "You should have called."

"I didn't want to bother anyone," Jenna said quietly. "Lora-Leigh was out at her parents' place, so I couldn't ask her for a ride, and I don't really know the other girls well enough yet to ask them for favors like that."

She followed Roni into the living room and plopped down next to Lora-Leigh as Roni took a seat next to Beverly. "Hey," she whispered to Lora-Leigh. "In five seconds or less before we get in trouble, how did it go with your mom this afternoon?" Lora-Leigh'd announced to her and Roni this morning over brunch at IHOP that she was going to make a trip out to her parents' to give her mom the shrug. She'd played off the whole thing as no big deal, but Jenna knew she'd been nervous. And now, as she caught a glimpse of the disappointment Lora-Leigh was trying so hard to hide, Jenna's heart went out to her. Whatever had happened, it didn't look good.

"Dad was there," Lora-Leigh said quietly, "but Mom was lunching with Dean Lower's wife."

"But she knew you were coming, right?" Jenna asked. "You said you called home this morning."

"Oh, yeah, she knew," Lora-Leigh said. "Can you say *avoidance*? The downside, I had to leave the shrug on the kitchen counter for her. The upside, I did all my laundry for free."

"I bet she'll be calling you as soon as she gets home, gushing over the shrug," Jenna encouraged.

"My mom doesn't gush," Lora-Leigh said. "She kvetches. But here's to hoping for a breakthrough."

Jenna giggled, but she and Lora-Leigh quieted as Marissa began the meeting, "Hey, y'all. Tonight, let's start with a Tears and Cheers and Jeers session, where we share triumphs, challenges, and funny stories."

Jenna tried to listen as the girls shared stories and experiences from the last week. Minnie Montiero had aced her German test and gotten chosen as a Latimer Belle, one of the university president's hostesses. Ashley Nardozzi shared a care package of sugar cookies her mom had sent, and Lora-Leigh and Roni shared their Dates from Hell with Chris and Ben, making everyone laugh. But as other sisters reported boy troubles, parties they'd attended, and university committees they were part of, Jenna's concentration faded. The truth was, she was having trouble concentrating on anything except Tiger.

It had only taken about ten seconds last night for Jenna to realize that a postgame date with Tiger was better than any game date she could have had. He'd actually told her she looked great in her band outfit. Shocker. "I love a girl in uniform," he'd teased. That alone earned him major brownie points. They'd found a corner table at Morgan's and had talked and danced the whole night. At two A.M., when Roni and Lora-Leigh finally called it quits, Jenna had reluctantly stood up to go home, too. But before she could move away, Tiger had pulled her back down onto the seat next to him.

"You know, we never tested out that theory," Tiger said.

"What theory?" Jenna asked.

"That brass players have great lips," Tiger whispered, leaning toward her. "Let's find out."

As his lips met hers, Jenna melted into him, her breath flying away. She didn't want the kiss to end . . . ever. But when it finally did, she glanced shyly at Tiger. "So what's the verdict?" she whispered.

"It's not a theory," Tiger said with a grin. "It's a fact."

Now all Jenna could think about was the way his lips had felt on hers, so soft and so sweet. She was still smiling at the memory when Roni elbowed her.

"Hey," she whispered. "Betsy's talking about Homecoming. You told me before you wanted to volunteer for something. Now's a good time."

"Oh," Jenna said. "Thanks."

Betsy went over the schedule for the float-building and marching in the parade, and Jenna decided she'd go with float-building since she'd already be marching in the parade with the band.

After Betsy was finished, Beverly took the floor to make an announcement to the new members.

"Sometime around Thanksgiving break, we'll be having our Big Sis/Little Sis reveal," she said. "Y'all should be thinking about who you want as your Big Sister. Consider all of the girls in the house, except the seniors, who'll be graduating. Also, especially consider the Rose Buds you've had each week. The closeness you'll have with your Big Sister comes from sharing interests, spending time together, and 'clicking.' She's your mentor, your friend, your family. It can be a bond for a lifetime. She will also be with you through your initiation ceremony at the end of the semester." Beverly placed her hand on her chest. "My Big Sis is Philly Ellinger. She graduated last year, but we still talk all the time. I know we'll always be in each other's lives. When her grandmother passed away last December, I felt like I'd lost a family member, too. We're that close. I hope each one of you can experience the same thing with whomever you choose—and are chosen by—as your Big Sis."

Jenna saw the emotion in Beverly's face and couldn't wait for her own Big Sis. So many of the sisters would make great Big Sisters, she was sure. But one sister stuck out in her mind: Darcy Worthington. But if she wanted Darcy to choose her as Little Sister, it meant she had to participate in everything she could. And she would.

"Now," Beverly finished, "Roni has something to tell y'all."

Roni popped up next to Beverly. "We have *the best* swap coming up. Beverly told me that every year, there's a traditional swap between Zeta Zeta Tau and Phi Omicron Chi."

"The Foxes?" Megan Gleason squealed.

Did Jenna hear right? They were going to have a party with Tiger's house?

Roni nodded. "Each year, there's a Big Fat Greek Wedding swap. We stage a fake wedding, and the new members of each house act as the wedding party. We supply the bride, and the Phi Omicron Chis provide the groom."

As the other new members cheered, Jenna wrote the date for the swap in huge red letters in her planner. There was no way she was going to miss this one.

"We just need a new member to be the bride," Roni continued. "Anyone?"

Jenna's throat caught. Talk about a way to get involved. Before she could think twice about it, she said, "I'll do it!"

CHAPTER 7

Lora-Leigh thought she'd done everything she could to avoid DeShawn during her Monday classes, but today he was like a ragged, loose thread on a cheap hemline. He was everywhere she went, and he just became more irritating as the day went on. She'd managed to escape him in Western Civ, but he caught up with her in the art studio before class started.

"Hey, Curly," he said. "So you moved your seat in Western Civ?"

"No biggie," she said, dead calm in her voice, despite the butterflies taking flight in her chest. "I couldn't hear very well in the back, so I moved up."

"I'm not buying it." DeShawn harrumphed, hoisting his backpack off his massive shoulder and onto the floor. "Are you going to move your easel away from me, too?"

Lora-Leigh glared at him, the frustration she'd felt from the other night bubbling up inside of her again. "I'd love to, believe me," she snapped. "But there's no room."

He sighed, staring at his paintbrushes. "Look, I'm sorry about last week and the other night. I know I've been acting weird."

"You think? Now there's a groundbreaking discovery."

He took her hand and held it firmly so she couldn't pull away, his green eyes slicing into her. "I'm into you; you've got to know that. But I've got other priorities right now. Football season's over in January, but I have to keep my mind on the game right now. I have to make it the number one thing in my life. For my family."

Lora-Leigh thought about all he'd told her about his family and wanting to provide for them. And suddenly, everything clicked into place, and she felt like a complete and total idiot. "I get it," she said quietly. "I'm not happy about it, but I get it."

DeShawn squeezed her hand and smiled. "Let's not say it'll never happen. You have no idea how hard it is *not* to kiss you sometimes. I don't know how long my iron will can hold out."

Lora-Leigh laughed. "It depends on how hard I try to break it."

"Don't tempt me, Curly," DeShawn said. "So . . . are we good?"

Lora-Leigh thought for a second, then nodded. She knew the attraction between them would always be there, and that would be tough to deal with sometimes. But she had such a great time just being with him, too, and she didn't want to give that up. "Yeah, we're good."

"And you're not going to kick my butt if I sit next to you?" DeShawn said. "'Cause friends can sit together, right?"

"If you behave yourself and keep your hands off my easel, I won't kick your butt," she said.

"Kewl," DeShawn said. "Now can I look at your notes from Western Civ?"

"Slept through it again, huh?" Lora-Leigh laughed, then made a big show of sighing like it was a huge burden. "Yes, you can see my notes. But you owe me big-time, Pritchard. I'm not going to let you forget it."

"I know you won't." DeShawn smiled. "That's what I love about you, Curly. You'll always call it like it is with me."

Lora-Leigh smiled, knowing he'd always do the same for her. And at least now she knew where she stood with him. Friendship wasn't her first choice, but she'd take it, for now. And who knew? Somewhere down the road, that might change. A girl could hope, couldn't she?

Tuesday afternoon, Roni ran down the sidewalk and up the steps into the science building, her Stuart Weitzmans tapping on the pavement.

She wasn't very interested in Geography 101. Drainage ditches, hurricanes, and mountain and river formations didn't do much for her. The only plus to this class was that she got to see Lance. And considering how he looked in a henley and Abercrombie jeans, it was a big plus. Unfortunately, they didn't ever get the chance to talk during the lectures, so the most they could do was exchange brief smiles as they were sitting down or leaving. Of course, Roni had to practically pull a 360 with her neck to catch a glimpse of him in his back-row seat, so she couldn't smile at him too often. But that was okay . . . she didn't want to be too obvious. And in her lab, the class was too small and the T.A. too much of a dictator to get away with chatting. The twenty-three-year-old graduate student loved to lord his authority over the class of freshmen. But today they were outside doing "field research," as the T.A. called it, so maybe she'd finally get a chance to make face-to-face contact.

Lance wasn't here at lab yet, though. The rest of the class was gathered on the front steps of Gordon Hall, where the T.A. handed out their lab assignment for the day. Glancing at the paper, she read that today's task was to pace off the distance of the block the building sat on in order to draw a map to match the exact landscape.

Ugh . . . she should have worn sneakers.

A vibration on her hip alerted her to her BlackBerry. Roni checked the screen. It was a text message from Kiersten, and Roni could already guess what it was about. They chatted no fewer than three times a week about wedding plans now.

Did u see the photo of the wedding gown I emailed u last nite?
K

Roni pressed the silver buttons with her thumbs, tapping away at the small keyboard.

Yup. Prfct 4 u! I luv it!
VVG

Within moments, she had a response from Kiersten:

Think I'm going to buy it. It's my dream dress! We'll shop for ur dress over Thanksgiving, k?

Roni smiled and typed:

It's a date!

"GPS won't help you with this map, Ms. Van Gelderen."

Roni jumped a little at the voice of the T.A., who was peering over her shoulder.

"Oh, I wasn't..." she stammered. "I just had a, err, message from my ride home."

The teaching assistant sneered at her. "Take care of that stuff on your own time."

"Sorry," she said, straining to smile politely. When he wandered off to annoy someone else, she slipped on her sunglasses and made an attempt to do the assignment, counting her steps down the block.

But she couldn't concentrate. Whatever her true calling was, it was *not* Geography. That much she knew.

Once she'd finished counting the first set of steps, she stopped at the next corner, sat on the curb, and began her calculations and sketch. The nutty, earthy taste of fall swept in the air around her. Sunshine danced through the corner palm tree, casting a long shadow that covered her paper.

"Looks more like a dead duck than our building," she heard.

Roni's face burned. How obnoxious could this T.A. get? She knew better than to shoot back a sarcastic response, so she held her tongue until she could calmly say, "I'll start the assignment over, if you want."

"Nah, I like the dead duck. It's one of a kind."

Okay, what alternate reality had she stepped into? She looked up and blushed to see Lance perusing her map from over the top of his sunglasses. "Sorry, I thought you were the T.A." She giggled. "He's out for the kill today, I think. He's been on my case nonstop."

Lance took a step forward and eased down next to her on the curb. His thick, rich brown hair fell over his forehead in an unkempt, Santiago Cabrera way. "I doubt he has it in for you. Maybe he's into you."

"What?" Roni shrieked, slapping a hand over her mouth as the T.A. walked by, glaring at her.

"You never know. He might be secretly obsessed with you," he continued. "It wouldn't be surprising. You probably have lots of admirers you don't know about." He grinned mischievously, and Roni's breath got sucked right out of her.

She kept her eyes on her drawing, not wanting to give herself away too quickly. "Okay, just the thought of Dr. Demento liking me is grossing me out. I'd rather have him being rude to me than harboring a secret passion. Aside from him being a totalitarian, he's not really my type."

Lance raised his eyebrows. "Really? What is your type, then?"

"My type?" she repeated back. "Oh, you know, the usual tall, dark, and handsome type. White horse, shining armor, the works."

He looked down the length of his body, and then his eyes returned to hers. His smile quirked on one side. "Well, whattaya know? That seems to describe me perfectly. I left the horse and armor at home, though." He leaned toward her conspiratorially. "I don't want to start any rumors."

Roni couldn't help laughing at his self-confidence. "You know, tall, dark, and handsome describes over half the guys here at Latimer."

He snapped his fingers. "What, and don't tell me they stole the horse and armor idea, too? I knew I should've gotten a

Porsche instead. Funding was an issue, though." He laughed, but then his eyes shifted to look behind Roni, and his demeanor changed. "I think we better move on because the warden's looking this way."

Roni stretched her legs to get up, and Lance extended a hand to help her. He pulled her to her feet but didn't let go of her hand right away. A delightful shiver ran through her before he finally let go.

"Come on, you two," the T.A. said as he and six other students rounded the corner. "You still have the other side of the building to map out."

Roni felt a blush stain her cheeks as she continued her counting. Like she could concentrate on anything but Lance. The breeze whipping down the street picked up on his spicy cologne, something earthy and masculine. Very nice.

"So, listen, I know I'm competing with half the guys at Latimer, and I probably don't stand a chance," Lance said, and Roni could've sworn she saw the tips of his ears turning red.

He brushed his hair away from his face, then met her gaze. "But I was wondering if—"

"This isn't an episode of *The Science of Love*," the T.A. interjected, almost snarling. "You want a flirtathon, take it elsewhere."

Roni frowned. She was going to kill the T.A. if he'd just ruined her chances. She'd been this close. . . . She glanced at Lance while the other students snickered and whistled around them, but he was already backing away.

"Um, what were you going to ask me before?" she whispered, hoping he hadn't given up completely.

But he just shook his head. "Nevermind," he mumbled, clearly as embarrassed as she was. "We'll catch up later, k?"

"Sure," Roni said, watching her chance with him getting farther and farther away with every step he took. She risked giving him one last smile. Even if the T.A. was still watching, she didn't care. Lance gave her a small, hopeful smile just before he turned away.

As she finished her assignment in silence, all she could think about was: when? When would she and Lance have a chance to catch up? She hoped it was sooner rather than later. Because if she was reading him right, and he *had* been about to ask her out, then she couldn't wait to say yes.

Lora-Leigh took a sip of her mocha and squirmed in the Strumann Center armchair, trying to get comfortable enough to focus on studying for her algebra quiz. But it was no use. After her chat with DeShawn in Art, she needed to decompress. And she couldn't do that either, because something kept nagging at the back of her mind. Something she hadn't been able to stop thinking about since yesterday afternoon. She sighed, pulling her cell phone out of her bag. She might as well get this over with so that she could finally stop obsessing about it.

She quickly dialed her mom's cell and held her breath. *Please pick up. Please pick up. Please pick—*

"Hello?" her mom answered.

"Hi, it's me," Lora-Leigh said, a little too eagerly.

"Oh, hello, Lora," her mom said, not giving away even an ounce of emotion. "Is everything all right?"

"Oh, sure." Lora-Leigh forced lightness into her voice. "I

was just calling to see if you got the, um, package I left for you yesterday."

There was a pause, and Lora-Leigh dug her hand into the chair cushion, waiting.

"The package," her mom said. "Yes, I did. The shrug is cute, and so . . . bright. Thank you."

Hmmm. This was not exactly the glowing review Lora-Leigh had been looking for.

"I thought it would be perfect for you to wear to the faculty dinner," Lora-Leigh said.

"Yes, well, about that," her mom said. "It's a little too flashy for someone my age. I was actually going to see if you wanted to give it to one of your friends instead. I'm sure it would suit them much better."

Lora-Leigh gripped the couch, suddenly feeling uncontrollable anger pushing into her chest and tears of rage and hurt welling in her eyes. "You're unbelievable, Mom," she snapped. "How many times have I called and e-mailed you in the last few weeks and heard nothing back? I thought if I made you the shrug, it might help us get back to normal. But even that's not good enough. Nothing is. I don't know why I even bothered."

"Don't raise your voice to me," her mom said, raising her own in the meantime (of course). "If you think this hasn't been a difficult time for me, too, you're wrong. By turning your back on Tri-Omega, I felt like you were turning your back on me, as well. And now you're New Member President of that second-rate sorority. I'm so embarrassed I haven't even been able to tell Colleen and Bunny or any of my other Tri-O friends."

"ZZT is *not* second-rate," Lora-Leigh shouted into the

phone. "It's an amazing sorority. If you'd let go of your tunnel vision for a second and actually talk to me about it, you might be able to see that. And, as for the presidency, you don't need to be embarrassed about that anymore. Not that you care, but I ran for it for your sake. And I lost. Bunny Crenshaw will love to hear that." The words were spilling out of her now, and she couldn't stop them. "And you know what's ironic? My friend Camille told me I only lost by one vote. She was trying to make me feel better, but what she didn't know was that I lost by my *own* vote. I voted for my best friend, Roni, because in my heart I knew she was the better candidate anyway."

"Lora," her mom sputtered, "if I'd known—"

"Too late," Lora-Leigh cut her off. "I'm done trying. If this is how you want things to be between us from now on, fine by me."

Click. Lora-Leigh snapped her cell shut before her mom had a chance to say anything else. She didn't know how long she stared at it in her hand, needles of unwanted tears pricking her eyes, until she felt a soft hand on her shoulder.

"Lora-Leigh, are you okay?" Camille Crawford said, standing over her in concern. "I had to pick up some things at the Supe Store and heard you talking on the phone as I walked past."

"Great," Lora-Leigh said, wiping her eyes. "Every student in Strumann probably knows about my little family dram now."

Camille smiled. "So what? Since when do you care what anyone thinks anyway?" She sat down in the chair facing Lora-Leigh, pulled a bag of M&M's out of her purse, and tossed them to her. "I had a craving for chocolate, but you need an emergency infusion of it. Now eat slowly, and tell me everything."

A half hour later, Lora-Leigh popped the last M&M into her mouth and finished spilling the story about her mom.

"Wow," Camille said. "I mean, you told me before that things with your mom weren't going so well, but I had no idea."

"Yeah," Lora-Leigh said. "If I didn't find him so completely smarmy, I'd call Dr. Phil myself."

Camille laughed. "Let's hold off on the acts of desperation until we really need them. I think you and your mom both need time to chill and process all this. Once you've both cooled off, you'll have another chance to make things right."

"That's just it," Lora-Leigh said. "I'm tired of making the effort."

"I hear you," Camille said, "but you can't burn a mom–daughter bridge. You can drive each other nuts and fight all you want to, but at the end of the day, you can't deny the bond."

Lora-Leigh snorted. "Oh, I can burn the bridge."

"But you won't," Camille said matter-of-factly.

And as much as Lora-Leigh wanted to deny it, she knew it was true. But she still couldn't think about the shrug her mom had rejected without cringing. She definitely needed some downtime without the *Mommy Dearest* thoughts.

"Come on," Camille said. "I don't have any classes this afternoon, and I know someplace we can go that'll cheer you up."

"I'm done with classes for the day, too," Lora-Leigh said. "But I doubt there's anything that can cheer me up."

"Oh yeah?" Camille said. "How does the textile exhibit at the Latimer Metropolitan Museum sound?" She pulled a pamphlet out of her bag and read, *"Mantles of Merit: Chin Textiles from*

Mandalay to Chittagong. The first major exhibition devoted to the sophisticated textiles from the Chin peoples."

"I read about that in the *LU News* last week," Lora-Leigh said. "It sounds incredible."

Camille nodded. "I have to do a paper on it for my anthropology class. I was actually going to see if you wanted to go with me this weekend, but I think today is a much better day to go instead. What do you say?"

Lora-Leigh smiled. "I say we forget my pathetic sob story for the afternoon and become intimately acquainted with Chin fashion." She knew it wouldn't be easy to forget about her fight with her mom, but, at least for today, she had a great friend to distract her.

CHAPTER
8

By seven o'clock on the night of the Greek wedding swap, Jenna knew one thing for certain: she had cold feet. Horrible, bone-chillingly cold feet, and they weren't going away anytime soon.

"I can't go through with this," she said, attempting to turn around and head back to the ZZT house for the third time in the past five minutes. "I don't know what I was thinking. I don't want to be a bride. I'm not ready."

"Now, now," Lora-Leigh said in a tone that smacked of matronly saccharine. "You're just nervous about your big day. All brides get nervous. Don't you worry, I'm sure you'll grow to love your groom." She grabbed Jenna's arm and gently steered her back in the direction of Fraternity Row.

"God, Lora-Leigh," Danika said, "you sound so much like a mother you're even starting to scare *me*."

"We're going to have a blast," Roni said, slipping a reassuring arm around Jenna. "It's all a joke anyway, remember?"

Jenna tried to smile. It was little comfort, but at least it was something. And a big plus to the night was that she'd get to see Tiger. After the text message she'd gotten from him earlier, she couldn't wait.

Just to make sure it was still real, Jenna reached into her purse and pulled out her silver cell phone. She punched a couple of buttons and reread the message for the second time (er, okay, the *twenty*-second time):

thinking of u. c u 2nite —T

A smile flickered across Jenna's face as she snapped her cell shut, and Lora-Leigh gave her an encouraging nudge on the arm. "There's a smile!" she said. "I knew you'd come around."

"Uh-huh," Jenna muttered, deciding it was easier just to let Lora-Leigh keep thinking that she was really getting excited about the pending nuptials.

"So are we doing the ZZT buddy system tonight?" Roni asked.

"Yes," Lora-Leigh said. "Keesha and me, Danika and Sandy, Roni and Jenna. That cool?"

"Works for me," Jenna agreed.

As the girls made their way to the front door of Phi Omicron Chi, a new wave of panic suddenly swept over Jenna. What was she doing? There was no way she could do this. Fake or not, she was going to be the center of attention. . . .

"I think I'm going to be sick," she moaned.

"Ah, it's prewedding jitters," Lora-Leigh said. "How sweet."

A tall blond wearing a faux-tux T-shirt and a plastic fluorescent green rose boutonnière answered the door and immediately pulled Lora-Leigh into a massive bear hug. "Hey, Sorenstein!" he said. "Someone told me you were going to be in the wedding party tonight. Always a bridesmaid, huh?"

"You know it. Bring on the groomsmen!" Lora-Leigh said with a laugh. "These are my sorority sisters." She turned to the girls. "This is Mark Dickson. He and I went to Latimer High School together."

"Yeah, I heard you'd joined ZZT. What happened to Tri-Omega?" Mark asked.

"Would a Tri-Omega be caught in a cheap crinoline bridesmaid dress?" Lora-Leigh said. "I don't think so. Nope, Tri-Omega wasn't my style. I needed a place where I could be free to unleash my kitschy side every once in a while."

"I hear you." He laughed, then said, "Y'all come on in and enjoy the party." He handed Jenna a glass of bubbly. "Here, have some champagne," he said. "To celebrate tonight's nuptials."

Jenna took the cup from him and quickly sipped the bubbly froth to help soothe her nerves.

As soon as they walked from the foyer into the dining room, she saw that the room had been decorated to resemble the inside of a Vegas drive-through chapel. A pink heart-shaped sign hung over the mantle, reading WEDDINGS HERE, 24/7. Plastic Greek columns stood guard on either side, wrapped in green and salmon pink crepe paper, and bouquets of mismatched fake flowers hung from the ends of each aisle of folding metal chairs. The pseudo wedding cake stood off to the side, each of its three tiers piled high with Twinkies, pink Snow Balls, and green Jell-O shots.

"Omigod," Roni whispered, looking by turns amused and horrified. "I've never seen anything like this. It's so . . . garish."

"Let go of your inner Martha Stewart," Lora-Leigh said, elbowing her. "Embrace the tasteless and tawdry. It's brilliant."

"It's tradition," Darcy said, joining the group.

"I'm so glad you're here!" Jenna hugged Darcy enthusiastically, then eyed her chic skirt and halter with envy. "You're so lucky you get to wear normal clothes all night. I haven't even seen my dress yet, but I'm already scared to walk down the aisle in it."

"Don't worry. You don't have to do it with a straight face. It's all about having fun." Darcy put an arm around Jenna and led her toward the drink table, motioning the other girls to follow. "Come on. Let's have ourselves a little bachelorette party before the ceremony. There's more champagne this way, and there's a glass with your name on it."

Halfway through her second glass of champagne, Jenna felt herself start to relax. But even though she was having fun, she was a little disappointed that she hadn't seen Tiger. The rest of the ZZT new members and other sisters were still pouring into the ΦOX house. Jenna saw plenty of other Foxes, some dressed in real tuxes (à la Napoleon Dynamite), others in more faux-tux T-shirts, and even a couple in togas to really complete the Greek wedding theme.

Lora-Leigh stopped her in the middle of one of her scans of the room.

"I know who you're looking for," she said, "but Tiger's not here yet. I did some reconnaissance, though, and found out that his golf tournament this afternoon ran late." Lora-Leigh winked. "He'll be here in time to see the bride in all her glory, though."

Jenna was relieved until she remembered she had no idea what she was actually going to look like as a bride since Lora-Leigh'd kept the gowns a secret from everyone. Suddenly picturing a Bride of Frankenstein horror show, Jenna wasn't sure she wanted Tiger to see her at all. She didn't have time to obsess about it, though, because Heather and Roni signaled it was time for her to go get changed. She and Lora-Leigh met Sandy, Danika, and Keesha in the bathroom.

"Ladies, prepare yourselves for the unveiling," Lora-Leigh said once the door was safely shut. She unzipped the garment bag she'd brought with her with somber deliberation. "First, the bridesmaid dress I like to call Little Bo Cheap."

Jenna's nerves vanished under a wave of giggles as Lora-Leigh pulled a Pepto-Bismol pink monstrosity from the bag, complete with enormous princess sleeves and ruffles at the neck, wrists, and hem of the massive petal skirt.

"That's straight out of some eighties shop of horrors," Keesha hiccuped as she bent over laughing.

"Courtesy of Kaylee's Thrift Shop. Glad you like it," Lora-Leigh said. "It's yours."

She tossed it at Keesha, clearly enjoying this. The next dress, a chartreuse satin number with a balloon skirt that had an enormous bow stretching across the entire front and a stretch lace, long-sleeve bodice with metallic and sequined accents, went to Danika. Sandy's dress was just as hilarious, a yellow Little Horror on the Prairie, with a blue-and-pink flower pattern covering it and eyelet sleeves. But Roni's dress, Swan Flake, was the best—a powder blue dress with a pink off-the-shoulder band at the neckline and a huge swan appliquéd on the front of the skirt. By the time Roni had hers on, Jenna could hardly breathe, she was laughing so hard.

"What about yours?" Roni asked Lora-Leigh.

"Ah, the Gilded Grape." Lora-Leigh grinned and pulled out a royal purple, floor-length maternity bridesmaid dress. "I sewed a pillow in for effect. I'll be the trashy, knocked-up bridesmaid. And now for the pièce de résistance." Lora-Leigh pulled Jenna's dress out of the bag with an exaggerated flourish. "I found some separates at the thrift shop and pieced them together last night."

Jenna gasped as she stared at the white satin corset-style bodice and petaled tulle ballerina-esque skirt.

"I am not walking down the aisle wearing *that*," Jenna said, laughing hysterically now. "It's Frederick's of Hollywood at the ballet. I don't even show that much skin when I go to the beach." Between her giggles, a sobering thought struck her. What if her pump showed through the outfit? That would be even more embarrassing than wearing the dress itself.

"Don't go getting all Bridezilla on me." Lora-Leigh snapped her fingers and stamped her foot, sticking her nose up in the air. "You must trust the creator. And you vill vear vat I tell you to vear, and you vill like it!"

"Spoken like a true Fashion Fascist," Keesha said with a laugh.

"It's *supposed* to be funny, Jenna," Roni said. "Besides, you're going to look great in this. And it's way better than what the rest of us are wearing."

Jenna opened her mouth to protest, then shut it again. She couldn't argue with her there. So she closed her eyes, took a deep breath, and said, "Okay. Here comes the bride."

Jenna made the other girls wait outside while she changed

(she didn't want anyone catching a glimpse of her insulin pump). But five minutes later, she opened the bathroom door and was met with half a dozen gasps.

"You look absolutely beautiful," Roni said.

"Yes, I am the master," Lora-Leigh said, taking a few bows. "Thank you very much, thank you, thank you."

Jenna rolled her eyes, but she did chance a glance in the mirror while Sandy and Darcy pinned her veil in place. She had to admit she did look pretty good. The bodice showed off her tiny waist and slender neck, and the skirt elongated her petite legs and luckily had enough give at the hip to keep her pump hidden. As far as spoof bridal gowns went, it could've been much, much worse.

"Okay, I'm going to be your mother and my buddy Rob Breslin is going to act as your father and help me give you away," Darcy said. "Your groom, I just found out, is Mike Ryan. I heard he's a sweetheart."

Jenna tried to smile at Darcy's reassurance, but her legs still wobbled underneath her skirt.

She bit her bottom lip. "Roni, can you tell me if Tiger's out there?" *Please let him be there, please, please, please.* If he wasn't, she wasn't sure she could go through with this.

Roni stuck her head around the door. "Yup, there he is. Black suit, royal blue shirt, no tie. One word: H-O-T."

Jenna smiled with relief, but her pulse picked up a beat or two as she heard music coming from the adjoining room. All the guys started hooting and hollering, calling for the bride.

"Come on, bride!" Keesha said, pulling her along. "It's time!"

Her sorority sisters started the processional into the "church," where the brothers of Phi Omicron Chi were lined up on one side. Everyone was having a hard time keeping from laughing.

"Hey, who's the father?" one guy shouted to Lora-Leigh, and Jenna cracked up when Lora-Leigh winked back at him, staying in character, and said, "No clue. You wanna be?"

"Are you ready, daughter?" Darcy asked Jenna, and Jenna nodded, taking a deep breath between nervous giggles.

Jenna walked slowly down the aisle with Darcy and Rob, trying to control her laughter. Shauna was warbling to a tape of "Love Lift Us Up," and everyone was howling. It was purposely horrible. Up at the front of the room was a tall, skinny guy in a maroon tux with tails and a white T-shirt underneath that read DEAD MAN WALKING. HELP ME was painted in big white letters on the back of his tuxedo jacket. This had to be her groom, Mike Ryan. Seeing his outfit, Jenna felt a flash of sympathy for him. But he seemed to be enjoying himself, tacky tux and all.

Right before she reached the altar, she turned to the right, and her eyes met Tiger's. He didn't appear to be very happy with the festivities.

She attempted a quick wave at him as Darcy and Rob steered her forward.

A tall blond guy—who Darcy had told her was Scott-Eric Miller, president of Phi Omicron Chi—stood in front of them, wearing a black robe and acting as the priest. He talked in a fake accent, throwing in some Italian words here and there, which brought everyone to near hysterics.

Mike took her hand when she got to him and said, "Hey there."

"Hi," Jenna said. Well, at least they'd exchanged hellos. It was a start for a soon-to-be husband and wife, right?

Scott-Eric raised his hand, and the music stopped. "Dearly beloved, we are gathered here today in the sight of our Greek brethren to join this Zeta Zeta Tau, Jenna Michelle Driscoll, with this Phi Omicron Chi, Michael 'Sully' Ryan."

There was a lot of catcalling and hooting and a lot of "All right, Sully!" around them. She could hear her sorority sisters laughing, too.

"If there is anyone here who objects to this union, let them speak now or forever hold their peace," Scott-Eric said, trying not to laugh.

It was silent for a moment, and then Jenna heard a rustle on the right side of the room.

"Yeah, I've got a problem with it."

She turned and saw Tiger standing there. Something fluttered in her chest, and she immediately dropped Sully's hands. "Tiger?"

"I won't let you do this, Jenna," he said to her. "You can't marry MikeDaddy."

The brothers laughed and hooted again.

"MikeDaddy?" Jenna asked, and then looked at her groom.

Mike shrugged and smiled. "And I live up to every bit of my name, baby."

"He's the biggest player at Latimer," Tiger said. "Every swap. Every mixer. He's hooked up with two Tri-Omegas, a Delta Kappa, a Beta Xi, three Alpha Sigma Gammas, and last night, an Eta Lambda Nu down at Morgan's."

"MikeDaddy!" one of the brothers shouted out until they all joined in. "MikeDaddy!"

Mike spread his arms wide and bowed to the applause in the room. "When you got it, you got it." Then he turned to Jenna with a wink. "So who's your daddy?"

"Not you!" Jenna laughed and playfully pushed him away. Then she added, a little more gently, "No offense."

"None taken, mademoiselle." Mike raised his hands over his head in a mock victory. "Free again!" Then he smiled and stepped away. "You win, man," he said to Tiger. "She's yours."

Tiger didn't hesitate to step in, take Jenna's hand, and ask, "What about it?"

She thought her heart was going to burst. He'd busted up her fake marriage because he didn't want her kissing his fraternity brother. She would've thought the whole thing was cheesy, if it hadn't been so . . . so adorable.

"Of course I'll marry you!" she said.

Scott-Eric smiled at them both. "And the tradition continues."

The rest of the ceremony went by in a blur of hysterical laughter, tacky love songs, and fake wedding vows. Before Jenna knew it, she and Tiger had finished with the I dos and were being carried into the downstairs den for the honeymoon. They were dumped on the couch amid roaring laughs.

"Have fun, you two!" Mark called out as everyone cheered. Then the door was shut behind them, leaving Jenna and Tiger alone.

In the dimly lit den, Jenna was suddenly having a tough time breathing. She was close enough to Tiger to feel the heat from his body, and it was making her own temp rise.

Jenna's eyes locked with his. As he bent his head toward her, Tiger's lips met hers, and her breath quickened as she slipped her hands around his neck. His hands moved across her back and then down to her waist as the kiss deepened. She was sinking into his arms, forgetting everything else, until the moment his hand brushed against the insulin pump at her hipbone.

She pushed him away. "What are you doing?"

"What's that?" Tiger asked. "Your cell or something?"

"No! I mean, it's nothing, okay? Just forget it." She adjusted her skirt and stood up. "Honeymoon's over. Kissing is one thing; hands down my pants are another." She couldn't believe she'd just said that to him, but all she could think about was her 'betes. The 'betes that she hated now more than anything.

"Jenna, that's not what I was doing," Tiger said. "It was an accident. I'm sorry."

He reached for her hand, but she pulled it away. "Jenna, please . . ."

But she was already opening the door and squinting into the bright lights of the living room. She couldn't explain her 'betes to Tiger. She hated herself for walking away from him, but she didn't know what else to do. She couldn't tell him the truth. Not tonight . . . not ever.

"That was quick," Mike joked when he saw her emerge. "Trouble in paradise already?"

Jenna ran a hand over herself, making sure everything was in place. "Nah. Just too much of a good thing," she said with a forced laugh.

Mike let out a whoop and tackled Tiger as he came out of the den, and Jenna only glanced back once to see a frustrated and confused Tiger trying to ward off his buddies' jokes and handshakes so he could follow her. Jenna spotted Lora-Leigh, Roni, and Darcy over by the makeshift wedding cake and hurried over to them before Tiger could escape the guys.

When Darcy caught sight of her, a look of concern crossed her pretty face. "You don't look too happy as the blushing bride anymore. Everything okay?"

"Sure. I'm just . . . I need a drink, that's all." She didn't even hesitate before grabbing two of the Jell-O shots from the table and downing them in one gulp.

"Whoa. She left for her honeymoon as a girl and came back a woman," Lora-Leigh teased, grinning and toasting her with a Jell-O shot of her own. "Let's get this party started."

"I'm ready," Jenna said, picking up another shot. She was ready to forget about her 'betes. And she'd make sure she did. It was about time.

Lora-Leigh was the first to notice it. The wedding reception had been in full swing for about two hours now, and Jenna had been drinking for most of those two hours. Not that Lora-Leigh usually checked peeps on their drinking. She normally stood by her "party and let party" philosophy. But when levelheaded Jenna climbed onto the couch to shout-sing to "SexyBack," Lora-Leigh knew it was time to blow the whistle. She found Roni and Darcy on the dance floor and pulled them aside.

"Excuse me, Madam President," she said to Roni. "I think we have an . . . a . . . situation on our hands," she said. "Does the bride's behavior seem a little . . . anti-Jen to you?"

"I don't know," Roni said. "Looks like she's just having fun to me."

"Maybe a little too much," Lora-Leigh said. "I've never seen her drink this much before. And you know what's really bizandom, she's been avoiding Tiger like a pair of Payless shoes ever since the wedding."

Roni nodded. "I noticed that, too. I asked her if they had a fight or something, but she said she was getting an annulment. And every time he heads her direction, she heads for the bathroom."

"I love this song!" Jenna screamed, grabbing for Darcy and Keesha and pulling them up on the couch with her. "Dirty babe," she sang out. "You see these shackles, baby, I'm your slave. . . ."

Darcy tried this time, slipping an arm around Jenna and saying gently, "Why don't we sit down for a sec and have some water?"

"No water." Jenna shook her head vehemently. "More dancing!" Then she grabbed Lora-Leigh by the shoulders and spun her around, singing, "Oooo, get your sexy on!"

"It's on all the time, sweetie," Lora-Leigh quipped.

"Lore, I love you soooo much. You're the bestest there ever wuzzz," Jenna shouted, spilling some of her punch into Lora-Leigh's hair and taking a dangerous dip off the couch. Roni and Lora-Leigh grabbed her as she dropped her punch cup and crumpled into a heap of laughter.

"Oooh, my stomach feels all squiggy," Jenna said with a half-giggle, half-moan.

"And that's the signal," Lora-Leigh said. "Time to go."

"Jenna's my buddy tonight," Roni said. "I can walk her home to the dorm."

"I'm coming with you," Lora-Leigh said.

"Okay, I don't want to embarrass her, though, so let's do this subtly."

"Right." Lora-Leigh wrapped an arm around Jenna's waist and swung her toward the door. "Come on, Jen My Friend, dance with me."

Jenna bounced up and down to the music with her eyes half-closed, but Lora-Leigh could see the front door getting closer. At least they were making progress. As Roni reached for the door, Tiger rushed over.

"Is she all right?" he asked, his face creased with concern.

"I'm perrrrrfectly fine," Jenna mumbled.

"That's debatable," Lora-Leigh said, then turned to Tiger. "We're just taking her home."

"Let me help," Tiger said, already stepping through the door.

"No!" Jenna yelled, pushing him away. "I don't want your help."

Tiger dropped his hands and backed away, red in the face and clearly crestfallen.

"Maybe it would be better if we just took her, Tiger," Roni said softly. "She might be a little embarrassed."

"Sure," Tiger muttered. "Just tell her . . . I'm sorry. Whatever it was . . . whatever I did. I'm sorry."

"We will," Lora-Leigh said, then waved as she and Roni maneuvered Jenna through the door.

"I'm so tired," Jenna said.

"Okay, sweetie. We're going to take you back to the dorm to sleep," Roni said. "But we're going to take a little walk first."

The walk to the dorm wasn't long, but keeping Jenna from stumbling along the way was still a challenge. Lora-Leigh'd snagged a couple of water bottles on the way out of the ΦΟΧ house, and they stopped every few minutes to give some to Jenna. When they finally reached Tuthill, they steered Jenna to the back door of the building.

"Whuuuur are we?" Jenna asked, her eyes at half-mast. "Whattare we doin' back 'crc?"

Roni held her up while opening the door. "We can't take you in through the lobby, sweetie. The guard will see you, and next thing we know, you'll be getting your stomach pumped."

Jenna's eyes widened. "How do you know about my pump?" she said defensively. "Did Tiger tell you? That ass."

"What? I don't know what you're talking about...a stomach pump. You know?"

"Oh, right." Biting her lip, Jenna looked like she was trying to act straight.

Lora-Leigh shot Roni a question with her eyes, and Roni just shrugged. "She's seriously out of it" was all she could say.

"Something must have happened with Tiger," Lora-Leigh said as they took the elevator up to the seventh floor.

"Tiger," Jenna mumbled as Roni dug into her purse for her keys. "I really screwed things up with him. He probably hates me." Her eyes suddenly filled with tears.

"Are you kidding? He's so in like with you he would've carried you all the way home tonight if we'd let him," Lora-Leigh said, ruffling Jenna's hair. "Besides, no one could hate you. It's a statistical impossibility."

"Amber does," Jenna said as Roni opened Jenna's door.

"Shhh . . . don't wake her up. She doezzz'un like it."

"I'm not concerned about Amber right now," Roni said firmly.

Jenna smiled. "Me neither!" she declared.

"If she so much as blinks in your direction tonight, I'm going to fix her biatchitude for her," Lora-Leigh said. And she meant it. She'd had enough of Jenna stressing over her roommate sitch. She didn't deserve it. But, lucky for Amber, she was MIA. "Let's get you to bed."

She pulled off Jenna's shoes and helped Jenna find her pillow.

"Just lie down, Jenna. I'll put the garbage can next to the bed in case you get sick."

"Mmm-hmm . . ."

"And stay turned on your side, okay, sweetie?" Roni said.

"Okay, Mom."

Jenna rolled her head from side to side. "I made one helluva bride, donncha think?"

"You were perfection at its best," Lora-Leigh said, just as Jenna drifted off.

Roni checked the clock next to Jenna's bed. Midnight on the dot. She covered a yawn with the back of her hand. It was still relatively early, but after everything that had happened tonight, she was drained.

"You think she'll be all right?" she asked Lora-Leigh, peeking over her shoulder to check on Jenna, who hadn't moved once in the last half hour.

"She's going to need some Tylenol tomorrow, for sure," Lora-Leigh said. "But I think she's fine. We should head out before the she-devil gets home. The last thing Jenna needs is an Amber assault in the morning."

"Want to order pizza and hang in my room for a while?" Roni said. "I'm in serious need of a fourth meal right now. I won't be able to sleep, otherwise."

"Sure," Lora-Leigh said, standing up and pulling Roni to her feet.

They were almost to Roni's room when her BlackBerry suddenly buzzed, making her jump.

"Who could be calling this late?"

"Calls after ten P.M. are never good news unless they're drunk dials from hotties," Lora-Leigh said.

Roni pulled the phone from her purse and saw the familiar 617 area code and her parents' number. "Hello?"

"Veronica, you have some explaining to do, young lady."

Her pulse picked up hearing her father's voice. When she first saw the number, she feared someone was sick, in the hospital, or worse. Sounded like she was in for the worse. "Explaining about what, Dad?"

"I just got my American Express bill." His voice crackled with anger. "What the hell is Morgan's?"

"Morgan's?" Her eyes cut across to Lora-Leigh, who gave her a "busted" look. "It's a . . . restaurant here in Latimer."

Her father growled into the phone. "A restaurant in the sticks of Florida that charges three sixty-eight ninety-four for a meal?"

Roni tried a delay tactic. "Three hundred sixty-eight?"

"And ninety-four cents! Explain this . . . now!"

Her stomach plummeting, Roni remembered. It was the

night after the Mississippi game when she and her sisters were celebrating. Roni had wanted to impress them, so she had picked up the tab for the night. She didn't think her father kept such a close watch on his platinum card statement. After all, he never kept a close watch on her. But apparently, money was a different matter entirely.

"I took my sorority sisters out. You said I could use the card for whatever I needed."

"I meant for books or supplies. Not for some sort of wild party!"

Roni winced. She sensed tears welling up behind her eyes. "You know, this is the first time you've called me all semester, Dad. And all you care about is how much I'm costing you, not how I'm doing. Well, sorry I'm such a financial burden, but maybe you should have thought about that before you had a child."

"Don't you dare talk to me like that." Her father's voice was chilled and deadly.

But the words were rushing out of Roni's mouth in a torrent now, and there was no stopping them. "I'm sick of being your showpiece. If you want to call to have a real conversation with your daughter, then be my guest. But otherwise, don't bother."

With that, she snapped off the phone and tossed it back into her purse. Only then did she look up at Lora-Leigh, who, for once, actually looked genuinely shocked.

"I didn't know you had it in you, Boston," she said.

Roni just swallowed the lump in her throat.

"The 'rents can be such totalitarians sometimes," Lora-Leigh said with a hard laugh. "My mom's working at it right now, too. It's not fun to deal with that, though."

"I know," Roni said. "I'm just so done with the absent parent act. I had to tell him."

"You did the right thing."

"You think?" Roni said. Suddenly, she wasn't so sure, and the possible consequences of what she'd done started racing through her mind. Her parents could stop helping her with her expenses here at Latimer, or they could disown her. Or they could make her drop out of Latimer. No, they couldn't do that. Could they?

"You know," she said weakly, "I'm not as hungry as I thought. Can we do pizza another night?"

"Absolutely," Lora-Leigh said, understanding flickering across her face. She gave a dramatic yawn. "I think I'll just make like a wave and crash. See you later."

"Okay," Roni said, feeling her lower lip start to tremble dangerously. The tears would come any second, but she really wanted to be alone in her room when they did.

Lora-Leigh was thankfully already halfway down the hallway, but she stopped before Roni shut her door.

"Hey, Boston?" Lora-Leigh said. "I'm sorry."

"Thanks," Roni said. "Me, too."

She shut her door and let the downpour start, all the while wondering if she'd made the biggest mistake of her life. No, she decided after the flood of tears subsided. Honesty could never be a mistake. As she drifted off into an uneasy sleep, though, she could only think of one question. What was going to happen now? But no answer would come to her in the darkness.

I'm so late!

Jenna literally ran up the stairs to her room on the seventh floor Friday morning. She was still hungover from the Greek wedding and had a killer headache from all the champagne. She burst into the dorm room, tossed her book bag on the bed, and frantically tugged off the nice black pants she'd worn to class and pulled on her jeans. Then she did a mental check of Amber's mood: frigid, as always. But she decided to risk braving the latest ice age to ask Amber for a favor. It was a risk only the desperately hungover would take, Jenna knew, but she had to give it a shot.

"I'm going to be late for band practice, Amber," she said quietly. "Can you drive me over?"

"Still smarting from your wedding night, huh?" Amber frowned at her. "Why don't you get one of your *sorority sisters* to do it?"

"Come on, Amber! Please don't be like that."

"Don't be like what? You only have something to do with me when it's convenient for you."

Jenna pulled her sweatshirt on and whipped her hair into a ponytail, cringing at the lingering pain in her head. Her hands were shaking something fierce, and she was afraid she hadn't given herself enough insulin today. Without wasting time to check the readout, Jenna dialed in some insulin and turned back to Amber. "I'm not only nice to you when it's convenient."

"Like hell you're not," Amber spat out.

Jenna shook even harder now. She wasn't sure if it was the hangover, her 'betes messing with her, or Amber's acid words. "What is your problem? Why do you hate me so much?"

Amber spun around, giving Jenna her back. "I don't hate you."

"You certainly do a good job pretending you do." Jenna hated confrontation, but this was a long time coming. "You've treated me like crap ever since I joined a sorority and you didn't."

"I don't have time for this." Amber gathered up some books and reached for her keys.

"And I do? Every time I come in our room, I get nervous wondering what your attitude will be! Either you ignore me, or play music, or you're over there IMing to your friends about me. And all your friends are rude to me."

"They are not. They're just not your poseur sorority sisters."

Jenna had had enough. She poked her finger into her chest. "*My* sorority sisters treat me like a human being! They don't ignore me and ostracize me."

"Whatever," Amber said with a sneer. "Not everything is about you, Jenna."

Jenna grabbed her head. "I didn't say it was. I just want to be friends with you, Amber. We live together, and I don't want it to be so tense all the time."

"Maybe I don't want to be friends with you."

It felt like Amber had just ripped Jenna's heart out of her

chest. Her breathing increased to a searing pace, and she shook like a leaf.

"I'm not a bad person, Amber. I'm not," Jenna said, struggling to keep from crying.

Amber fell to her bed and put her head in her hands but didn't say anything.

"I'll find my own way to band practice. Thanks for nothing."

"Jenna, I—"

Jenna didn't hear what Amber said after that. She was already out the door.

"You're late again, Driscoll," Papa Skank said, bristling as Jenna stepped into formation with the other trumpets. "That makes two missed practices and three tardies in two weeks."

"I know," Jenna started. "I'm so sorry. I—"

"Don't give me any lame excuses," he barked. "You can stay after and polish the brass instruments instead. And the next time you're tardy, you'll be suspended from band activities until further notice."

"Yes, sir." Heat rushed over her face, and Jenna felt salty pinpricks in the corners of her eyes. Great. First her freakout with Tiger last night, then Amber's tirade, and now this. Just what she needed to top off her stellar morning so far. If she could just make it through band practice, then she could go and have a good, long, cathartic cry. Maybe that would help cure her splitting headache and her aching body.

She tried to steady herself by looking at Lora-Leigh and

Darcy, sitting on the small wooden bleachers ready to cheer her on. They'd been nice enough to drive her to band practice after her fight with Amber and had even offered to stay to watch her practice. Lora-Leigh had her sunglasses on and her hand over her eyes to get a better view of the band's formations. Darcy had a highlighter in her hand and was doing homework. For some reason, Jenna felt secure and protected with them nearby. There were more important people in Jenna's life than Amber, people who gave her as much as she gave them. Only one more semester living with Amber and she'd probably never have to see her again. She just didn't know if she could last that long.

She wished she wasn't still shaking from Amber's words and Papa Skank's scolding. She had to calm down and focus on the practice, but she worried that her quivering could be in part from too little insulin. Risking Papa Skank's wrath, Jenna ran to the bathroom and dialed in a little more, then went back to her section.

She drained the spit valve on her trumpet and listened for the drum major's next command. Now Jenna was sweating like some sort of farm animal out here on the practice field even though today was unusually cool by Florida standards. What was wrong with her?

"Band! Ready oblique! One, two, three!"

Shifting her feet in time to the drum cadence, Jenna executed the oblique shift—a forty-five-degree movement, half of a right flank with her upper body remaining facing the press box.

The drum major issued the next command. "Mark time, mark!"

Jenna marched in place, rolling smoothly from heel to toe without bouncing.

She was still shaking, though, and queasiness broke in massive waves over her, sweat rolling down her back and forehead. Her ears were ringing, and a black curtain of marching ants swarmed around the edges of her eyes.

What was happening?

While the drum solo played, she kept marching and followed along as much as she could, practicing the formation they'd do at the game on Saturday. But suddenly her knees buckled. Everything blurred, and she barely heard the first trumpet player in her section, Bridget, call her name as she wobbled and fell to the ground.

"Oh my God! Jenna!"

Lora-Leigh was off the bleachers in a flash when she saw Jenna fall to the ground and begin to shake.

"What's going on?" Darcy asked in Lora-Leigh's wake, but she didn't stop.

When she got to Jenna's side, Lora-Leigh gasped and put her hand to her mouth. Jenna had drool coming out of her mouth, and she was flailing around, fighting people off.

"I hate you! Stop it! Stop touching me!"

This was *not* Jenna. It was like she was possessed all of a sudden.

"Jenna! Can you hear me?" Lora-Leigh shouted, trying to get closer.

The curly-headed blonde from the trumpet section pushed Lora-Leigh back. "She needs air."

"She needs a hell of a lot more than air," Lora-Leigh screamed. "Someone get an ambulance!"

Just then Darcy was by Jenna's side, holding her hand. "Y'all . . . she's diabetic," Darcy announced. "She's having a seizure."

"She's *what?*" Lora-Leigh's mouth fell open. How did she not know this? How could something so important about one of her best friends have escaped her?

"Mr. Zamoida's called the ambulance, and they'll be here in a minute," a guy holding a trombone said.

Lora-Leigh moved in and held Jenna's hand tightly as she thrashed around on the grass. Her eyes were rolled into the back of her head. Lora-Leigh's fear crept up her throat. "Hang in there, Jenna. Help's on the way."

Finally, Lora-Leigh heard the siren in the distance. She wished Jenna had told her about her condition, if only so she could have been prepared to help in just this sort of incident. But now she wasn't going to leave Jenna's side.

The paramedics moved in quickly and got Jenna on a stretcher. She batted and swatted at them, fighting with all her strength as they tried to put in an IV. Lora-Leigh held Jenna's hand steady while the two men worked in tandem. They explained that Jenna needed glucose in her system.

"We're going to take her to the emergency room," one of the EMTs said.

"I'm going with her," Lora-Leigh said emphatically.

"Are you family?"

Without even a second's hesitation, Lora-Leigh nodded. "Her sister."

Following the stretcher, Lora-Leigh called out to Darcy, "Get Roni and meet us at the hospital!"

"I will!" Darcy ran to her car.

Once inside the ambulance, Lora-Leigh took a seat at Jenna's side and reached for her hand.

"Lora-Leigh?" Jenna asked weakly.

"Hey, sweetie."

"Wh-wh-where am I? What's going on?"

"You've had a seizure, Jenna. I'm in the ambulance with you."

"Oh. Where are my sunglasses?" Jenna asked, looking around.

"Sunglasses? I'm freaking over here, and you're worried about your sunglasses?" She attempted a smile, but her heart pounded ferociously in her chest. "Don't worry we'll find them later."

"What's going on?" Jenna asked again.

The EMT adjusted the IV. "You've had a diabetic seizure. We're giving you glucose and getting you to the hospital so the doctor can look at you. Okay?"

Her eyes closed again. "You can't tell anyone about my 'betes. You can't."

Lora-Leigh noticed some dried drool on Jenna's face. "Do you have something I can clean this off with?" Lora-Leigh asked the EMT.

He tore open an antiseptic packet. "I've got it. You keep holding her hand."

Lora-Leigh smiled at the EMT and then returned her gaze to Jenna. "We're getting you help. Just hang in there, Jenna. Darcy and Roni are meeting us at the hospital."

Rolling her head side to side, Jenna said, "Amber's so mad at me. So mad. I told her how mean she was."

"Kudos, girlfriend! It's about time that demonatrix got a talking-to!" Lora-Leigh said through a haze of tears and laughter. "You're gonna be fine, Jenna. I just know it."

CHAPTER
9

Lora-Leigh met Darcy and Roni in the waiting room of the Latimer Medical Center emergency room. After what felt like an eternity, the doctor came in to where the girls were waiting.

"Are you with Miss Driscoll?" the doctor asked.

"Yes, sir," Darcy said, jumping to her feet.

"Well, it looks like she accidentally dialed in too much insulin and had an overdose, which caused her seizure. She was lucky she wasn't by herself when this happened."

Lora-Leigh relaxed only a little bit when she heard this. "Is she going to be okay?"

"She will," the doctor said. "However, I want to keep her for a few more hours, just for observation. And, of course, we'll need to call her parents."

"I can do that," Darcy spoke up.

"Very well. If you'll excuse me." The doctor walked back through the emergency room double doors.

Lora-Leigh turned to Darcy and Roni and let out the breath she'd been holding in for what seemed like hours now. "God, and I thought tapered jeans were the scariest thing I'd ever seen." She looked down at her hands, which hadn't stopped shaking since the minute Jenna'd collapsed. "I—I—I thought she was dying. Right there in front of us."

Roni took her hand and gave it a reassuring squeeze. "She's all right. I'm just so glad that you were there with her when it happened."

"Me, too," Lora-Leigh said. "But why didn't Jenna tell anyone about her condition? If I weren't so worried about her, I'd be pissed at her right now."

"We don't have to understand her motives yet," Roni said. "We just need to support her moving forward."

"I know. You're right," Lora-Leigh said. "Do you think they'll let us see her?"

Darcy nodded. "I'm sure they will."

Lora-Leigh tightened her grip on Roni's hand. "We've got to let Jenna know what she means to us."

Roni's calm nature spread to Lora-Leigh. "We will."

Jenna woke up to the feeling she was being watched. She slowly lifted her eyelids and stared up at a tiled ceiling. Where was she? Last thing she remembered was being at band practice and feeling shaky. Had she fallen?

"She's awake," she heard someone whisper.

Swallowing hard, Jenna turned her head and saw several silhouettes in the doorway making their way into the room.

"Where am I?" she asked.

Darcy's friendly face appeared next to her. "You're in the hospital, Jenna. You had a seizure a few hours ago."

"Oh, no . . ." she groaned. She didn't remember a thing, although her entire body was sore and exhausted, like she'd just run a marathon.

"Hey, you," Lora-Leigh said. "You ever scare me like that again and you can forget about that knockoff Prada skirt I promised to make you."

Jenna smiled weakly and struggled to sit up in her hospital bed. Roni propped a pillow behind her to help.

"I'm so embarrassed," Jenna said in a warbly voice.

"Don't be," Roni said simply.

A tear escaped from Jenna's eyes.

"Why didn't you tell us, Jenna?" Lora-Leigh asked.

She swallowed hard, her throat raw from the ordeal. "I didn't want y'all treating me differently or pitying me like everyone back home did. It was always 'oh, Jenna can't do this,' or 'Jenna can't do that.' Here at Latimer, I had a fresh start." She dropped her eyes to look down at the sheet. "Until now."

"Nothing's changed," Roni insisted. "Well, that's not true. Everything's changed. We're here for you, whenever you need us. But we're not going to treat you differently because of your illness. You'll always be just Jenna, and we love you."

"Thanks, Roni. You don't know how much that means to me."

"You just have to promise to be straight with us about everything from now on, okay?" Lora-Leigh said. "My delicate constitution can't take the trauma."

Jenna laughed just as the hospital room door opened. A thin, blond doctor with black-framed glasses came in.

"I'm Dr. Pearson. I hear you had a nasty incident this morning?"

"I guess so," she said. "I really don't remember much of it."

"That's perfectly normal, Jenna." He peeked over his glasses at a folder in front of him. "We've been monitoring your glucose, and it seems everything has leveled out. What made you give yourself two large doses of insulin?"

"I was rattled," Jenna said. She certainly wasn't going to admit to the hangover, but she would admit to the frustrating fight with Amber. "My roommate and I had an argument, and I was shaking because of it. I thought it was my diabetes, so I dialed in. And then I got to band practice, and I guess I forgot that I'd already given myself insulin, and that's when it happened."

Dr. Pearson frowned. "You should keep a journal of your dosage, Jenna. That way things like this won't happen. You've got to take more responsibility for your body."

"I know," Jenna said, picking at the bedsheet with her fingers. "I will."

He pricked her finger and ran the litmus paper across the blood while questioning her on her daily routine. Jenna glanced over at Darcy, Lora-Leigh, and Roni and then explained her monitoring practices. When he asked about her schedule, Jenna told the doctor she'd pulled a half-dozen all-nighters in the last month and then gave the list of all the school papers and tests, band practices, and ZZT activities she'd had lately.

"Jenna," Roni gasped. "I didn't know you had that much going on. I knew you were busy . . . but that's . . ."

"Lunacy," Lora-Leigh said, shaking her head.

"What about your diet recently?" Dr. Pearson asked Jenna. "Any big changes?"

"Um." Jenna hesitated, blushing. "I've been eating out a lot more than I did at home. I guess I haven't been eating so great, come to think of it."

"Well, that will definitely need to change right away," he said firmly. He did some more poking and prodding, checking out nodes and glands, and then wrote some stuff in her file.

"I want to take some more blood to be on the safe side. But, Jenna, I want you to stop burning the candle at both ends. With the schedule you have, you're not letting your body rest enough," Dr. Pearson said. "I want to give you a B12 shot and a flu shot while you're here, for prevention."

He drew two vials of blood from her and then administered the shots.

The doctor turned to her sorority sisters. "Since you're her friends, I want you to make sure she gets extra rest. Jenna, if you feel you can't sleep in your dorm room for any reason, the university can put you up at the Health Center for a couple of nights."

"No, Dr. Pearson. I'm okay. I just need to take better care of myself."

"We'll make sure she does, Doctor," Darcy said.

"I'm going to release you," he finally told Jenna, "but be careful, Miss Driscoll. Freshman year can be overwhelming. Someone like you can live a perfectly normal, healthy life, but you have to take care of yourself so you'll be here for sophomore year."

Jenna smiled at her sisters. "Thanks, Dr. Pearson."

She got dressed and took the mandatory wheelchair ride out of the hospital to Darcy's waiting Cherokee.

"Let's get you home," Lora-Leigh said.

Jenna shook her head. "I don't want to go to my room...with Amber. I want to be with y'all."

"That's what she meant," Roni said. "Let's go home to ZZT."

"Are you sure about this?" Jenna asked Roni for the hundredth time.

And for the hundredth time, Roni answered, "Yes."

In fact, she'd never been so sure of anything before in her life. Since she'd hung up on her father on Thursday night, she'd been doing a lot of thinking. She hadn't heard from either of her parents since the fight, but that hadn't surprised her. Her father had probably stared at the Amex bill for another five minutes after their argument, then had written the check with a flick of his wrist and returned to his latest case research. She could just imagine her mother clucking her tongue and saying something like, "This is what's to be expected from a less than adequate college experience: an ungrateful, feral child."

She'd lain awake the last two nights wondering what she should do, but suddenly, she'd woken up this morning with it all brilliantly clear in her mind. Now she sat in the living room at the ZZT house with Jenna, Lora-Leigh, and Beverly, her Amex card and a pair of scissors on the coffee table in front of her. She was glad she had all of the girls here for moral support, and she was especially relieved that Jenna was feeling up to it. She seemed to be doing much better since being released from the hospital. The color was returning to her cheeks, and her face looked more relaxed and happier than it had in weeks.

"You know, you don't have to go through with this," Lora-Leigh said. "You could take us all on a mad shopping spree on Worth Avenue and rack up some truly profane charges on Daddy's card. Palm Beach is only an hour's drive from here."

"Wishful thinking," Roni said.

"Yeah, I figure that was my only shot at an authentic pair of Jimmy Choos until I'm a famed, egocentric designer with millions." Lora-Leigh shrugged.

"Sorry to disappoint you." Roni giggled through her nervousness, relieved that Lora-Leigh was there as comic relief. "But I have to do this. I'm tired of hoping that someday my parents will change and then being disappointed over and over again. They are the way they are, and I just have to accept it. But if they can't make time to be a part of my life, then I don't have to follow their rules anymore."

She took a deep breath, picked up her credit card in one hand and the scissors in the other, and, with a few quick strokes, sliced her card into pieces.

"Farewell, fortune," Lora-Leigh said. "Hello, Independence Day."

Roni hurriedly slipped the credit card pieces into the envelope addressed to her dad, then stood up.

"I'm going to drop this in the mailbox before I lose my nerve," she said.

"But what will happen when your dad gets the card in the mail?" Jenna asked. "Thanksgiving is coming up in just a few weeks."

Lora-Leigh gave a short laugh. "That's gonna be one memorable Turkey Day in the Van Gelderen household."

Roni looked down at the envelope in her hands. "I already thought about that," she said quietly. "And I don't think I'm going to go home for Thanksgiving this year. I was going to call Kiersten later and see if I could stay with her."

Lora-Leigh whistled under her breath. "I've got to hand it to you, Boston. That takes some serious *cojones*."

"Thanks," Roni said with a smile. A comment like that from Lora-Leigh meant something. She suddenly felt braver than ever and knew that, with her friends by her side, she could get through this.

Out at the mailbox, she quickly reached into her pocket and pulled out the letter she'd written to her dad last night:

Father,

You don't have to worry about your Amex from now on. I won't be needing it anymore. And I'll be paying you back in full for the amount of the last bill as soon as I have the money.

Sincerely,
Veronica

The note was short, but Roni hoped it sent the message loud and clear. Veronica Ven Gelderen was breaking free of her parents' manipulation tactics once and for all. If they wanted to make the first move to reach out to her, then she'd listen. But she was pretty sure that wouldn't happen anytime soon. And she promised herself she wouldn't set her hopes on it either. She was done with getting crushed when her expectations fell through. This was her time to take control of her own life, with or without her parents as a part of it.

Jenna sat in silence in her resident advisor's room, trying to talk her heart into thundering a little less loudly in her ears. It was no use. She'd been avoiding looking over at Amber, but she could still feel her presence next to her on the couch, radiating bad vibes. Even though she'd been feeling much, much better since her seizure, this meeting was sending waves of panic and nausea through her again. And this time, it had nothing to do with her 'betes and *everything* to do with Amber.

"So, Jenna," her resident advisor, Tricia, continued, "you've been sleeping at the ZZT house since last Friday instead of here at Tuthill?"

Jenna nodded. When Darcy'd explained Jenna's situation to the other actives at the house, the girls decided to do something that they'd never done before: invite a new member to stay in the house. They made it clear that it was only temporary and that Jenna still wouldn't be allowed upstairs (she slept on the pull-out sofa in the living room instead). But Jenna'd been so relieved to escape Amber's moods for a couple of days that she'd slept like a queen, even on the lumpy sofa mattress. The rest had given her a clear head again for the first time in weeks, and the old Jenna—the take-charge Jenna who'd known how to juggle being the family chauffeur with her school and social life back home—was back and had a plan for action. She'd called her RA as soon as she'd felt up to it and set up this meeting for her and Amber to "discuss" their living arrangement. Tricia'd already spent an hour talking to her and Amber separately, and now they were coming together for a "joint consult," as Tricia called it. It was an über-awkward sitch, no doubt about it, but it had to be done.

"I just wasn't comfortable coming back to Tuthill," Jenna told Tricia now. "Amber and I have been having a lot of conflicts lately."

Amber snorted next to her, but Jenna steadied herself and kept going. "It's not that I don't like her . . . I do." Well, at least that used to be true, before Amber changed from her energetic, bubbly former self into a first-rate witch. "We're just so . . . *different*," Jenna finished, settling on the word that seemed the most diplomatic.

"You can say that again," Amber grumbled.

Tricia nodded, then flipped through her RA handbook, reviewing her notes for a few moments before finally looking up. "Well, normally I wouldn't suggest a change of roommates for either one of you without a few more meetings to try to work things out. But, in this case, I think the best thing is for both of you to move on to a more positive arrangement." She smiled at them, and Jenna felt the tiniest ray of hope.

"I'll review my floor plan over the next week or so and see if I can find places for both of you with new roommates," Tricia continued. "Okay?"

Jenna nodded and sensed a movement on the couch next to

her that she interpreted as a nod from Amber, too. Phew! At last, something they both agreed on.

"We won't be able to make the switch until after the winter break," Tricia said, "so you'll have to hang in there until then. But I know you can do it."

Sensing a peppy RA "it's all about attitude and compromise" speech coming, Jenna tuned out and focused on the word that was suddenly screaming euphorically through her head: *free!* Soon, she would be totally and absolutely free of Cynthia Amber Ferris . . . forever. She'd be able to start over again with a new roommate—a roommate who could possibly even turn out to be a true friend instead of Resident Evil, as Lora-Leigh had dubbed Amber postseizure. Jenna blew out the breath she'd been holding as the weight of worry from the past few weeks fell away. And only then, when she was sure she had that smile bubbling inside her safely under control, did she chance a look at Amber.

But once she did, she saw she shouldn't have worried. Because—could it be?—a bona fide, honest-to-God smile was spreading across Amber's face, too. Gone was the perma-scowl that Jenna'd seen for months. Of course, Amber was probably just smiling maniacally at the prospect of getting rid of her, but suddenly Jenna didn't care. She'd made the right decision in coming to Tricia—a decision that was good for both of them. And that was all that mattered.

As she and Amber left Tricia's room ten minutes later, Jenna shouldered her bag and searched for something to say to break the silence.

She finally mustered up a "Well, I better get to class. . . ."

"Sure," Amber muttered, already turning away. But then she hesitated. "Look, Jenna, I'm . . . I'm sorry about what happened to you the other day." She kept her eyes on the carpet, but Jenna could see her cheeks reddening underneath her fiery hair.

"Thanks," Jenna said, amazed that she'd actually heard the word *sorry* escape Amber's lips without being accompanied by a sneer.

"I know I've been a little tough to put up with lately."

A little? That was the understatement of the millennium, but in the interest of maintaining the awkward peace they seemed to be aiming for, Jenna decided to let it go. "That's all right," she said. "I know you've been disappointed about not getting into a sorority."

Amber frowned. "It's not just that. This first semester's been harder for me than I thought. I miss my friends from home. This campus is so huge. I guess sometimes I just feel lost here." She shrugged, waving her hand dismissively. "Whatev. That's my problem, not yours."

"But I didn't know. You could've talked to me about it," Jenna said. "Anytime."

Amber rolled her eyes. "Are you kidding? It wasn't an option. Not when I saw you running around to all your social events and having so much fun. You were the *last* person I wanted to talk to."

"Oh," Jenna said, nodding as everything fell into place. "I think I get that." And she did. With her 'betes, she'd always viewed her own friends' freedom with the smallest touch of jealousy. She'd never admit that to any of them, but there it was. And Amber must have felt the same way. "You know, we've got next semester to start over fresh with new roommates. Do you think that will help you feel better about LU?"

"I don't know," Amber said. "Maybe. I'm going to talk to my parents about it over break. We'll see what happens."

"In the meantime, do you think you can tolerate me as a roomie for a few more weeks?"

"As long as you don't wax poetic about ZZT every hour on the hour." Amber snorted.

"I'll try not to," Jenna said.

"Then we'll survive until break," Amber said.

"Definitely," Jenna said with a smile.

CHAPTER
10

Monday afternoon, Roni bent over the schedule for the Homecoming events, willing herself to concentrate. She'd asked Beverly to meet up with her at the ZZT house to go over all of her responsibilities for the next few days leading up to Homecoming. But the truth was, she didn't really need hand-holding with the schedule. Betsy'd had it all planned out for weeks, and Roni was just executing the plans. What she needed was a distraction. Ever since Lance had been a no-show in her Geography lab yesterday, Roni'd been trying to quash her disappointment. She'd actually, unbelievably, been looking forward to the yawn-worthy lab, hoping that she and Lance would finally be able to finish the conversation they'd started last week. And maybe, just maybe, he'd ask her out this time. But Lance had never shown up. Roni'd even made an extra trip to the natatorium this morning to see if she could catch him at the pool. But no such luck.

Now, as she and Beverly reviewed all the Homecoming

details, Roni was busy with her own list of should haves and could haves. She should have given Lance her number weeks ago! Why hadn't she at least done that? Now he had no way to reach her. *Stupid, stupid, stupid!*

"Roni?" Beverly jolted her out of her mental talking-to.

"Yes," Roni said, shaking off her thoughts of Lance and refocusing. "Right. So here's what the Homecoming T-shirt looks like. We just got the first sample in this morning." She pulled a blue-and-white T-shirt out of her bag and held it up to Beverly. "Janet Herlitzer did an amazing job sketching out the design for these, and they came out great."

Beverly looked over the T-shirt, which had the ZZT crest in the center with the slogan ZZT: MAKING MEMORIES THAT LAST A LIFETIME. She smiled. "This is fantastic, Roni!" she said. "It fits in perfectly with the Homecoming theme."

"I double-checked our order to make sure we had all the girls' sizes right," Roni said. "The rest of the shirts should come in by Wednesday of this week."

"Great," Beverly said. "Now what about the float and book drive?"

"Betsy already gave me the schedule for the float construction. It's right here. Each girl will take a one-hour shift, and we'll work in teams of five each. We start working on it tomorrow." Roni showed Beverly how she'd mapped out a timetable of hours and girls. "Heather and Betsy already ordered all of the supplies, so we should be all set. And the sign-up sheet for the book drive booth is posted by the front door. Most of the new members signed up earlier in the semester, but a few more signed on this week, too. We'll have more than enough people to work the booth."

"Wow," Beverly said. "Is there any detail you haven't taken care of?"

Roni grinned. "I'm just so glad I could help out as the New Member President."

"I think you secretly love being a taskmaster," Beverly teased. "I'm going to have to warn your Big Sis about that."

Roni's ears perked up at the mention of her Big Sis. She was dying to know who she'd end up with, or even the littlest hint about the big reveal. She figured it was worth a try. "So, Beverly, when is the Big Sis/Little Sis reveal?"

Beverly laughed. "I can't tell you *that*."

"Sure you can. You tell me everything."

"But this is off-limits. When it comes to that event, you're not the New Member President. You'll have to stay in suspense with the rest of your sisters."

Eyes locked on Beverly's, Roni blurted out, "I hope I get the person I want."

Raising a brow, Beverly asked, "Who would that be?"

Roni hesitated, her heart speeding up. She wanted so much to tell Beverly that she'd chosen her, but she knew she couldn't. It was so tempting, but finally she shook her head. "Nice try, but I'll never tell. Unless you tell me who you picked first."

Beverly laughed. "I'm sworn to secrecy, just like all the other actives."

"Oh, come on," Roni teased. "Spill it." But just then her cell rang.

"Saved by the cell," Beverly said with a laugh. "Answer it. I want to grab a Diet Coke from the kitchen anyway."

Roni checked her screen and saw that it was Kiersten calling.

She smiled with relief. She'd sent her a long e-mail yesterday telling her everything that had happened with her dad, and she'd been hoping to hear back from her.

"Kiersten!" she said. "I'm so glad you called."

"Oh, Roni," Kiersten said. "I didn't check my e-mails until this morning. But I'm so sorry about your fight with your dad. Are you okay?"

"I'm great, actually," Roni said. "My instincts tell me I did the right thing. And it's just so . . . freeing not to be obsessing about them for once."

"I'm glad you're happy, and I'm so proud of the decision you made. You're such a strong person, Roni. I know you're going to be just fine."

"Thanks," Roni said, feeling renewed confidence at getting Kiersten's nod of approval for standing her ground. "I think I'm going to need to find a job soon, though."

"With your background and personality, I bet you'll find something right away," Kiersten said. "But I wanted to talk to you about something else. You asked about staying with me over Thanksgiving. Roni, I . . ." She sighed. "You know I'd love to have you, but . . ."

"You can't?" Roni said, her spirits sinking.

"My parents invited my future in-laws over for Thanksgiving dinner. They're flying out for the weekend," Kiersten said. "And you know Phillip only has a studio, so I offered to let them stay with me because I have the extra room. And this is the first time my parents will meet his, so we're both a little nervous about it to begin with."

"Don't worry about me!" Roni said, striving to make her

voice sound cheery even though a leaden weight was settling over her. "I already had a few friends invite me to their homes." That was a lie. She hadn't even broached the subject with anyone because she'd thought Kiersten was a sure thing.

"Really?" Kiersten sounded completely relieved. "I'm so glad, because I was so worried I'd be leaving you high and dry."

"Nope," Roni said. "I have lots of options. But the only thing is, if I don't come to Boston for Thanksgiving, when will we go dress shopping?"

"I thought about that," Kiersten said. "You know I already picked out my dress, but I also did some research and found the chicest Watters and Watters bridesmaid dress. I was going to take you to try it on when you came home in a few weeks, but now I'm thinking I can just order it for you instead."

"Okay! That would be terrific," Roni said. "I'll get you my measurements this week."

"Perfect," Kiersten said. "And I promise we'll go shopping together for other wedding goodies when you come home for winter break."

"I'd love that," Roni said.

They talked for a few more minutes, and Roni tried her best to sound relaxed about everything. But as soon as she'd hung up, her feigned cheeriness made an immediate exit. So far, between her blowup with her dad, Kiersten's news, and Lance's disappearance, this was definitely not her week. Now what was she going to do about Thanksgiving? There was no way she was going groveling back to her parents' place, but at the same time, the prospect of staying here on campus by herself was equally depressing. The dorms stayed open for the few desperate souls who couldn't go home or didn't want to go home for the long weekend, but if she had to eat Top Ramen Noodles on Turkey Day . . . well, she might as well open the door to the pity party knocking at the back of her head right now.

Roni let out a long sigh just as Beverly walked back into the room.

"Whoa. I sense a mood shift," Beverly said. "Happiness to hara-kiri in under five minutes. What's wrong?"

Roni looked at Beverly, wanting more than anything to tell all. But if she did, she knew Beverly would invite her to her family's for Thanksgiving. And Roni already knew that Beverly was counting on spending most of that time with the boyfriend at home she'd been dating long-distance since she'd started at Latimer. He went to Baylor, so the holidays were the only times they got to see each other. And Roni wasn't going to mess with that. Not a chance. She didn't want to be third-wheeling it (an awkward role to begin with) at someone else's expense.

So, Roni decided to tell a half-truth. "You know my friend Kiersten?"

"The one who's getting married?"

"Right," Roni said. "Her engagement party is this weekend, and I'm just bummed I'm missing it." That was true. But she'd known she was going to miss that party for a while, so she'd dealt with her disappointment over it already.

Beverly patted Roni's hand. "I'm so sorry. I know how much she means to you. You'll get to see her in just a few weeks, right?"

"Right," Roni said. It would be six weeks until she saw Kiersten instead of the three until Thanksgiving, but she wasn't going to share that part with Beverly. No, she'd keep her nixed

Thanksgiving plans to herself until she'd weighed her other options. What those other options were, she didn't know. But she had only three weeks to find out.

Jenna bolted down the front steps of Tuthill Tuesday afternoon, unleashing a real, relaxed smile for the first time in weeks. She'd moved back into her room last night, and so far, living with Amber had turned from hellish to moderately tolerable. Amber was still a walking ad for Midol with her mood swings, but at least now she didn't always unleash them on Jenna. Instead, she plugged into her iPod and turned on the thrash metal. They were making progress. In fact, Jenna'd just left Amber in their room studying, and for once, when she'd said, "See you later," Amber'd actually replied with a relatively amicable "Later." Jenna'd take what she could get until next semester (six weeks and counting!).

As she hurried across University Avenue toward Billado Hall for her English Comp class, her cell beeped with a text message:

How goes the exorcism today? LLS

Jenna grinned. Lora-Leigh had already joked that she'd buy Jenna a crucifix and holy water if things on the Amber front didn't improve. Jenna typed:

I declare Tuthill Hall . . . clean. :) JD

Ding dong the wtch is ded! LLS

Jenna was too busy laughing to notice the shadow in her path until —*smack*!

"Oh my God! Jenna!" A familiar voice loomed above her. "Did I hurt you?"

Jenna glanced up from the ground, where she'd landed, none too gracefully, with books and papers sprawled everywhere, to see Tiger, hovering over her in a huffy combination of embarrassment and concern. Her heart catapulted upward, and guilt and relief washed over her simultaneously. It was so great to see him. She'd missed him the last few days. But there was so much he didn't know . . . and so much she hadn't been ready to tell him. Until now.

"I'm fine, no worries," Jenna said as Tiger helped her to her feet. He didn't release her hands right away, and she clung to the tiny hope that maybe that meant he didn't hate her as much as she'd feared he did.

"I've been wanting to talk to you since the party," he said. "I called your cell a few times, but it went straight to voice mail. Didn't you get my text messages?"

Jenna's cheeks flamed with shame and embarrassment. "I know," she said quietly. "I'm sorry. I just didn't know what to say. A lot's happened since the party."

"Maybe you can tell me about it, then?" He leaned closer. "I know you probably hate me, but—"

"What?" Jenna cried, staring at him in disbelief.

"You were so mad at the party," Tiger said. "I took things too far when we were alone, and I—"

"Stop," Jenna said suddenly. Then she did something she'd always been too reserved to do before. She took his hand. "Stop right there. You didn't do anything wrong. It was all me."

"Okay," Tiger said. "I think you just lost me."

Jenna smiled and motioned toward the staircase in front of Billado Hall. Together, they sat on the steps.

She bit her bottom lip. She'd promised to turn over a new leaf, no longer hiding her condition or how it affected her life. She was the New Jenna. The one who was balancing her life and her priorities better than ever. The New Jenna, who wasn't going to keep her 'betes from the people in her life anymore. Taking a deep breath for confidence, she said, "That night, when we were kissing, your hand brushed against my insulin pump."

"Your what?"

"See, Tiger, I've got..." *Just tell him.* "I'm diabetic."

He smiled at her and squeezed her hand. "Hey, diabetes is no biggie. Not like it used to be years ago. Right?"

"Well, I have the insulin pump, so that makes dosing easier." Jenna sighed. "But I've only had diabetes for a year now. And I still hate that I have it. For the longest time I didn't want you to know about it. I didn't want anyone to know. So when you accidentally touched the pump the other night, I panicked. I was so embarrassed, and I didn't know how to tell you. So I just ran. But I shouldn't have snapped at you like I did. That was horrible. And I'm so sorry."

"Hey," Tiger said softly, leaning closer, "it's okay."

"No, it's not. I wanted to call you, but I was afraid you'd hate me," Jenna said. "And then I got sick, so I couldn't call. I just haven't been doing a good job monitoring my diabetes, and I sort of had a seizure. I was in the hospital."

Tiger's mouth dropped open. "Jenna! Why didn't you tell me? I would have come to see you . . . or sent flowers."

"That's really sweet, Tiger. I should have told you. It was

just that everything happened so fast. And since then, I've been working out some things with my roommate and meeting with my academic advisor to try to organize my time and schedule better to get back on track."

"But you're okay now?"

"Yeah," she said, trying to tamp down the thrill of feeling his fingers sliding against hers. "I'm fine. I had to tell my parents what happened, but I promised them that I was taking better care of myself, so they're fine with it. And all the girls in ZZT know about my diabetes now, too, so I don't have to hide anything anymore. They're great about it."

"I will be, too," he said. "If you let me." He leaned over and planted a warm kiss on her cheek. The electricity zipped through her.

Then she heard the clock tower chime three o'clock. She jumped to her feet. "I'm going to be late to English!" She grabbed her backpack. "Can we talk more later?"

"Definitely. But wait, Jenna," he said. "I know we're already married and all, but how would you feel about a dinner date this Thursday?"

"Isn't that doing things a little out of order?" Jenna teased.

"Dates are always a good way to spice up a marriage, don't you think?" he said. "To keep the romance alive?"

"Well, I'm very pro-romance." Jenna laughed. "That sounds great."

He smiled and said, "So I'll pick you up at a quarter to six." He started to turn away, but then instead took a step closer to her. "Oh, and I'm really glad you explained what happened at the party during our 'honeymoon.' I was just worried that I'd done something wrong. Like maybe the kissing was too, I don't know, wet, or dry, or . . . horrible."

Jenna laughed. "The kissing"—she quickly brushed her lips against his before she lost her nerve—"was perfect."

Then she turned and ran to her class, her heart dancing happily. She glanced back only once to see Tiger standing there, smiling.

Lora-Leigh had seen more than a dozen LU Homecoming parades while she was growing up, but the last few years her parents had dragged her to them against her will, arguing that she needed to put in an obligatory appearance as the dean's daughter. But this year was different. This year, Lora-Leigh was building the ZZT float with her sisters. She wouldn't just be a bored onlooker; she'd be riding the float she'd help to make, and that changed everything. Plus, she wanted ZZT to win the float competition on Friday (especially if it meant beating the Tri-Os). She knew that in just two days, out in the crowd somewhere, her mom would be watching the parade, too. And Lora-Leigh wanted the ZZT float to be flawless—no, better than flawless—when she saw it. That was why she'd suggested to Roni and Beverly that they skip the new member meeting tonight and round up all the sisters, new members and actives alike, to finish the float.

Now she dipped her brush into gray paint and focused on the portrait of John and Emma Weiland, the founders of Latimer University, that she was painting for one of the eight larger-than-life photo frames on the float. She was copying it from a photo Minnie had found at the LU Historical Society, and so far she had their outfits perfect, but she needed to work on Emma's eyes and hair. She wanted to get the shading just right....

"Lora-Leigh," Camille said, plopping down beside her to offer her a soda, "you haven't moved from that spot for the last two hours. Do you always go catatonic when you're creating a masterpiece?"

"Hey, there's a reason why most artists are tortured souls," Lora-Leigh said. "Perfection just isn't good enough for us." She stretched her neck and took a swig of soda. "Besides, this is nothing. You should see me when I'm sewing. Sometimes I skip two meals before I even remember I'm supposed to be hungry."

Camille laughed as she stuffed crumpled brown tissue paper into the chicken wire they'd used to build the picture frames. "I wish I had your talent, but I don't think I could pull off the starving artist image. I'd be gorging on Ben & Jerry's before I even finished one sketch."

Across the street, the Beta Xis had made a funny LU Evolution-style float, with papier-mâché figures showing how the Red Raider football uniforms, the Marching Raiders uniforms, and the Red Raider mascots had changed over a hundred years. It was looking pretty cool, but the Tri-Omega float was the one that was the real jaw-dropper. The Tri-Os had constructed a miniature model of LU's original Sorority Row from 1923. Roni was amazed at how huge and intricate it was. Of course, the largest and most impressive house on the float was the original Tri-O house. They'd made sure that the immaculate plantation-style mansion stood out like a beacon of glory among the other, smaller houses.

"I wonder if the Tri-Os need any help over there," Lora-Leigh said, nodding across the street. "I could put some of my artist skills to work on their float. Something a little more deconstructionist would be great. All I need is an axe. . . ."

"Be nice, Lora-Leigh," Roni scolded as she stapled some glittery fringe around the edge of the float platform.

"Yes, Madam President," Lora-Leigh muttered.

"Come on," Roni said. "Jenna and Keesha need some help with their picture. Their painting of Billado Hall is starting to look like the Kremlin."

"Lora-Leigh to the rescue," Camille said, waving her away. "I promise to make sure no one touches Emma Weiland."

"Thanks," Lora-Leigh said. She walked to the back of the float with Roni to where Jenna and Keesha were trying—and failing—to paint a historic picture of the LU campus.

"Okay, ladies, make way for the master," Lora-Leigh teased, playfully shooing them away. "Give me five minutes to fix the dome on Billado, and then you can take over again."

"Please, save us," Jenna said. "Whenever I try, it just looks like finger painting."

"Well, no wonder," Lora-Leigh said, elbowing Jenna. "You've had a one-track mind ever since you made up with Tiger. You're a lost cause."

Jenna blushed and giggled, but she didn't deny it.

"Enough said." Lora-Leigh smiled, then grabbed some brushes and set to work, giving directions as to which paint colors she needed and how to mix them.

"So, Roni, since the actives are out of earshot," Keesha whispered, "give us the lowdown on the Big Sister reveal. We're dying here."

"Hey, I'm as much in the dark as you guys," Roni said. "I'm guessing it'll be before Thanksgiving, but who knows?"

"Whenever it is, I know Lora-Leigh's going to get Camille Crawford," Jenna said. "Y'all were kindred spirits from day one."

"That would be brill," Lora-Leigh said.

"I hope I get Betsy Bickford," Keesha said. "She was my last Rose Bud, and I loved spending time with her."

"Well," Sue-Marie Weiss said. "I want *your* big sister." Keesha's real-life big sister, Kwana, was also a ZZT. Lora-Leigh'd seen her and Sue-Marie hanging out together a lot.

"I always wanted an older sister," Roni said. "My friend Kiersten is like my big sis already, although now she lives five thousand miles away, which isn't easy. But since I came here, Beverly and I have become really close. I can call or text her anytime, and I love hanging out with her." A smile lit up Roni's face. "Maybe, if I'm lucky, Beverly will be my Big Sis."

Lora-Leigh smiled at Roni, hoping, for her sake, that she'd get Beverly, especially since Roni didn't have much in the way of a real family these days. But, come to think of it, neither did Lora-Leigh.

Lora-Leigh put the finishing touches on Billado Hall and stood back to inspect her work. "Well, the dome is still a little lopsided," she said, "but I'm not a miracle worker."

Keesha, Jenna, and Roni all grinned. "It looks so much better," Jenna said. "Thanks."

The girls went back to their assigned jobs, and Lora-Leigh headed back to her workstation. One thing was for sure: there was no way the Tri-Os were going to outshine ZZT this time. Lora-Leigh would work on this float all night if that's what it took to get everything just right.

CHAPTER 11

As soon as Lora-Leigh saw Jenna's panicked face and the discarded clothes strewn haphazardly around her side of the room, she knew she and Roni had arrived in the nick of time.

"Okay, step back from the clothes very slowly," Lora-Leigh said. "We'll get through this together."

"Everything looks awful," Jenna said, collapsing onto her bed.

"Nothing could look awful on you," Roni said consolingly. "Besides, Tiger's seen you in lots of these clothes already, and he must've liked the way you looked in them. He's still crushing on you big-time."

"But this is different," Jenna said. "I want to look to die for."

"So the gang's all here," Amber said, holding her hand up in a half-wave without shifting her eyes from her computer screen.

Lora-Leigh stared at Amber, biting her tongue to keep from saying anything. Anyone who had treated Jenna the way she had, deserved a little catfight. But Lora-Leigh would hold back, for Jenna's sake.

"I'm sorry, Amber," Jenna said, worry shining in her eyes. "It's a wardrobe crisis of mass proportion. My date with Tiger is tonight, and I've already rejected the contents of my entire closet...*twice*. I need a fashion intervention ASAP."

"And you can't make a decision without your entourage, of course," Amber said, standing up and grabbing her books. "I was heading to the library in a few anyway. Later."

As soon as the door was safely shut, Lora-Leigh snipped, "So the Princess of Darkness still reigns, huh?"

"Hey, she's speaking to me without gnashing her teeth," Jenna said. "For her, that's a concerted effort. Really."

"As long as you can relax and get some rest for the next couple of weeks before break," Roni said.

"Things are way better than they were. Trust me," Jenna said. "But relaxing is the last thing I'm going to be able to do if I don't find something to wear!"

Lora-Leigh grinned. This was where she came in. "Ask, and it shall be given to you." Lora-Leigh reached into her bag and pulled out a burgundy sweater dress with a plunging neckline and fluted sleeves. "Not too tight at the waist, so your pump won't show. But a little bit of cleavage and a lot of chic."

"It's perfect," Roni echoed. "It'll look amazing on your petite figure."

Jenna undressed quickly, and Lora-Leigh noticed that, for the first time, she wasn't trying to hide her pump from them. She slipped the dress over her head and looked in the mirror, beaming. Lora-Leigh smiled proudly as she watched Jenna vamp in front of the mirror. Her creation looked amazing on Jenna, if she did say so herself.

"Did you make this?" Jenna said. "For me?"

Lora-Leigh nodded. "I've been working on it since you were in the hospital. My mom doesn't want my designs, so I thought I'd target a younger market this time."

"You still haven't spoken to her?" Roni asked.

"Nah, but—hey—I've got you guys. I dish everything to you anyway. Who needs her?" Lora-Leigh shrugged.

"You do," Jenna whispered, then suddenly grabbed Lora-Leigh in an impulsive hug. "Thank you so much for the dress. I love it."

"I'm glad," Lora-Leigh whispered hoarsely. Those were the words she'd wanted her mom to say to her, but she was happy to hear them from Jenna, too. She let her friend engulf her in the hug. Even though it still cut through her that she hadn't heard from or spoken to her mom in over a week, she couldn't talk about it too much out loud, or the waterworks started building behind her eyes.

"You know, after tonight," Lora-Leigh said, pulling away, "I predict that you're on your way to girlfriend status with Tiger."

"I agree," Roni singsonged.

"I don't know," Jenna said uncertainly, then smiled shyly. "But I think I'd like that."

"So," Lora-Leigh said, "has the crisis been averted?"

Jenna took in her overall appearance one more time, then nodded. "Yup, I'm ready. I feel beautiful, thanks to y'all."

"You are," Roni said with a hug.

One final touch—her ZZT new member pin—and Jenna

was ready to go. Lora-Leigh and Roni walked her downstairs to where Tiger was going to pick her up. Lora-Leigh smiled as she and Roni headed back inside Tuthill, glad that she'd been able to help Jenna tonight. That was what she loved most about designing clothes—the idea that she was creating something that would make someone feel special and beautiful. If only her mom had realized that about the shrug she'd made, then she might have understood what Lora-Leigh was trying to tell her, the apology she was trying to make. But Lora-Leigh couldn't explain that to her now. And, more importantly, she wasn't sure she wanted to.

Jenna dipped another piece of chicken into the cheese fondue and smiled at Tiger. He'd taken her to So Fond of You, a tiny restaurant on the other side of Latimer made from an old steam engine. Jenna and Tiger had a dining suite in one of the old nineteenth-century passenger cars all to themselves. Between the plush velvet rail booths, the soft candlelight, the white twinkling lights strung like a canopy of stars above them, and the warmth of Tiger's hand in hers, this was the most romantic date Jenna'd ever been on, and she was loving every minute of it.

"This is delish," she said between bites. "I've never been to a fondue restaurant before."

"I thought you might like the hands-on dining experience, since you love to cook," Tiger said. "And I was hoping you wouldn't be too tough a food critic."

"I give it four stars," Jenna said. "Charming ambience, a delectable palette of flavors, and good company."

"Are you talking about me or the waiter?" Tiger teased.

"The waiter, of course," Jenna said with a laugh.

"I guess that makes sense. He's the keeper of the chocolate fondue, after all. You want to stay on his good side. And speaking of which." Tiger flagged the waiter over. "Could you bring us the Chocolate Dream for dessert?" he asked him.

The waiter nodded and disappeared as Jenna felt a familiar nervousness sweep over her. Chocolate—just the thought of it made her mouth water. But she'd promised her doctor that she would be a lot more careful about her diet, and she'd been watching her sugar intake ever since she got out of the hospital. She knew she could adjust her pump if she needed to, but she'd been trying not to abuse it like she had been the last few weeks. She sighed, already dreading what she was about to say.

"Um, Tiger, I'm sorry," she said quietly. "I don't think I should have the chocolate fondue tonight. It might mess with my 'betes too much." She cringed, hating the fact that she was sabotaging the romantic mood with her high-maintenance body.

"This kind of chocolate won't," Tiger said with a reassuring smile, giving her hand a squeeze. "I thought about that beforehand, and I bought some sugar-free chocolate and brought it with me. The waiter's already taken care of it. "

Jenna lifted her eyes and stared at him in disbelief, her self-consciousness fading away. With that one thoughtful gesture, Tiger had made her feel more at ease than any guy she'd ever met.

"I didn't want to tell you earlier 'cause I wasn't sure if you'd feel awkward about it," Tiger said. "I hope it was okay that I did this."

"It was more than okay," Jenna said with a smile. "It was perfect."

"Good," Tiger said, looking relieved. Just then, the waiter returned with the chocolate and a whole plate of strawberries. "Dig in," Tiger said. "You can eat the whole pot if you want to."

"Maybe I will." Jenna giggled, dipping one of the strawberries in.

Two hours later, Tiger pulled into the parking lot at Tuthill and turned the radio down low. Jenna sighed, reluctant to get out of the car and put an end to such a wonderful night.

"Thanks so much for dinner . . . and everything," Jenna said, feeling her cheeks warm again.

"Thanks for saying yes," Tiger said, leaning over to give her a whispery-soft kiss. "You know, Homecoming is this weekend."

Her breath caught as their fingers entwined. "I know. We've got a whole new halftime program to do. Some pretty cool formations."

"You want to be my Homecoming date?"

Jenna's smile stretched her cheeks to maximum capacity. "But I'm in the band." Meaning, she wouldn't get to dress up, get a white mum corsage with her sorority letters (or his frat letters) on them, and sit in the stands with him or her sisters and their dates.

"So? We can hang out after the bonfire, and you can come over to the house for our after-party."

"I'd really like that," she whispered.

He brushed her hair away from her face and brought her lips to meet his. "I really like *you*," he whispered into the darkness.

It was at least another fifteen minutes before Jenna glided up to her dorm room, her lips still warm from his kisses.

❖

"Hurry, everyone!" Roni yelled, feeling adrenaline coursing through her. "The parade's about to start." This was it. All the work she'd done for the past few weeks on Homecoming was coming down to this—this parade and the book drive tomorrow. She sprinted through the parking lot of the biology building, getting the new members in line around the float. Hollis Hendricks and Emma Cox were up front with the banner they'd made that read:

> ## ZZTs ♡ THE RED RAIDERS

The rest of the sisters, all wearing their Homecoming T-shirts, followed. Heather Bourke had the top down on her VW Beetle, and some of the officers of the house piled in with red-and-white school pom-poms.

The Sigma Sigma fraternity was in front of them in a parade of pickup trucks decorated with streamers. The guys were throwing LU key chains out to the crowds of students, university faculty, and Latimer residents gathered on either side of the road.

"Everything ready?" Beverly asked, coming up to Roni and giving her a reassuring hug.

"I hope so," Roni said, taking a deep breath. "Let's do it."

The parade kicked off to the roaring cheers of the crowd on University Boulevard, and Roni stepped into place, walking behind the ZZT float with Lora-Leigh, Danika, and Sandy, smiling and waving and making sure everyone stayed in place.

Soon, Hollis and Sue-Marie started the chanting, and Roni chimed in with everyone else. "I said it's great . . . to be . . . a ZZT; I said it's great . . . to be . . . a ZZT; I said it's great . . ."

In the background, Roni could hear the Marching Raiders, and she thought of Jenna. She wished Jenna could have walked with them, but she was where she needed to be. The Marching Raiders were last in the parade and would do a mini-concert at the review stand in front of the library, which was full of important alums, officers of the university, the football coach, and the mayor of Latimer.

The parade wound along University Boulevard, a vibrant collage of at least a dozen colorful floats, ticker tape, and hundreds of students. As she walked, pride swelled inside her. She'd had a hand in this; she'd helped to make it happen. She'd never participated in anything like this back in Boston. In fact, her parents never even liked her watching the Macy's Thanksgiving Parade on TV. They'd always said cattle drives like that were for simpletons. But today, Roni wasn't just a student at LU; she was part of the fabric of ZZT and of the university itself. And it felt amazing. As the ZZT float finally came to a stop in front of the library after the two-mile route, she was exhausted but elated.

"That was awesome," she said, linking arms with Lora-Leigh.

Lora-Leigh laughed. "You know, I used to make fun of people like us when I watched the parade with my parents in high school. But you're right. It was awesome, mostly because our float was the highlight of the parade. In short, it kicked ass."

"Definitely," Sandy agreed as she joined them. "But now

I'm starving. Let's check out the snack cart over there to see if we can grab some chips or something before the rally and bonfire."

Megan Gleason grimaced. "There's no way I'm going to eat junk food tonight. I've sworn off it until after Thanksgiving. I'm saving up the calories for my mom's Cajun fried turkey. I could put on five pounds in a day just by eating it."

At the mention of Thanksgiving, Roni felt her bubble of happiness burst. That was the last thing she wanted to think about. She still hadn't figured out what to do or where to go, and time was running out. It wasn't in her blood to invite herself over to someone else's home for the holiday. It just didn't seem proper, and even if she was blowing off her parents right now, the decorum they'd taught her to live with was a lot harder to ignore.

"Come on, let's get some grub and meet up with the sistahs for the rally," Lora-Leigh said, throwing her arm around Roni and snapping her out of her thoughts.

Roni smiled. She'd deal with Thanksgiving later. Or maybe she wouldn't deal with it at all. She'd just stay at Latimer and pretend that Thanksgiving wasn't happening in every house on every corner in every state. Yes, that's what she'd do. Absolute denial. And until then, she'd enjoy being surrounded by her friends.

When the rally started, Roni forgot all about Thanksgiving in the thrill of watching the football players file onto the stage as the band blared out the fight song and the cheerleaders somersaulted through the air, pumping up the crowd.

"Reeeeeeeed Raiders! Reeeeeeeed Raiders! Fight! Fight! Fight!"

Roni screamed the school cheers at the top of her lungs as the captain of the football team lit the three-story teepee-shaped wooden bonfire. Then she sang the LU alma mater arm in arm with Lora-Leigh, Danika, Sandy, and Allison Carlton.

At one point, as she watched the flames dance in front of her, her attention shifted to just beyond the fire, to a figure in the background standing tall against the flickering light. Somehow, his eyes found hers across the crowd. His brown hair was mussed from the warm November breeze, and his face was lit up by the firelight, making him look drop-dead gorgeous. A thrill coursed through her as Lance McManus started walking toward her, smiling.

"Hey, stranger," he said. "I know you were looking for the white horse, but he's not really into the whole bonfire scene. Reminds him too much of fire-breathing dragons."

Roni grinned at him while she quickly introduced him to Lora-Leigh and the other girls. Lora-Leigh, who caught on right away to who he was, said, "Well, we're going to go in search of Beverly and Camille."

"Okay, I'll catch up with you in a few," Roni said, sending her a silent thank-you with her eyes. As the other girls faded into the crowd, Roni turned back to Lance. It was so good to see him, but she had to play it cool. She had no idea where she stood with him now; he'd been MIA for so long. "So what happened to Geography 101?" she asked. "Couldn't handle Dr. Sylvester and his minion anymore?"

"I think I could've survived the semester with the right company," he said with a smile. "But I had to switch around my classes because of my swim team schedule. Now I'm in

Dr. Hornby's class on Thursdays. And his T.A. is even more maniacal than Dr. Sylvester's. Consider yourself lucky."

Roni laughed. "Well, I've been trying to drive our T.A. slowly insane with my lack of enthusiasm for plate tectonics, but it'd be nice to have a partner in crime."

"Sorry I can't be there to help you plot his demise." Lance smiled again. "But aside from the T.A. and his devious ways, there's another conversation we started that we never got to finish. I would've called you, but I didn't have your number. . . ."

"If you have a cell with you, I can fix that right now," Roni said. There was no way she was going to miss this opportunity again. Lance pulled out his cell, and the two of them swapped numbers.

"So," Lance said, "does this mean you don't mind if I call you?"

"I'd like that," Roni said breathlessly.

He leaned closer. "And what if I asked you out?"

Roni grinned. Finally! "I'd like that even better," she said.

"Great!" Lance said, looking relieved in a very cute, boyish way. "I'm pretty swamped with meets and finals between now and winter break, but I can call you over the break, and we could get together when classes start next semester."

"Definitely," Roni said. She was the tiniest bit disappointed that they wouldn't have their first date for another month and a half, but she'd waited this long to see him again, so she guessed she could wait a little longer for a date. Besides, they could get to know each other better over phone and e-mail until then.

"Well, I better go find my friends," Roni said reluctantly, not wanting to say good-bye but knowing she had to. "The rally's almost over, and we're going back to the ZZT house after this."

Lance nodded. "So I'll see you soon, okay? And I'll call you."

"Is that a promise?" Roni asked, her pulse quickening.

"It is now," Lance said with a grin. He gave her hand a quick squeeze and then walked away, looking back over his shoulder to give her one more disarming smile.

Roni practically floated back to Lora-Leigh, who was, of course, waiting with a sly smile.

"Okay, we need the four-one-one on that tasty find, pronto," she said. "He was the mystery man you told us about from your Geography class, right?"

Roni nodded; then, feeling euphoric, she told her everything.

"You know, this is the first guy who I've actually wanted to call me in a long, long time," she said.

"And you're going to get your wish," Lora-Leigh said. "You're gonna get Lanced-A-Lot next semester, girlfriend."

Roni laughed as her friends teased her. She joined in the rest of the cheers and songs as the rally came to an end. And all the while she kept on smiling, high on the knowledge that something was going to happen with Lance. Maybe not right now but . . . eventually. And that was more than enough for her.

Lora-Leigh was taking a dozen romance paperbacks from some Delta Kappa new members who'd stopped by the ZZT book drive booth, when the warm, tangy scent of Old Spice cologne mixed with Pierre Cardin aftershave hit her nose. She smiled. She knew her dad was here before she even turned around.

"I'm so impressed with what you girls are doing for the Latimer Library," he was saying to Marissa as he checked out the mountain of boxes and crates of books that were filling more than three-fourths of the booth by now. "One of the best Greek Homecoming projects this year, I think."

"Thanks, Dean Sorenstein," Marissa said, glancing over at Lora-Leigh with a smile. "It's because we've got great new members. I believe you know one of them?"

"Now, who would that be?" he said teasingly, his eyes twinkling.

"Hey, Dad!" Lora-Leigh said.

"Well looka here." He smiled, giving her a giant hug. Lora-Leigh pressed her face into his chest, so relieved that she and her dad could still be normal around each other after all that had happened with her mom. "Are you enjoying your first Homecoming as an LU student?"

She nodded. "Definitely." It had been a great weekend so far. The ZZTs won second place for their float (but they still beat out the Tri-Os, ha, ha, ha), and the book drive and Friday's parade participation combined earned the chapter the title of Most Enthusiastic from the LU Panhellenic Association. And she was going to the game this afternoon with Mark Dickson, her friend from high school, and hanging with him at the Fox after-party tonight, too. It was just a friend-date thing, but she'd always thought Mark was a fun guy, and she knew they'd have a good time together. And Jenna would be at the Fox party, too, with Tiger (of course), so that would make her night even better.

"Think we'll win the game this afternoon?" she asked her dad.

"We've got some pro scouts here today," he said, "so I'd say for the sake of the players, winning is what they need to do."

Lora-Leigh's stomach suddenly knotted with nerves. Did DeShawn know there would be scouts at the game? If he did, she was sure he'd be battling for blood on the field today to catch their eyes.

"Excuse me, Dean Sorenstein?" Marissa interjected. "Could you pose for a picture with us?"

"That's what I'm here for." He smiled.

While the photographer took a picture of him with Marissa and the other sisters who'd coordinated the book drive, Lora-Leigh watched her dad. He certainly was in his element. She understood now why he wanted her to attend Latimer University. It was what he was proud of.

After the picture, her father reached for her arm. "It looks like you've really come into your own here," he said. "I'm happy to see you making the most out of your first semester. And"—he paused, glancing around at her friends—"it looks like you joined a great sorority, and the right one for you. Despite what your mother thinks."

Lora-Leigh blew a curl of hair out of her eyes. "Can you tell her that, please?"

"You know your mother," he said. "She won't listen until she's good and ready. She is one hardheaded woman." He winked. "Like someone else I know."

"Me?" Lora-Leigh snorted. "Never."

He smiled.

"Tell Mom I'll see her next Thursday at Thanksgiving," Lora-Leigh said.

He nodded and started to turn away, then stopped. "Just so you know . . . she's going to start cooking on Wednesday afternoon."

"Is that a hint?" Lora-Leigh said with a smile.

Her dad shrugged. "Just relaying the information, that's all."

But Lora-Leigh knew her dad better than that. In dad-speak, the translation was, it would be a good thing to head home right after class ended on Wednesday to see her mother and . . . talk.

"See ya, Dad," she called out to him as he walked toward the Gamma Gamma Rho fraternity.

She turned back to the booth just as someone else stepped into her line of vision—a five-eleven, two-hundred-and-five-pound mass of muscle in a sleek Kenneth Cole suit that made him look like a walking *GQ* ad. DeShawn's eyes connected with hers even at this distance. And "just friends" or not, she couldn't stop her stomach from free-falling every time she set eyes on him.

"Well, if it isn't the sisters of Zeta Zeta Tau," DeShawn said as he approached with several of his football buds, all in suits and ties.

"And if it isn't the entire offensive backfield of the Latimer University Red Raiders," she countered. "Shouldn't you be resting up for the game?"

"We're headed to the stadium right now, but we wanted to stop here first," he said. "We brought a bunch of used books. Just show me where to put them."

Lora-Leigh led him to the back table, where he set down the boxes. "Thanks, DeShawn," she said.

"Just wanted to help out my girl," he said, tugging her curls.

His girl. Lora-Leigh's breath caught. Oh, he was killing her.

But she knew where things stood, and she had to respect that. She stretched her hand out to him in what she thought was a pure friend way and said, "Hey, have a great game today. I'll be cheering for you."

He clasped her hand in his larger one and stroked her thumb, ever so slightly. "Thanks, Curly," he said. "I'll be looking for you in the stands."

He pulled away and walked off with his friends, and as he did, Roni sidled up next to Lora-Leigh. "Friends," she said. "I don't think so. You're not fooling me."

Lora-Leigh knew Roni was right. *We're not fooling anybody,* she thought. *Not even ourselves.*

"First and ten, do it again, go, go, go!"

Lora-Leigh nearly spilled her Diet Coke on her soft wool pants as she screamed at the Red Raiders. The score was tied 10–10 in the fourth quarter.

"Homecoming's supposed to be a gimme game," Lora-Leigh groaned, putting her head in her hands.

"Easy there, Sorenstein," her Homecoming date, Mark Dickson, said. "I had no idea you were such a Red Raiders fan."

She shrugged, not wanting to admit who exactly she was such a fan of.

"Lora-Leigh's one of our most spirited new members,"

Camille Crawford said. Lora-Leigh and Mark had set her up with one of the other Foxes, Mike Muti, so she and Mike were sitting with them.

"I don't know about most spirited, but I'm definitely the loudest." Lora-Leigh laughed. "That's what I'm talking about!" she screamed as Latimer's tight end hauled in a screen pass from quarterback Coy Peterson and ran for a first down before being tackled. "Gooooooooo Latimer!"

Camille leaned toward Lora-Leigh and whispered, "Enjoying your view of the backfield?"

Lora-Leigh laughed and turned back to the game just as Peterson snapped the ball, then passed it to DeShawn, who took off running.

"Go DeShawn!" she yelled.

He hurdled a diving defenseman, his massive thighs powering him forward. Lora-Leigh clutched Camille's hand, jumping up and down . . . until . . .

Crunch!

She heard the hit from her seat. A high-low with the two safeties, one taking DeShawn's feet out from under him and the other delivering a helmet-to-helmet hit.

"Come on, ref . . . where's the freakin' flag?" someone yelled.

"That's bull!" Mark screamed out when no penalty was called.

Camille squeezed Lora-Leigh's hand tighter. "He's gonna be okay."

She watched DeShawn try to get up and put weight on his right leg, but it buckled under him. The trainers rushed onto the field while the ref called an injury time-out. DeShawn pulled off his helmet, and Lora-Leigh could read the pain all over his face. His eyes were intense, his teeth clenched, and the vein in his neck was straining against his muscles. The crowd cheered when he was helped off the field. He gazed up into the student section to give them a thumbs-up.

Lora-Leigh's throat went dry when she thought this injury might end DeShawn's chances as an NFL hopeful. *Please be okay, DeShawn . . . please*, she silently chanted in her head.

She watched him pace the sidelines, first limping in pain and then slowly walking more steadily, seemingly cursing under his breath for allowing it to happen.

"He looks all right," Lora-Leigh finally said, letting out a long breath and squeezing Camille's hand.

She had to admit to herself that the whole platonic friendship thing was just not working out, at least on her end. She liked him . . . a lot. But there were only a few football games left in the season—and a possible bowl bid for the team—so Lora-Leigh would respect DeShawn's wishes to keep things on a friendship level. For now.

As she looked back on the field, DeShawn's eyes shifted up through the student section, connecting with hers, and he smiled.

She mouthed, "Are you okay?"

He nodded and then winked.

Oh, yeah . . . once football season was over, she was officially putting an end to their friendship.

CHAPTER
12

The atmosphere at the Zeta Zeta Tau house seemed electric Sunday night when Roni walked in with Lora-Leigh and Jenna. Beverly had finally announced to the new members during lunch that tonight would be the traditional Big Sis/Little Sis reveal, and since then, Roni hadn't been able to think about anything else.

The foyer of the ZZT house was lit up with festive colored lanterns, and appetizers and fruit were laid out on a banquet table decorated with a white linen tablecloth, flowers, and blue confetti. Overhead hung a huge hand-painted banner of a large teddy bear (ZZT's official mascot) holding the paw of a smaller bear that read:

Anything for my little sister

Actives and new members milled around, visiting and rehashing all the Homecoming parties and hookups, but Roni noticed that everyone was speaking in hushed, expectant tones, wondering what would happen next.

"I'm getting goose bumps," Jenna said to Roni gleefully. "Oh, I want to be Darcy's Little Sis so bad."

"You will be," Lora-Leigh said, and Roni knew she was right.

Darcy was already acting like Jenna's Big Sis and had been for a while, and Roni was almost certain they'd be matched up. And Lora-Leigh and Camille seemed like the obvious pair, too. Now she just had to hope that she'd get the sister she wanted, too. But she was as much in the dark about tonight's proceedings as the other girls.

Now Beverly stepped up to Roni and said, "We're ready, if you want to gather all the new members in front of the closed living room door."

Roni nodded, her heartbeat speeding up, and quickly got them together, then did a head count to make sure everyone was there. "We're all set," she said to Beverly.

Beverly opened the door, and Roni's mouth dropped as she stared at the room. It was completely covered in a spidery web of . . . yarn? Yarn everywhere, weaving in and out of chair and table legs, up around lamps and candlestick holders, through the cushions of the couches in vibrant yellow, red, orange, green, blue, every color imaginable.

"I'm not cleaning this up," Lora-Leigh joked.

Beverly climbed up onto a chair, avoiding the stringwork around her feet. "As y'all know," she started, "at Zeta Zeta Tau we are family. Through good and bad, thick and thin. However, there's always that special bond you have with one person in the house. Tonight, we want you to make that connection to your Big Sister. She's someone who has chosen you over everyone else. Each piece of colored yarn has a tag attached to it. Find the tag with your name and then follow the yarn until you reach the end and your new Big Sister."

"When can we start?" Bonni asked.

Beverly held her hands up and shouted, "Go for it!"

Roni clambered over to the couch along with the other twenty-nine girls, trying to get to the string that had her name on it. The melee of voices blended together in high-pitched giggles and squeals sounding out through the large living room. Pulse racing like she'd just done ten laps of backstrokes, Roni broke through an opening between Jenna's elbow, Madison Sabatini's left knee, and Keesha's head. She managed to make out VERONICA VAN GELDEREN on a black-and-white string.

Roni nabbed the card and ran smack into Courtney Goodson. Their strings were interlocked, so they danced around each other, unweaving the tangled mess before each turned in opposite directions to continue along the maze of netting.

"Up over the lamp and under the footstool," Roni muttered to herself, her heart pounding away with each loosening of the string. "Around the white couch, over the painting of the founders and underneath the bookshelf."

"Watch out, Boston!" Lora-Leigh hollered as they barely avoided a head-on collision. Her crimson string was entwined with Roni's, and they had to switch yarn to unscramble the chaos.

"Sorry!"

Roni's black-and-white string continued into the TV lounge,

where Sue-Marie Weiss, LaDonna Griffin, and Rachel Hughes were jumbled together behind the couch.

"That's mine!" Sue-Marie shouted.

"Don't get your panties in a twist, Weiss!" LaDonna said with a giggle.

The new members slowly untangled, eventually all meeting up with their strings at the double doors leading into the dining room and lounge. The doors were slid apart just enough for the girls to see that all of their strings converged at the opening.

When they were all sorted out and ready, there almost seemed to be a collective gathering of breath. Roni could barely contain her emotions and anticipation, wondering what waited for them behind the partition. As the New Member President, she decided to take the lead. She pushed the doors apart—with help from Courtney and Megan—to reveal the candlelit dining room, cleared of tables and chairs. Each girl's string led to one of the ZZT actives—a Big Sister, holding a candle and waiting for her Little Sister to arrive.

Roni watched, her heart thundering, as the rest of the new members rushed toward their Big Sisters. The new pairs were united with hugs, laughter, and tears of happiness: Jenna with Darcy, Lora-Leigh with Camille, Sandy with Marissa, Ashleigh with Melody. Finally, with shaking hands, Roni looked to see where her own string was leading, into the farthest corner of the room. Then she let out an ecstatic laugh as she catapulted across the room to where Beverly stood, arms spread wide.

"Hey there, Little Sis," Beverly said, hugging her. "I was hoping you'd pick me."

"I was hoping you'd pick me!"

"This is for you," Beverly said, handing Roni what looked like a small boat oar. The wood was beautiful, stained and glossed, with the ZZT crest in the middle. Roni's name was written out in calligraphy on the face, and there was a picture of her and Beverly together at the bottom.

"A paddle from your Big Sister. And here's a silver paint pen. You can have all the sisters sign it."

"I love it so much, Beverly," Roni whispered through her tears. "Thank you."

One by one, the Big Sisters paired up with their newly chosen Little Sisters, handing each of them a gift bag, their first ZZT teddy bear, and their own specially decorated paddle—a long-lived sorority and fraternity tradition. For the rest of the night, the girls autographed one another's paddles, ate yummy food, sang sorority songs, and just enjoyed the company of their family.

My chosen family, Roni thought, quite contentedly. *And my chosen sister*, she thought, glancing at Beverly.

"Only one more big hurdle now, Roni," Beverly said with a gleam in her eye. "Soon you'll be fully initiated."

Roni beamed. It was hard to believe that her experience with ZZT could get any better. But she knew it would once she was initiated, and she couldn't wait.

Jenna'd just finished packing for her trip home for Thanksgiving when there was a knock on her door. She opened it to see Tricia, her resident advisor, smiling mischievously at her.

"Jenna," she said, "can I come in for a sec?"

"Um, sure," Jenna said, wondering what this might be about.

"Was I playing the music too loud?" She hurried to turn it down, just in case. Amber was gone for the afternoon, studying at the student center, so Jenna'd taken her few hours of freedom to relax and crank up some of her own music for a change.

"Nope, the music's fine." Tricia's eyes settled on Jenna's duffel bag. "Going out of town this weekend?"

Jenna blushed. Now this was embarrassing. "Actually, no," she muttered. "I was packing for Thanksgiving. I know it's still a week away, but I had some gifts for my sisters lying around, so I decided I'd just get a head start on my packing." She grinned sheepishly. "I guess I'm a little excited to be going home."

"I used to do that freshman year, too," Tricia admitted. "As much as I wanted to get away from the fam when I started college, I ended up missing them. I was always so ready to see them over breaks, but I was even more ready to say good-bye to them after the breaks."

Jenna laughed at that. She might not get tired of the Little Js over Thanksgiving, but after shuffling them around to their activities for six weeks over winter break, she knew she'd be ready to get back to school, too.

"I was actually coming by to talk to you about your roommate situation for next semester," Tricia said. "I think I might have found you a new roommate. Or, I guess I should say, she found me."

"That's great!" Jenna said. She'd been hoping to get the roommate sitch in place before the semester ended. "Do you think we'll get along?"

Tricia smiled. "I think I can safely say that I know you will."

"So when can I meet her?" Jenna said, the idea of a fresh start sending flashes of excitement through her.

"Now, if you want. She's waiting in my room."

"I'd love to," Jenna said, already hoping that they'd hit it off right away and be cyber-chatting over the holidays, getting to know each other. She followed Tricia down the hall to her room. But when Jenna walked through Tricia's door, it wasn't a stranger she saw smiling back at her.

"Roni?!?" Jenna cried with a mixture of happiness and confusion.

"Surprise!" Roni laughed, rushing to hug her.

"But how?" Jenna asked.

"Well, I'm not even sure my parents will still foot the bill for my room and board next semester," Roni said. "I e-mailed them to let them know I wouldn't be home for Thanksgiving, but never heard back." She shrugged. *C'est la vie.* But if I end up having to pay my own way, I'm definitely going to need a roommate. And I knew you needed one, so—*voilà!*—here I am. Besides, having a single dorm room was getting kind of lonely."

"Roni can move in with you at the beginning of spring semester," Tricia said to Jenna. "But since she's staying here over Thanksgiving weekend, she said she wanted to get a jump start on packing up some of her things. I wanted to run everything by you before that. So is this going to work out?"

Jenna beamed at her friend. "It's going to be perfect!" But something about what Tricia had just said was nagging her. "Wait a sec. Roni, you're staying here over Thanksgiving?"

Roni let her dark hair slip into her eyes and muttered, "I was hoping you hadn't heard that part."

Jenna crossed her arms, instinctively shifting into oldest sibling mode. "Well, I heard. So what's going on? Fess up."

Roni blushed and glanced sideways at Tricia, and Jenna took the hint. Roni obviously wanted to talk to Jenna about this in private, so Jenna quickly thanked Tricia for organizing the roommate switch, assured her that everything would work out great, and then pulled Roni out into the hallway.

As soon as Tricia's door shut, Roni told Jenna about her plans for Thanksgiving with Kiersten falling through.

"But why didn't you tell me and Lora-Leigh?" Jenna said when Roni'd finished.

Roni shrugged. "Lora-Leigh's got her own issues to deal with at home right now. I didn't want to add to them. And I knew how excited you were to be spending time with your sisters and everything. I just didn't want to be a nuisance to anybody."

"Stop right there," Jenna said, gaping at Roni. "There is a time and place for your Miss Manners side to make her appearances, but it's not in the presence of a best friend. Got it?"

Roni giggled. "Are you actually scolding me?"

"Yes," Jenna said. "First of all, you should have told us. If I could tell you about my 'betes, then you are required to divulge any crisis of mass proportion to me. And Lora-Leigh, too. Second of all, you could never be a nuisance, except by trying so hard *not* to be one. And third and most important . . ." Jenna dropped her lecturey tone and smiled, putting a hand on Roni's shoulder. ". . . You're coming home with me for Thanksgiving."

Roni smiled. "Thanks for offering," she said. "That's so sweet of you."

"So say yes," Jenna said.

Roni seemed lost in thought for a minute. Finally, she shook her head. "Up until five minutes ago, I thought I would've jumped at the chance to go home with you. And I'd love to meet your family. But you know what? I think I'm going to stay here in Latimer."

Jenna opened her mouth to protest, but Roni raised her hand to stop her. "I want to stay here," Roni said. "I can start looking for a job for next semester. I have a feeling I'll need one. And actually, I'd like to have some time to myself over the long weekend. I've spent so many holidays making small talk with my parents' social and political 'friends'—people I barely know. It'll be a relief to have a quiet break to do whatever I want to do, whenever I want to do it. I've never had that before."

Jenna watched Roni's eyes light up at the thought of a solitary weekend of R&R. "I just hate the thought of you being alone," she said.

"But being alone will be a break for me," Roni said.

Jenna nodded slowly. "I think I get it. But don't think you're off the hook. If you stay here, I'm still calling you every day. And I'm bringing back leftovers for you, too."

Roni laughed. "I think I can handle that."

"So you want to come down to my room so we can figure out how we'll arrange it when you move in?" Jenna said. "I know I still have to live with Amber for a few more weeks, but this will give me something positive to focus on when she gets antisocial on me."

"Sure." As they headed to Jenna's room, Roni stopped her. "Hey, what is your stance on snoring?"

Jenna giggled at the picture of prim and proper Roni rattling the room with some horrific version of sleep apnea. "Snoring?" she said. "I think I could tolerate it on a case-by-case basis."

"That's a relief," Roni said. "Then we'll get along as roommates just fine."

Jenna gave her a half-hug. "I'm sure we will." And she was.

Lora-Leigh'd been sitting in her parents' driveway for the last twenty minutes, trying to get up the courage to go inside. The dorms had closed at noon on Wednesday, and the campus had quickly turned into a ghost town. They'd all be back by Sunday, though, and ZZT Initiation was barely more than a week away.

But she couldn't think of that now, not when this weekend was her penance. A good dose of guilt had bathed her all week when she thought of her mother and how they hadn't spoken at all in the last several weeks. But how many times had she tried to reach out to her mom already and been snubbed? She sighed and checked herself over in the rearview mirror for the hundredth time, then slowly got out of the car with her duffel. It didn't matter how many times her mom had pushed her away. Even if it meant eating crow (*again*), she had to make things right with her mother once and for all.

When she slipped her key into the back door, the aroma of cranberries and apples wrapped around her. The cinnamon and allspice practically curled a finger into the air, inviting her deeper into the kitchen.

"Thomas? Did you get the marshmallows for the sweet potato casserole?" her mother called out.

Lora-Leigh came through the laundry room and smiled weakly, half-prepared to duck if any plates were hurled at her. "It's me, Mom. Not Dad."

Hannah Sorenstein stood in front of the oven wearing a crisp white blouse, slacks, and an apron. Of course, she had her traditional Tri-Omega pearls on. "Hello, Lora," she said, already turning her back again to focus on her cooking. "If you came home to do laundry, I can throw in a load for you as soon as I'm done with this stuffing."

"No," Lora-Leigh said, taking a deep breath to brace herself for this dreaded confab. "I came home for Thanksgiving."

"Oh," her mom said. "When I didn't hear from you, I thought maybe you'd be spending the weekend with your ZZT friends."

Ouch. Lora-Leigh cringed. Her mom was definitely not going to make this easy.

"No," Lora-Leigh said again. "I wanted to spend this weekend with you and Dad and Scott. How many times have I tried to talk to you about this? To get you to understand." She sighed. "I love you, and the fact that I chose ZZT doesn't change that. Tri-Omega was right for you. It fit who you are. That's how ZZT is for me." She stepped in front of her mom and put her hands on her shoulders, forcing her to make eye contact. "It comes down to this. If ZZT isn't good enough for you, then neither am I."

Lora-Leigh dropped her hands and turned away, dreading the biting response she knew had to be coming. But her mom surprised her when her mouth suddenly crumpled at the corners, and she put her hands over her eyes. "Oh, Lora-Leigh," she said. "I'm so sorry . . . about everything I've said and done. I never meant what I said about ZZT being second-rate. I'm sure it's a fine sorority." She clucked her tongue, shaking her head. "I hate myself for the way I've been acting. It's just you and I are so different. We were at each other's throats so much these last few years when you were in high school. Tri-Omega was the one thing I always had that I thought I would share with you. I thought we could at least have that in common, but now..."

"Now we have the fact that we're both in sororities in common," Lora-Leigh said, her eyes welling up against her will. Suddenly, it was all crystal clear to her—why her mom had pushed her so hard to join the Tri-Os, and why she'd been inconsolable when she hadn't. "We're still connected by the whole sorority life thing, even if we're not in the same sisterhood. And right now, I'm here because I want to spend time with you, just you. I missed you."

"I missed you, too," her mother said quietly. "It's nice to have you home. It's been too long."

Lora-Leigh grabbed some of the potatoes that were washed and out on the counter and began peeling them, needing something to do to break through the weightiness of the conversation. "You know, my friend Roni is staying on campus this weekend. She's not going home to Boston, so I was wondering if she could come over for turkey dinner tomorrow. Would that be okay?"

Hannah nodded. "Of course. We can't very well leave the poor girl alone for the holiday, and we always have room at our table for friends, provided your brother doesn't eat us out of house and home."

"I've already told her about your kugel. No one makes noodle kugel like you do."

Her mom smiled a bit as she mixed the onions and celery into the stuffing. "Well, of course I'll make kugel for her." Her mom paused, seeming deep in thought as she fidgeted with the kitchen towel she was using to wipe her hands. "Just tell me one thing, honestly. Are you enjoying your new member semester?"

"I'm loving every second of it," Lora-Leigh said. "I never expected it to be like this. I mean, I used to think sororities were completely laughable. But the friends I've made are better than any I've ever had before. And I love my big sister, Camille. I want you to meet her, too. And the philanthropy project we did for Homecoming was amazing, and our float—"

"Was beautiful," her mom said.

"You saw it?" Lora-Leigh asked.

Her mom nodded, smiling. "I recognized your artwork in almost every one of the picture frames."

Lora-Leigh blushed. "Listen, Mom, I never thanked you for making me go through sorority recruitment, but I want to now. These have been the best months of my life." Her voice cracked on the last word, and her mother put her hand up to her mouth.

"That's all I ever wanted for you," her mom said. "And I have something to thank you for, too. That shrug you made me. Every woman at the faculty dinner complimented me on it. They were dying to know where they could buy one like it."

Lora-Leigh stared at her mom, a tumult of emotions racing through her. "You mean you actually wore it?"

"Of course I did," her mom said. "I know, I know, I said it was too flashy. But then I decided to give a new look a try. I've never felt as much pride as I did telling everyone at the dinner that the shrug they were all fawning over was made by my own daughter. I even took a picture of it for your portfolio for your FIT application."

Then, before Lora-Leigh could even think, her mother stepped forward, pulled her into her arms, and hugged her tightly, not saying a word. Lora-Leigh closed her eyes and hugged back until her father walked into the room and cleared his throat. "Well, isn't that a sight for sore eyes. My girls have made up."

CHAPTER
13

As Roni sat down to dinner at the ZZT house on Monday night with Jenna, Lora-Leigh, and the other sisters, she smiled, realizing how glad she was that all of her friends were back from the Thanksgiving weekend. She'd had a quiet, relaxing weekend to herself, sleeping in, watching sappy romantic comedies, and sitting for hours at The Funky Bean reading *Pride and Prejudice* (one of her all-time favorite books). She'd had a wonderful time with Lora-Leigh and her family on Thursday, too. And even though Lora-Leigh'd warned her beforehand about her brother being a goofball and her mom being overbearing, Roni'd actually thought Scott was a charming brother and Hannah Sorenstein was a devoted, loving mother. She was so glad to see that Lora-Leigh and her mom had finally made up, and Mrs. Sorenstein had been so kind and welcoming to her, too. But even though Roni'd had a great weekend, it felt good to be surrounded by her ZZT sisters once again and be back in the groove of school.

As she took a tentative bite of Miss Merry's jalapeño-and-potato casserole and listened to her friends catching up on news after the long weekend, her BlackBerry buzzed. After checking her e-mail, she discovered that she had something else to smile about:

From: k_douglas@bostonemail.com
To: veronica.van.gelderen@latimer.edu

Hi sweetie!
I hope you had a wonderful Thanksgiving with your friend Lora-Leigh. All went well with the big meeting of the respective in-laws. Everyone seems to be getting along fine (phew!). Just wanted to let you know about a potential holiday job for you. I was out looking for ideas for wedding favors and came across this adorable chocolate boutique, How Sweet It Is, on Newbury Street. It's a mom-and-pop store run by the Madame and Monsieur Beauchamp (oui, oui, they are from France). They have a hot chocolate bar in the back, and they make their own chocolate on-site. Roni, this place is perfect for you! Sophisticated and cozy, and the owners are fabu! They're looking for help for the holiday rush, so I gave them your name and résumé. Expect a call from them next week sometime. I hope this will help you get your feet on solid ground after the family feud. Can't wait to see you in a few weeks!
Love,
Kiersten

Roni slipped her BlackBerry back into her pocket and looked up to see both Jenna and Lora-Leigh staring at her expectantly.

"Okay, Boston," Lora-Leigh said. "I'm sure there's some sort of rule against a smile that bright. What's with the Cheshire cat act?"

"I think I have a job lined up for the holidays!"

"Congrats, girl!" Jenna said. "See? You don't need your parents to foot the bills. You're on your way to full-blown autonomy."

Roni nodded. "And I stopped by the natatorium on Saturday to see if they needed anyone to help out there next semester. They have an opening for a lifeguard, so I applied. If I get that job, too, I should be able to pay off my dad's Amex bill and maybe even have some left over for another trip to Morgan's."

"Cheers to that!" Lora-Leigh said, clinking her soda glass to Roni's.

"Now, if Lance would just call you, you'd be all set," Jenna teased.

Roni blushed but played it cool. "He'll call when he's ready. Besides, right now I just want to focus on our Initiation coming up. I'll have plenty of time for Lance after that."

"Did I hear someone say Initiation?" Beverly said, sitting down at the end of their table. She reached for the Sweet'n Lo and opened the packet into her iced tea.

Darcy sat down next to her and did the same. "Are y'all getting nervous about Initiation?"

Jenna blurted out, "I haven't thought of it because I've been so busy finishing up my Shakespeare paper and hanging with Tiger."

"Well, you *should* be getting nervous about Initiation," Camille chimed in from the other side of Lora-Leigh. "It's this weekend, you know."

"We know," Roni said. She and Beverly had gone over the schedule just last night.

Sandy piped up. "I'll admit it. I'm scared."

Camille let out a sinister laugh, and Roni thought again how perfect she was as Lora-Leigh's Big Sis.

Lora-Leigh scoffed. "It's not like y'all are gonna make us parade up and down Sorority Row naked or eat dog food."

"Dog food?" Jenna shrieked. "I'm not eating dog food."

"My mom had to eat dog food when she got initiated into Tri-Omega," Lora-Leigh said.

Roni snickered. "Another good reason not to be a Tri-Omega."

Jenna turned to Darcy. "Do you know what they're going to do to us?"

Darcy wiped her mouth with her napkin. "I can't tell you anything about Initiation, but you need to take it seriously. When I was in your shoes, I was a nervous wreck."

As if on cue, Marissa tapped her glass at the front of the dining room and stood. "Hey, everyone! I wanted to make some announcements about Initiation on Saturday night. Please bring a flower with you to the ceremony. It can be your favorite flower, or one that has special meaning to you. No new members should wear makeup to the ceremony on Saturday. You mustn't wear any jewelry except your new member pin. That means the earrings are out, Lora-Leigh."

"But they're my keystone." Lora-Leigh groaned. "It'll be like amputation."

Roni noticed all the new members snicker, but the actives stayed straight-faced.

Marissa continued. "The time before Initiation is very solemn, an opportunity for meditation and quiet. You need to contemplate this final decision, thinking of how you fit into the house and what you have to offer. The history of ZZT is important to all of us because it's a reminder of where our sisterhood came from. We expect every one of you to respect our founders, our creed, and the secrets you will soon learn. For this reason, we ask for a period of silence on Saturday afternoon leading up to Initiation."

Roni shifted her eyes to Beverly, who smiled at her.

"One more thing," Marissa said. "You must be on your best behavior because Friday night, the chapter will vote on every one of you to make sure you qualify for Initiation."

A unified gasp tiptoed throughout the room. Roni felt the harsh grasp of fear around her heart. She'd tried to be the best new member ever, never missing a meeting and always volunteering to do stuff. But the thought of ZZT rejecting her after so much time was enough to make her body shake. It wouldn't happen, though. She'd proven herself. Everything was going to be okay. She hoped.

She tried to quell her panic as Marissa officially ended dinner and escorted Mrs. Walsh, their housemother, out of the room.

"See y'all later," Darcy said, standing up to go. She and Camille stifled laughs, but they left the new members sitting there with their mouths hanging open.

"They're just messing with our heads," Lora-Leigh said.

"You don't know that for sure," Sandy said. "I'm even more scared now."

Roni tried to be the voice of reason, but she was nervous, too. "We have nothing to worry about," she said, making her voice sound as convincing as possible. "They're our sisters, and they love us."

"Are they really going to vote on us?" Jenna asked.

"I don't know." Roni sighed. "Beverly never mentioned it. But they can pretty much do anything they want."

"So what do we do?" Sandy asked Roni.

Roni wrapped her arms around both Sandy and Jenna. "We keep doing what we've been doing. Be good to each other, and just see what happens on Saturday. I can't wait to be a full-fledged member."

"Me either," Jenna echoed.

Lora-Leigh smiled. "Damn straight."

Saturday night, Lora-Leigh didn't know what was killing her more . . . the silence in the room or the fact that she'd had to take out her good-luck earrings (all six of them) for tonight's Initiation ceremony.

"Okay, so maybe I can live without my hardware for a few hours. Maybe," she grumbled. "But I swear, if they ask us to drink blood or speak in tongues, I'm so outta there."

Jenna stifled a giggle, but Roni frowned. "Shhh . . . We're supposed to be silent," she fussed. "Contemplative and reflective."

"Right, I'm reflectin' on my bare naked earlobes."

"You've *got* to be quiet, Lora-Leigh," Roni said firmly.

"Y'all are gonna get us in trouble," Jenna whispered in the darkness.

"With who? No one's here but us," Lora-Leigh smarted off. The three of them were sitting in Roni's room, awaiting the arrival of the ZZT sisters who would bring them over to the house—*finally!*—for tonight's initiation ceremony.

"Y'all," Jenna whispered meekly, "what if I didn't pass the vote today?"

"We all passed the vote," Roni said.

"There was no vote," Lora-Leigh said. "It was all a mind game."

"I'm so nervous." Jenna bit her bottom lip.

"There's no reason to be," Lora-Leigh said, even as she heard the deafening pounding of her own heart. "It's going to be brill. Something we'll always remember." At least that was what her mother had told her in the note she'd dropped off at Tuthill for Lora-Leigh earlier today. When Lora-Leigh'd returned to her room after studying at the library for finals, there'd been a package waiting for her on her bed. Inside was a note from her mom along with an ivory scrapbook with gold lettering on the front reading ZETA ZETA TAU. Even now, remembering the note made Lora-Leigh's eyes fill up unwillingly:

My Sweet Lora-Leigh,

I'm so proud of the choices you've made. Here is a scrapbook to start saving your own precious sorority memories. They will stay with you all of the days of your life.

Much love,
Mom

Now that she and her mom had made their peace, Lora-Leigh was finally ready to become a full-fledged active in Zeta Zeta Tau, without guilt or worry, with only a free spirit. The only problem was, she didn't know how much longer she could wait for the ceremony or stay quiet. (The staying quiet part was already failing miserably.)

Thankfully, at exactly eight P.M., there was a knock on the door. Lora-Leigh opened it to three sisters wearing sunglasses, black fedoras, and black trench coats. Lora-Leigh thought she recognized Heather Bourke underneath one of the fedoras, but she couldn't be positive.

They stepped inside, and the girl in the middle spoke. "Sisters Van Gelderen, Driscoll, and Sorenstein. Your presence is requested at the Initiation ritual for the Alpha Lambda chapter of the sisterhood of Zeta Zeta Tau national sorority. Do you hereby accept the invitation?"

"We do," the three girls said in unison.

"Do you come of your own free will?"

"We do."

"Will you fully participate in the rituals of ZZT?"

"We will."

"Then come," the girl continued. "Let us traverse the final path of the neophyte and enter into the cleansing home and eternal bonds of sisterhood."

Neophyte? Lora-Leigh couldn't stop herself. "When is the human sacrifice?" she joked.

An unattributable snicker rang out in the darkness.

As they made their way out of Roni's room, Lora-Leigh could see one of the girls was none other than her Big Sister, Camille. She knew her immediately from the dark, black, curly ponytail. Camille leaned over and whispered, "Behave yourself, Sorenstein. I'm watching you."

"You should be," Lora-Leigh whispered.

This was going to be a night she'd never forget.

Roni stood in the foyer of the ZZT house, which was lit with tall white taper candles in glass candelabras. She watched wax trail down the small candle in her hand, onto the protective glass holder, trying to keep her hands from trembling too much. The new members stood quietly in alphabetical order—she was behind Amy Tubbs and in front of Sue-Marie Weiss and Claudine Woodson, the last of the bunch—and listened carefully to the instructions of Beverly, who was dressed in a silver robe with a long Excalibur-like sword tied at her hip. Tonight Beverly wasn't Roni's Big Sister, but The Knight, who would guide them through Initiation. Tonight Roni wasn't the New Member President. She was simply another new member who would take her final step into the full sisterhood.

She couldn't wait to get her initiate pin, to move into the house next year, to maybe one day be an officer. There was so much to look forward to.

A thick white satin rope was extended for everyone to grab on to, with Beverly at the front. "Follow me in silence, please," Beverly instructed. "Hold ye steadfast to the rope uniting you with your sisters. Ye are about to enter the ritual world of Zeta Zeta Tau. Everything you witness, hear, and absorb is part of the history, preservation, and secrets of our great sorority. Do you so swear to keep the secrets of ZZT?"

"I swear," Roni said, almost the first one in the group to do so.

They moved slowly behind the grand staircase to a hidden

panel that opened to stairs leading down. She hadn't even been aware that there was more to the ZZT house.

They snaked downstairs to a large, black iron door, lit only by candelabras on either side. Beverly—or rather The Knight—pulled a skeletal key from her robe and opened the door. The smell of piquant incense and oranges spiked the air, prickling Roni's nose as she followed the group into a dimly lit chamber draped all in white curtains. On the floor were bulky satin pillows, and each new member took a cushion. Roni crossed her legs underneath her and wove her fingers together as she waited for what would happen next.

Ten sisters, each clad in flowing white chiffon robes that reminded Roni of ethereal goddesses of ancient times, stood around them in a circle. Roni recognized Melody Montgomery, Louise Campbell, and Hallie Stoops at the front of the room.

"We are The Sorceresses, here to march you through your rebirth," Melody said, reading from a mammoth tome in her arms. Roni listened to Melody as she explained that the new members had to be symbolically cleansed of their previous lives and reborn into the sisterhood of ZZT. As she spoke, the other Sorceresses handed out steaming-hot white towels.

"Take one and cleanse yourselves," Melody said. "This will purge you of the impurities of your former life and prepare you for entrance into the secrets of the sisterhood."

Roni took a warm towel from Hallie and drew the cloth over her arms and down her bare legs. She glanced around to see Jenna washing her face and Lora-Leigh scrubbing under her armpits. That girl couldn't take anything seriously.

Roni breathed in deeply, exhaling some of the nervousness

that had built up inside her. Around her, her fellow new sisters listened intently as Melody continued.

"Do you accept your neophyte passing and virtual rebirth into the sisterhood?" she asked.

"I do," the new members answered.

"Do you solemnly swear allegiance and loyalty not only to the letters *Zeta Zeta Tau* and the women who stand with you, but to all women of the sisterhood who have worn these letters and will wear these letters?"

Roni gazed across the room and saw Lora-Leigh wink at her. "I do," she said, together with her sisters.

Suddenly Beverly drew her silver sword and slashed an opening in the draped fabric at the back of the room, revealing another chamber.

"Come, for you are neophytes no more and are on your way to receiving the sanctified rituals of Zeta Zeta Tau," she said. "You have moved into the realm of The Apprentice."

Roni followed along into a sanctuary-type room with small pews where all the girls sat in order. Beverly set a very large, deep crystal vase in the middle of a round table, draped with a smooth white cloth, at the front of the room. Surrounding the vase was a host of white votives, casting a golden dance of light across the table.

"Each one of you was asked to bring a flower tonight," Beverly said. "One by one, we'd like you to come forward, place your flower in the vase, and tell your sisters how this flower reflects your values, personality, and what you bring to ZZT."

Roni watched in silence as Danika added a green orchid and Sandy a calla lily. Other sisters added peonies, carnations, and more and more roses. The bouquet grew and bloomed with vibrant reds, pinks, yellows, and purples.

"Jenna Driscoll, please come forward," Beverly said.

Jenna walked up and placed a sunny white Gerber daisy into the mix. "Daisies are some of the hardiest flowers, and they always make you smile." Jenna looked up at her sisters with tears in her eyes. "I try to be that way, but for the first part of this semester, I held back a part of myself because I was scared about how you'd treat me." Her face flushed, and Roni was sure she was thinking about her diabetes. "Well, now I know I can share everything with you, and I'll always be loved, no matter what. Starting now, I want to help be the backbone of ZZT, and I want to bring the same happiness you've given me to all of you."

As Jenna sat back down, Roni caught her eye, giving her a reassuring smile.

When it was Lora-Leigh's turn, she walked to the front of the room clutching her flowers, a bouquet of wild crimson clover, and placed them in and around the other more brilliant and vivacious flowers.

"Some people think clover is an eyesore," Lora-Leigh said, looking down. "It's not always welcomed where it puts down roots. But it makes this amazing blanket of color in the fall that's totally unique." She touched the velvety petals of the clover. "I found a place to grow here. So I hope I can offer whatever part of me you think is useful to the sisterhood."

Finally, Roni's turn came, and she quietly took her place at the front of the room, holding an orange tropical flower. "This is a bromeliad." She ran her hand over the exotically shaped bloom. "Bromeliads adapt to their growing conditions whether they're indoors or out. I feel very much like this flower. I was planted in the wrong environment for the longest time. Now I'm blooming in my new environment here at ZZT because you're allowing me to. You give me the strength and courage to be who I am." With her last statement, she placed her flower in the middle of the arrangement.

As Roni passed by Jenna to sit down again, Jenna reached out to squeeze her hand.

Beverly picked up the vase and held it high. "I hold a bounty of beauty in my hands. You're all unique and special, just like each of these flowers. However, when placed together, these flowers represent a blooming bouquet. The sisters of Zeta Zeta Tau have also joined together to generate a sisterhood of strength and talent and unique qualities more special as a group than separate. Take the memory of this night with you," Beverly said. "Let it seep into your hearts, becoming part of you, as you are part of us."

With that, Beverly gave each girl a scroll to hold on to until further instructed.

Roni fingered the crinkly papyrus, dying to unfurl it and see what it said. She was overwhelmed at the emotions circling around her, overcome by the ceremony and traditions that had been passed down for more than a hundred years, since the founding of ZZT. It was an honor to be able to partake of this ritual, especially with these girls, her friends, surrounding her.

Roni tried to memorize the scent of mint and orange in the air, the flickering candlelight on the white curtains, the expectant faces of her sisters. All of this she wanted to cement in her mind forever. To draw strength from it. To fall back on whenever she lacked confidence. To cling to whenever she felt like nothing but a supreme disappointment to her parents.

Right here, right now, she basked in the warm glow of sisterhood, anxious to cross the final bridge awaiting her. As the happy tears flowed from her clear eyes, she saw Beverly smile at her from across the room.

"And now, sisters," Beverly said. "It's time to don your ritual robes for your final embarkation."

Roni stood, took a deep breath, and followed her new member class as they walked behind the white curtain.

Jenna struggled with the heap of emotions tumbling through her as the rest of the new members tugged off their white blouses, skirts, and dresses. She was washed in relief that she no longer had to hide her 'betes from her sisters, whom she loved and trusted. Everything was out in the open, and she was free to just be herself.

"Do you need some help with your robe?" a soft voice asked from behind her.

"Oh, Darcy!" she whispered. "It's you!"

"I have a special robe for you," Darcy said. "So you don't have to worry about your pump. There's a slit right here on the left in case you need to get to it."

"I can't believe you did that." Jenna flung herself onto her Big Sister. "That's so thoughtful."

She eased her T-shirt over her head, stood in her white cotton bra and panties, and clipped her insulin pump to the elastic waistband of her underpants.

"Okay, ready?" Darcy asked in a whisper.

"As ready as I'll ever be." She bit her lip. "I'm so nervous I think I'm going to pass out."

Darcy shook her head. "Now don't go and do that. You'll miss all the fun." She draped the soft fabric of the robe over Jenna's shoulders and belted the waist in a small knot. "Deep breath. You'll be fine. I'll be right behind you."

Rejoining her new member class, Jenna left the secret underground area and climbed up the back stairs of the house into the TV lounge room. The adjoining door into the formal living room opened, casting forth a bright orangey-yellow glow, and Jenna's knees shook with excitement. This was it. She was about to be let in on the treasured secrets of the wonderful world of Zeta Zeta Tau.

Darcy escorted her into the room where the remaining sisters were clad in chiffon robes, wearing wreaths of baby's breath on their heads. Marissa stood in front of a round mirrored table that held a jeweled chest and a long, silver sword. She was dressed in a vibrant blue satin robe with white trimming on the edges and sleeves. An ethereal white satin hood covered her red hair.

Marissa spoke solemnly from under her hood. "As Grand Imperial Merlin of the Alpha Lambda chapter of Zeta Zeta Tau sorority, I welcome you to your final initiation and receiving of the rituals." Then, flanked by two other sisters in light blue robes, she began reading from a massive, ancient-looking book with worn pages and a gilded spine. Marissa talked of sisterhood, of how the sorority was founded and how it had grown through the years, nurturing young women to great accomplishments through philanthropy and social service. Jenna hoped she would be one of those success stories someday, too.

Sure, the fall semester had been intense—her 'betes a burden and her classes challenging, but she'd made it through. And now she was more in control and less afraid. Not to mention she was part of one of the best sororities on campus and had the most amazing Big Sister. And then there was Tiger and the promise of something more with him. So much had changed in her life the past few months, and so much had changed *her*, too.

As Marissa kept reading, Jenna smiled at the sisters around her. They would each bring so much to ZZT, and together they formed a cohesive bond of sisterhood that would last forever.

". . . and in taking this oath, I vow that I will never disparage another sister of Zeta Zeta Tau," Marissa finished.

"I do so vow," Jenna uttered in unison with her sisters.

Kwana Johnson, Keesha's real older sister, stepped forward with a large scroll that looked exactly like the one Jenna and the new members were holding, along with their candles. "Open with me, if you will, the scroll of truth and read in harmony the Creed of Zeta Zeta Tau."

Jenna's vision blurred with tears, and she blinked hard to focus on the curly cursive writing. She cleared her throat and pledged in unison with all in the room:

> *We do hereby solemnly strive for these things:*
> *A clear visualization of the world around us and our part*
>   *therein,*
> *That with cordial and humane actions,*
> *We may spread peace, happiness, and joy to others,*
> *And convey the true meaning and value of proper sisterhood,*
> *An enjoyment of life's bounties,*

But also an appreciation of the struggles we must overcome.
Determination, perseverance, tenacity,
And a striving to better ourselves,
That without acrimony or hostility,
We may learn from our challenges,
Grow from our mistakes,
Develop with our accomplishments,
And celebrate with fervor the triumphs to come.
Help us to infuse this creed within our souls,
That we too may be
Victorious in all we do.

Kwana stepped aside, and Marissa reached for the sword with her right hand. "The sword is the beloved symbol of Zeta Zeta Tau. As you see from our crest, the sword stands over the world, which is made of mother-of-pearl. Our motto is taken from the words of the great William Shakespeare: 'Why, then the world's mine oyster, Which I with sword will open.'"

Which I with sword will open . . . Jenna repeated in her head. She had overcome so much already and knew that with the help of her loyal, amazing ZZT sisters, no struggle would slow her down. She would draw her strength from this group of extraordinary women.

Slowly, each new member approached the table, took the sword, and opened the jeweled box with the tip of it. Inside were hundreds of pearls, and one was given to each new sister by Kwana, The Jeweler.

Peggy Moderance, The Florist, stepped forward and presented each new member a white rose. "The official flower of our beloved ZZT is the white rose. This variety is a hybrid of two varieties of roses that were believed to be incompatible, an exquisite flower. But it's a pale reflection of the meaning of our sisterhood, where women from every walk of life come together in friendship."

Jenna beamed as she accepted her pearl from Kwana and caught Darcy's tearing eyes as she returned to the group. She'd wear the pearl on the lovely platinum chain her mother and stepfather had given her as a high school graduation present, bringing together her old family with her new one.

She watched as Lora-Leigh took her pearl, amazingly staying straight-faced throughout the ceremony, and as a teary-eyed Roni took hers and grasped it to her chest. Finally, after oaths were administered, chants repeated, and many songs sung, Marissa presented each new sister with her initiate pin: a silver sword of ZZT impaled through a pearl. Jenna gazed down at hers, pinned on the left side of her chest, just over her heart, and felt her pulse tapping away against it.

All of the sisters gathered about the round, mirrored table. Each new initiate placed her candle in the center, enhancing the glow of the candlelight beaming throughout the room. The rest of the sisters congregated around, fixing their eyes on the mirror.

"We are all one," Marissa said. "In fraternal love, in sisterhood, in friendship, joy, and fellowship."

And as the heartwarming, moving candlelight ceremony came to a close, the sisters of ZZT raised their voices in harmony and sang:

"Remember Zeta Zeta Tau,
Remember what we say,
Remember how proud you should be to wear our silver sword
ev'ry day.
Remember whatever happens, our sisterhood is true.
Remember Zeta Zeta Tau . . . and we will remember you."

Jenna felt a tug behind her and knew it was Darcy. To her left, Lora-Leigh reached over and took her hand and then joined her own with Roni's. The bond transmitted between them like electricity. Friendship for the rest of their days.

GREEK ALPHABET

ENGLISH SPELLING	GREEK LETTER	PRONUNCIATION
Alpha	A	*Al-fah*
Beta	B	*Bay-tah*
Gamma	Γ	*Gam-ah*
Delta	Δ	*Del-tah*
Epsilon	E	*Ep-si-lon*
Zeta	Z	*Zay-tah*
Eta	H	*A-tah*
Theta	Θ	*Thay-tah*
Iota	I	*Eye-o-tah*
Kappa	K	*Cap-ah*
Lambda	Λ	*Lamb-dah*
Mu	M	*Mew*
Nu	N	*New*
Xi	Ξ	*Zigh*
Omicron	O	*Ohm-i-kron*
Pi	Π	*Pie*
Rho	P	*Roe*
Sigma	Σ	*Sig-mah*
Tau	T	*Taw*
Upsilon	Υ	*Oop-si-lon*
Phi	Φ	*Fie*
Chi	X	*Kie*
Psi	Ψ	*Sigh*
Omega	Ω	*O-may-gah*

GREEK ORGANIZATIONS
—— LATIMER UNIVERSITY ——
Latimer, Florida

ORGANIZATION	GREEK LETTER	CLASSIFICATION
Alpha Sigma Gamma	ΑΣΓ	Sorority
Alpha Mu	ΑΜ	Fraternity
Beta Eta Psi	ΒΗΨ	Fraternity
Beta Xi	ΒΞ	Sorority
Chi Pi	ΧΠ	Fraternity
Delta Kappa	ΔΚ	Sorority
Delta Sigma Nu	ΔΣΝ	Fraternity
Eta Lamba Nu	ΗΛΝ	Sorority
Gamma Gamma Rho	ΓΓΡ	Fraternity
Kappa Omega	ΚΩ	Fraternity
Kappa Tau Omicron	ΚΤΟ	Fraternity
Omega Omega Omega	ΩΩΩ	Sorority
Omega Phi	ΩΦ	Fraternity
Omicron Chi Omega	ΟΧΩ	Sorority
Phi Omicron Chi	ΦΟΧ	Fraternity
Pi Epsilon Chi	ΠΕΧ	Sorority
Pi Theta Epsilon	ΠΘΕ	Fraternity
Psi Kappa Upsilon	ΨΚΥ	Sorority
Sigma Sigma	ΣΣ	Fraternity
Tau Delta Iota	ΤΔΙ	Fraternity
Theta Beta Gamma	ΘΒΓ	Sorority
Zeta Theta Mu	ΖΘΜ	Fraternity
Zeta Zeta Tau	ΖΖΤ	Sorority

For more about
the sisters of
Zeta Zeta Tau, read

SORORITY 101:
The Formal